Stripped to the Bone

Brad leant back and thought about Annie. She was so delicious and unfathomable. She was a beautiful dark tunnel he perpetually wanted to penetrate. He wanted to penetrate her to the core and get at her mystery. Why did she wrap him up so much? Why was he obsessed by her? He smelt her everywhere. Before they had fucked he imagined he saw her everywhere; now he tasted and smelt her – in his coffee, on his tie, in his car, at the bar. She pulsed through his pores.

Stripped to the Bone
Jasmine Stone

BLACK LACE

Black Lace books contain sexual fantasies.
In real life, always practise safe sex.

First published in 1999 by
Black Lace
Thames Wharf Studios
Rainville Road
London W6 9HA

Reprinted 2002

Printed and bound by Mackays of Chatham PLC

ISBN 0 352 33463 0

Prologue

*T*here she sits, nine-year-old Annie with her curly hair pulled back severely; sits cross-legged on top of her bed; sits with half-closed eyes (the hairstyle is so tight that closing her eyes all the way is painful); sits under a red scarf hung from the overhead light, pretending to be in a trance. Crushed in a red glow lies the Ouija board.

'Will I be rich?' she telepaths.

The Ouija board moves rapidly to 'Yes'.

'Will I be famous?'

The Ouija board again moves quickly. 'Yes.'

'Will I have love?'

The Ouija board pauses. Annie knows she's the phantom mover yet tries to force the board to choose 'Yes' or 'No'. She traces the letters on the board, slowly: L ... O ... V ... E ...

Without paying the least attention, the planchette comes to rest on the question mark.

It's a boring game, Annie decides. Too much waiting.

Chapter One

When Annie was in ninth grade, her body had the gawkiness of a daddy long-legs – knobby dangling limbs with an insignificant torso. Boys would come up to her and give her dog tags or tell her she was a pirate's dream: a sunken chest.

To an imaginative eye, Annie's face had the promise of beauty. Alabaster skin and a full, pouty lower lip. Her dark blue eyes turned slightly downward, giving her a soulful look beyond her years, and her curly black hair flew about her like a halo of shadows. Unfortunately, Annie was surrounded by those whose lofty visions were quite limited by pubescent hormones. Teenage boys could not see beyond her exaggerated disconnectedness.

Annie didn't have the good fortune to be part of a group of girlfriends who would shield her from the boys' taunts. She simply stood in her own little sphere and let their short-sighted observations wash over her. Sometimes, Annie imagined what people would say about her if she died. Hence, when the far-away stare came over her face, a funeral was being created far away in her mind.

Nancy, her older sister, thought the cruel words should make Annie upset, but they didn't.

'Annie, this will pass. Just trust it,' Nancy consoled.

'Who cares?' replied Annie. Her eyes focused out the window on a bare tree which grew in front of their family's home.

'I know it bothers you. It *has* to bother you.'

'Sis, I don't care. Why should I?'

The question disturbed Nancy, for it was secretly what she yearned to know herself. To understand the point of the worrying, the concern. Just thinking God would take care of it all didn't suffice. She put her hand on Annie's forearm and lightly rubbed the smooth white skin.

In a slightly haughty voice, a voice she used to show she was the older sister and did know what she was talking about, Nancy said, 'Annie, you should care just because you *should*.'

As was typical for Californian public schools, the point of attending for most students was social, not educational. Their high school, located in the Richmond area of San Francisco, was no different. It was of vital importance to students attending to move in a group which resembled oneself in dress, character and values – and to stay with that group as a necessary passport to a semblance of normalcy while the hormones raged.

Most of the students at their school were children of immigrant Russians or American-born Chinese. The few white-looking students, the group most likely to accept her, seemed stamped from a mould Annie couldn't fathom. They slouched or slithered, holding their bodies in contorted ways, making themselves shields against the fog, their parents and other students. There was no one at the school to connect with, to buffer her feeling of aloneness. Annie believed from time to time that she might have been friends with the Russian children. Their gestures, melodious language, wolf eyes – it all appeared so familiar to her that she wanted to ask them, 'Do you think we might have common blood?' But this group was entirely closed up; it seemed to Annie that even bacteria couldn't penetrate its inner core.

Since she had no friends to complicate plans, Annie easily disappeared during the breaks between classes. Her school was near Golden Gate Park and she would slip out to wander for a few minutes between the twisting eucalyptus trees and squash vines. She would breathe in this bit of man-made nature and quietness, and feel restored and whole. Or, during longer breaks, she would run to the beach and gather up all the whole sand dollars she could find, even though their modest home had no room for collections of things you could walk to the beach and see. Then she would return to class on time. Annie was not one to flaunt breaking rules, merely step around them.

Her bouts on public transportation were usually more enjoyable than her time in public school. On the bus, she could silently witness how comfortable everyone was with being disconnected from others. The passengers rarely noticed her. She had the feeling of observing everything, everyone, from a space about three yards outside of her body. It gave her eyes the quality of at once looking inward, and at something far away in the distance.

One day on the bus, a group of young boys got on, looking mean and chewing their gum as if they meant to insult someone with their masticating. The other passengers averted their heads but Annie, in an unusual move, stared right at them. They didn't return her glare but stared through her. Annie did not mind the invisibility but *did* mind what she saw. They had taken a doll from a retarded girl in the front row of the bus and were holding it just out of her reach.

The adults on the bus said nothing. Annie said, 'Give it back to her.' The boys looked at her and through her again and continued taunting the retarded girl who was now crying and looking very confused.

The passivity of everyone on the bus made Annie feel nauseous. She yelled, 'Give it back to her,' again. The bus driver heard the commotion at last and turned around. He kicked the boys off the bus, who were still carrying the girl's doll, holding it up and laughing down the street as the bus pulled away. It hadn't occurred to Annie to comfort the girl. Instead, she stared long and hard at the other passengers who pretended they didn't see her. Yet it was not difficult to notice in the awkward shifting of hands on magazines, the adjustments of Walkmans, the repeated movement of fingers through hair: they felt her watching them and they were uncomfortable, if not ashamed.

From then on, Annie knew she was not backdrop material any more, though the feelings of disconnectedness never left. She also knew, despite the day's events with the boys and the doll, that when Annie got on the bus the next day, few passengers would remember her. For the most part, she was just another swirling colour that streamed in and out of an orange vehicle. Not background material but not in any way headed for the limelight.

And though she never did, Annie looked forward to seeing the boys again. She wanted to have them try and take something of hers. She imagined every possible situation where she could kick them until they cried. Cried that they should never have taken that doll. Cried that they had looked through Annie and not at her. Cried that she was lost to them for ever.

It excited her to think of those boys frustrated and refused by a gawky ninth-grade girl who now believed her stare capable of opening up faultlines. At her funeral, if she just happened to die right now, there would be those boys, standing in the back, with horror-stricken faces. The crowd on the bus would let them know that the woman in the coffin was noble and they were dirt. Forever dirt.

* * *

6

Within a few years, Annie did not need to dream of skewering others with her gaze. At sixteen, she was suddenly discovered by every straight male within the San Francisco Bay Area. The body which once looked like a sketch done by an artist in a great hurry now became a fully fleshed-out work of art. Her dangling arms possessed a curve which didn't seem to stop at the fingers or shoulders but continue out like an idea one longed to follow. Her breasts weren't large but were a sensuous round shape that echoed her shoulders, cheeks, thighs.

Those soulful blue eyes had grown larger. They seemed to be made of sparks and when Annie applied the slightest bit of mascara to them, even the boys who had stared at her breasts, dreaming of cupping them or rubbing them or seeing their nipples, had to stare straight into those eyes. They gazed into them and wondered how an iris could capture the colour of morning the moment before the sun clears the ocean. They longed to crush the colour into their hearts for ever, letting the blue purify the *other* thoughts they had of pounding their young boyhoods into Annie until she could no longer stand.

Whereas before it was perceived that Annie was alone because she was ungainly and ugly, now most thought she stood alone because of her beauty. No one wanted to get close enough to touch her because she had surpassed the line between acceptable beauty and exceptional beauty. Combined with that same aloofness and other-worldly gaze, she now made everyone a bit afraid.

Chapter Two

'You're not going out of the house dressed like *that*, are you?' asked Nancy.

'I don't see what's wrong with it,' replied Annie in a flat tone.

'Why don't you just wear a big sign that says, "stare at me"? It would be easier.'

'Come on, Sis. The heels are high but so what? I didn't get a tattoo or anything. I never tell you what to wear.' Annie eyed Nancy and added under her breath, 'Not that it'd matter.'

'What's that supposed to mean, Ms Latex? I'm only concerned for your soul, Annie. That's all.'

'Nancy, look. God is not going to let you into heaven because you only wear beige. Now, are you going to drive me? Otherwise, I need to call and tell them I'll be in late.'

Nancy drove, trying to show how reluctant she was at every stop sign or street light. When it turned red, she would sigh and then sigh again when it turned green, moving at a top speed of Tai Chi to shift gears. Annie didn't show any signs that Nancy's deliberate slowness was irritating.

In fact, the silence in the car, brought on by Nancy, had no effect on Annie. She seemed pleased to be riding in a quiet bubble. She sat in her black latex bustier, a velvet choker dividing her long neck into two luscious sections. A semi-precious ruby hung from the choker and rested in the cleavage thrown up by the bustier. Her skirt was see-through and full of layers of various pastel gossamer material. A young modern renaissance woman. Or a witch.

If her funeral happened right now, Annie imagined she would be lain out in such an outfit and Nancy would at last see the beauty of the style. Nancy would stand in front of the group gathered, Mother holding her hand, and say, 'I could not see how she understood, but my sister really knew how to put together an outfit which would last for ever. Goodbye, dear Annie. God will be happy to have some colour in His realm.'

Though Nancy knew God and a small group of church-going friends would call it covetous, idolatry or just plain petty (they could only comprehend what God might say through a nineteen-year-old's vocabulary), she was distraught and envious of her younger sister's new-found beauty. When Annie was the ugly duckling, Nancy delighted in consoling and telling her that things would only get better as she got older. Funny though. Annie never seemed to need the sympathy. She listened to her sister, those drooping eyes staring without comprehending. It had infuriated Nancy that Annie didn't seem to be hurt at all by those comments the way Nancy had been hurt by them. For Nancy, the meanness had cut into the quick of her heart and left her feeling she would never be lovable. She could never look in the mirror again without hearing the titter of boys handing her a razor. Though her moustache was as faint as could be, Nancy, even in adulthood, viewed it as one step away from a beard. Though not in any way ugly, at twenty-one she had married the first guy who had professed his love for Jesus and kissed her with his eyes open.

If she had been more honest with herself, her empathy for Annie was closer to a comforting of her own past wounds more than any real interest in helping her little sister.

Nancy hadn't counted on things getting better for Annie before they got better for Nancy. It was positively evil to have a younger sister who was so suddenly, so stunningly beautiful. More boys talked to Nancy now, but with the intention that they might get to know her younger sister. Nancy never wanted to hear, 'Are you Annie's sister?' spoken to her ever again, with that horrible ingratiating tone that said they couldn't give a damn about her.

Equally infuriating it was to have a sister so independent. While Nancy had begun to work for a neighbourhood church, Annie had got a job at a clothing boutique on Union Street. For some reason, their parents thought it perfectly fine that Annie was working while still in high school – something they had never permitted Nancy to do. Then again, Nancy would never have got a job first and then told her parents she was working. When Nancy was sixteen, she had asked for permission and permission had been denied. Annie never asked for permission to do anything. Consequently, Annie did anything she wanted to. And now that Annie was beautiful, her parents seemed as afraid of her as everyone else was.

It was in that same sixteenth year of Annie's life that her parents announced they were moving to Florida.

'We've had it with the bay ... gay and bay ... you know, kids,' their father said, his thick eyebrows rising on every syllable. He had a touch of an Irish lilt in his voice. Annie thought he acquired it in San Francisco, at Molly Malone's Pub. She was sure he was not from Ireland no matter how many times he mentioned his poor miserable childhood back there and how he escaped to make a better life for himself in the States. Annie hated his references to gays in San Francisco. It was all 'ho, ho, ho' and some insipid joke shared with the family in an attempt to feign closeness. His favoured joke, told daily, was to comment while bending over to pick something up, 'Would have to leave that right where it is if this were the Castro or prison. Otherwise, I'd be a soprano.' Try as hard as she might, Annie could never quite imagine her father saying, 'Annie, it's too late but forgive me for all my racist, homophobic jokes,' at her funeral.

Annie thought that her father, more than likely, secretly envied the freedom of the gay lifestyle. Only that could explain his frequent comments on it. Both her parents were terribly prejudiced and conventional.

'You kids'll love it in Florida,' said their mother, her arm resting on their father's for the first time Annie ever remembered seeing. Her mother had more of a Slavic beauty though she swore she had no idea what was her background. She said she was adopted. Annie didn't believe this either. It seemed a much too convenient way of avoiding real conversation – something both her parents did rather well. Not that Annie was a big fan of the art of talking, her role models notwithstanding.

While Annie smiled at the news, Nancy sat staring at the dish of mashed potatoes in front of her, willing the potatoes to erase what she had just heard. Where was *she* going to live? She wasn't moving. The church needed her. She began to say so when Annie spoke.

'Hey, that's great. I'm not coming with you though.' Annie spoke without a hint of regret.

Her parents looked at each other and then back at those shining blue eyes and said in a trance, 'Well, OK.'

Nancy hit the table with her knife and fled the dining room.

* * *

11

Annie knocked. 'Come in,' said a hoarse Nancy.

'Listen, looks like you're upset about Mom and Dad's news.'

'I'm not upset.'

Annie sat down on the edge of the bed and laughed lightly. 'Sure.'

'Well, aren't you upset? They're leaving your junior year of high school. You are going to have to go.'

'No, I already said I'm staying.'

'But . . . where are you going to live? Where am I going to live? And,' she put in as an afterthought, 'what about your studies?'

'Who cares? High school is a big joke anyway. I don't learn much there. Learn more at the boutique from the customers.' Annie smiled, the light in Nancy's bedroom hitting her cheeks in a way that made her look Asian.

'Those upscale snobs? Annie, they're just rich losers. You know where the real power lies.' Nancy looked up at the ceiling and Annie rolled up her eyes so far in her head that she thought she saw a horizon.

'Jesus! Can't we have a conversation without you referring to someone on the roof?' Annie began to leave the room.

Nancy called behind her, 'There are more things to this universe, Horatio, than meet our eyes.'

After slamming it, Annie called through the closed door, 'It's "There are more things in heaven and earth, Horatio, than are dreamt in your philosophy". Just read it in school yesterday. Seems like you would've remembered the heaven part.'

After hitting her pillow fourteen times and feeling she was not nineteen years old but three, Nancy calmed down enough to wonder why on earth she still loved her little sister.

Annie figured that she had saved up enough money to move into an in-law apartment in the Sunset area, about a mile across from her family's soon-to-be-sold home, across Golden Gate Park. Most of the landlords looked rather sceptically at a beautiful sixteen-year-old promising that she could indeed pay the rent.

Thankfully, her beauty, which had been proving a handicap in this situation, was lost on a near-sighted Chinese man who said, 'I like you. You move in tomorrow. I don't need references. I just need see person and know. You good person.'

Annie loved her new freedom away from the family, though her beauty made her feel less free in another way. Now when she boarded the orange bus, heads turned and men smiled. She was always offered a seat, for people treated her beauty as something fragile. She no longer felt invisible.

Annie knew this should have been disturbing but she felt more outside of herself than ever. She could look at herself in a mirror and marvel at what her face had become. She appreciated her own beauty in a detached way, understanding that she had little to do with it. If she were Nancy, she might have got down on her knees and thanked the good Lord ... But she was Annie and felt she had no one to thank. She merely looked for things to add to her rulebook for reference.

Pasted on the inside of her diary was the list which so far read:

1. Life is not to maul and pad over until it's sore and stagnated.
2. Living comes from doing.
3. If you must take advantage, take advantage of those who are more fortunate.

When Fred walked into the boutique one Saturday, Annie was sipping a *latte* from next door. The smell of hot milk and coffee swirled around her and Annie

13

thought it heaven. A light drizzle was falling upon the huge front glass of the boutique and she could just hear the slight brushing of the water. She was the only one in the store and was loving the quiet. Her landlord had gained 200 pounds and now the attempted tiptoeing he was wont to do late at night had turned into a dance of ill-mannered elephants on the parquet floor above.

Fred was so quiet she only noticed him because of the cold draught he brought inside. Annie smiled but didn't offer the usual, 'May I help you?' She knew she could help people and didn't need anyone's permission for that.

'Hi,' said Fred, his eyes locked on to hers, 'saw you from the street.'

'I didn't see you from the street,' replied Annie.

Fred thought about this for a second. He wasn't sure what more he could say. Her lovely eyes had simply drawn him into the store.

'I am, uh, looking for a present for my sister.'

'Older or younger?' asked Annie.

'Older,' said Fred. The place grew startlingly quiet for him. After a long second, he heard what he said and started to laugh. 'Oh hell. I don't know why I'm in here. I just saw you and I wanted to come inside.'

Annie finally set her coffee down. She had been staring at him through the steam up until then. She was seventeen now, would finish high school in two months, and had never kissed a boy. Never. Her beauty scared any high-school boy from asking her out. Everyone had assumed she went out, but in truth, Annie spent her sunsets walking the cliffs of Ocean Beach – alone.

She guessed him to be about twenty. He looked like a nice guy. No one was around, the shop and street were deserted due to the rain. The earthiness of the coffee made her feel comforted inside. She looked into Fred's eyes. They were a vivid hazel and opened wide. Annie noted that he didn't look afraid, only very excited.

'Do you want to kiss me? I've never been kissed.' She said it so matter-of-factly that Fred had to translate from the words to the tone and back to the words again to understand what was being asked.

'You want *me* to be the first to kiss you?'

'Yes.'

He hesitated then kissed her, placing his cold hands on her face. Annie felt the moisture of the coffee leaving her mouth and travelling into his darkness. It was quite pleasant and she began to laugh. A sweet laugh which surprised her the way it resonated warmly in the empty store.

Fred laughed too, without understanding why. He became caught up in Annie's childlike mood following her gleeful discovery. He relished, as most men do, being the first at something, particularly love.

They kissed for nearly a half-hour, standing in the same spot in front of a row of long lilac-blue Jacquard dresses. Thankfully, no one entered the boutique. Although not written in the store policy, Annie had the good sense to understand that what she was doing was highly unprofessional and risky. She absolutely had to keep the job in order to finish up high school.

Afterwards, Annie promised to herself that she would not risk a job again just for a kiss. A first kiss OK, but after that, never.

Fred was not only the first to kiss her but the first for everything else. Annie liked the way he made her melt inside. He made her feel her beauty. Now it didn't seem an unreal thing that had suddenly sprung upon her but a thing which mesmerized both her lover and herself. To see his hands upon her body and to know they were etching the curves with a form of worship made Annie feel grounded. Fred helped her settle into her own skin and appreciate it.

She took him on those walks around the cliffs. They saw the Golden Gate Bridge hit with the pinkness of an

15

April sun. She showed Fred the place atop the steep steps where she felt she could hear something twice removed from its source, just beyond the range of her hearing.

'It's like a portal or a door to another dimension,' she insisted. 'Listen. You can hear "Sigool" or something like that. Definitely an "s".'

'Oh, how sweet to be seventeen again and believe in something!' Apparently Fred's twenty years had taken most of his imagination clean away.

'But I *don't* believe!' Annie had replied, seeing no evident contradiction.

She felt him laugh at her, though his face betrayed nothing. He looked lustful at best, perhaps bemused.

Fred grabbed her and put his hands on her face. 'Kissss me in your sssss,' he shouted. For an odd second, he wondered if what he heard were the trees whispering half-words, but then Annie kissed him and he could only hear the ocean and the whip of her hair around his ears. She was so delicious, a sweet mouth full of sea air.

The fire raced inside Annie. She forgot in an instant that Fred couldn't possibly understand what she meant about the portal. Nearly forgot her newly forming philosophy that it was possible, even natural, to hold two opposing ideas in one's head. Like how she wanted to hold Fred for ever *and* push him off the cliff at the same time. Watching his body slip into the unruly ocean below.

There were others who came after Fred. She met Charles in a Black American Literature class in college and he took Annie, on her twenty-first birthday, to a bar in an unfamiliar part of the city. Unfamiliar to her. To Charles, it seemed his natural residence. He had hoped to shock her with the goings-on inside the bar but Annie enjoyed watching all the sex around her. She had no desire to participate but took in everything: the large girl in the corner who might be rather fun in bed but would not get a chance in the outside world because of her size;

a drag queen whose stuffed breasts blinked 'Love ya' and 'Mean it' who was gladly being fondled by every man in sight; the huge boxes of condoms with happy faces and signs encouraging safe sex or no sex; the friendliness of people who were introducing themselves after having anonymous sex; a room for men only; another room for punishment and punishers.

She went into that last room with Charles. They watched a couple, the man with his back against a wooden beam and a woman in thigh-high white stockings pressing her naked breasts into his chest. Another couple circled around them, hitting both couples on their exposed arses. The woman was getting hit more because she had no beam to protect her. Her partner stroked her hair and kissed her cheeks softly as she was paddled. The punishers were laughing and then broke away to screw discreetly in the corner. The man of the punished couple then grabbed his woman's arse and sat her up on to his cock.

Annie and Charles wandered around the other rooms. She smelt the tart smell of mingled sex juices and found they went perfectly with her cold glass of Chenin blanc. All these disconnected bodies connecting up and then falling away again. Some of the women looked sad.

Charles said, 'Like it?'

Annie stared at him and said, 'I like sex. Let's go home.'

After Charles, she added to her rules:

4. In sex, only two rules apply: no one gets hurt and no one cheats.
5. Be open to everything but don't let everything open you.

At the funeral, Fred and Charles might gather together and murmur to each other about what a fantastic lover Annie had been. Fred would talk about Annie's firsties with him and Charles would talk about his firsties with Annie. She imagined Nancy there, holding her mother's hand and wondering who the two gorgeous men were in the back. Nancy would make a speech about how she'd have liked to have known her sister better. Would anyone care to enlighten her? The two men would come forward, whisper in her sister's ear and Nancy would faint.

Fred and Charles were good beginnings for a woman with Annie's needs. They gave her distance and worship. Most of her lovers did, with two exceptions: one who needed to touch her soul and another who tried to destroy it.

Chapter Three

*A*fter two years in the Sunset, Annie was able to afford moving to an area where the average age was thirty-something and the average income, excluding hers, was six digits. She moved there because she needed more light. She had grown tired of dressing in the Sunset area's fog and then riding over to the sun-enshrouded clothing boutique. She thought it better the other way around: living in light and working in the shadows. Once she saw it this way, she had to move. Besides, her landlord had taken to juggling wooden balls late at night and he wasn't good at it. Now it was like having a very inconsiderate elephant upstairs, shaking an overly ripe coconut tree.

She needed sleep.

The unfettered look of Nob Hill had also impressed her. No visible power lines, no trash, no street people – just smiling, happy, well-dressed young men and women. The public transportation there ran on time, as opposed to the unreliable buses throughout the rest of the city – something German tourists could never get over being amazed at. If the Nob Hill line was a mere thirty seconds late, cell phones came out, speed dials were pressed, and demands were conveyed to the transport's high office. These beautiful people were determined to get what they knew their good looks and salary promised: a classy, high-cut life with no interruptions or delays. It was all hurry up with them and looks of impatience at anything which seemed out of sorts with the angles they had prescribed for themselves.

Annie's leather pants and general latex style of dressing didn't quite fit in with the crisp pastels of the others, but Annie possessed that handsome face which made others forget to notice her outfits. A strange situation for a clothing salesclerk but one she enjoyed until boredom made her change jobs.

It was a good move and she lived in Nob Hill seven years until she broke a few too many of her own rules.

Whiteness spilt off the walls in Annie's small Nob Hill flat, embracing her duvet. Coming from the Marina and glinting off the white-stoned buildings which lined the streets, the dusty morning light seemed to sanctify the room. Lately, Annie needed this feeling of purification and looked forward to each morning. There were times when her dreams sliced through the twilight and she woke feeling her heart forcing her to forget something. When that happened, she made herself go back to sleep, pulling the dim whiteness of the morning and the warmness of her down comforter into her. That fleeting hollow feeling completely evaporated as soon as she left her bed and tasted her first sip of very dark, very rich coffee – nearly the consistency of blood.

Now twenty-five, Annie's current job at Nepravina Advertising dragged her out of bed earlier than any of her previous jobs had. Besides the light, she eventually found other ways to enjoy the early morning hours. An automated coffee maker which ground the beans first helped, as did a kitchen with eastern exposure and a radio station playing twentieth-century classical music. (She'd grown to love the gulag sound in Shostakovich.)

At the office, she appreciated the smell of damp hair on her colleagues, how coffee lingered on clothes, and the different ways people worked themselves into a day. Carol the waif arrived with some piece of her outfit missing – a vest, a scarf, a lapel pin – which she would put on after canvassing the office for opinions she didn't heed; Marty usually came with sheet lines still creasing his face; Peter made coffee slowly, checked his e-mail slowly, read the newspaper slowly, and then, at ten o'clock, went into a panic; Sasha turned on her computer and then inhabited the bathroom for an uncomfortably long period – apparently believing that the new computers took the same amount of time to warm up as 1950s TVs had.

During the first few months at Nepravina Advertising, Annie's alarm clock had cut right through her heart but, with time, she woke before it went off and then let herself drift back into that borderland between sleepy consciousness and waking reality. She wished she could spend more than an hour every morning in that twilight world, for it was where she got her ideas for advertising and any other creative endeavours she might embark upon during the course of the day. Annie felt there was a secret creativity dwelling in those hours that, had she no work, she might find something there, something she was trying to remember. Annie knew she was good at things, but she felt those early hours contained the secret to her being great.

She had been working for this advertising agency for over a year, though, to Annie, it seemed longer, the newness wearing off at about the same rate it had taken her to adjust to her alarm clock. She never worked anywhere longer than a few years. From her work at the clothing boutique, she found she could master anything, given time. Which is why she had to change jobs every few years – out of boredom. If all her bosses gathered together at her funeral, Annie imagined they would compare notes and come up with the same conclusion: Annie was a first-rate employee and nearly impossible to replace.

At the clothing boutique, she had found the exact formula to put a customer together with an affordable and wearable outfit. She knew colours and the people they represented: brown for a background person, red for risk-takers, white for a transcendental mood, plum surely a colour for suicide, and black – sexy yet basic. The store simplified things for her since it only sold monochrome clothing. Annie did not like dealing with patterns and florals. They were too conflicting, out of balance – excessive in their overuse of colours.

Her move from clothing adviser to a job in a legal firm was not as much of a leap as it appeared. Annie discovered that putting cases together with the right lawyers, staff, research and, of course, clients, was something that few eighteen-year-olds, or anyone for that matter, could do. Annie asked the right questions for all sides and then let her intuition dictate who would work best with whom. It hadn't been what her job title specified but the lawyers at the firm were so pleased with the results that they gave her a raise and free reign of the office. Her older boss particularly liked that she never asked a new client, 'May I help you?'

The legal work soon became too easy for her and the problems of the clients too predictable. It was a family law office and the impetus for the clients coming there was that they were sure they were getting screwed. Most of them were selfish and cared more about hurting the other party than reaching an equitable settlement where the children would most benefit. This disturbed Annie, for her idea of living was to solve a problem and keep on moving. Certainly not to intentionally hurt someone. To carry a lawsuit out over two to three years, and then to whine about it indefinitely in front of the child victims, struck at her sense of the proportion of things.

She traded the legal assistant's job for a stint at designing websites – where she lied shamelessly on her résumé about her work experience in the field. Up to then, the only thing she had mastered on the computer was the spreadsheet. After she sent in her résumé, based on one she'd glanced at for a moment in a bookstore, she called her sister to ask about the jargon. Nancy had married by this time and was living with her husband in Silicon Valley.

'You are not going for a job you know nothing about. They'll find out,' her sister had protested.

'They're a corporation. By the time they realise I don't know what I'm doing, I'll know what I'm doing. Please, Nancy, give me some lingo for the interview.'

'I don't like this. You know I'll have to ask Phil. I'm not sure how he feels about the ethics of this.'

'What ethics, Sis? Come on. I'd lie for you in a heartbeat. You know I would. It's just a job.' Annie felt certain this would cut to Nancy's heart. Her sister never wanted to be seen as selfish. It took precedence over being moral.

'I'll do it, Annie, but you know how I feel. There are some ways to do things and then there are Annie's ways.' Nancy's tone was serious, a bit reprimanding. What could Annie expect? Nancy was her older, still religious sister and sometimes forgot she wasn't also her mother too.

'Thanks, Sis. I won't forget it.'

'No, please forget it. Please completely forget it.'

The interviewers appeared to have not even looked at her résumé and no one asked Annie to prove any skills. Each man, there wasn't a woman for miles, seemed a perfect representation of a special class of computer geek. The man on the far left end had greasy hair and very heavy black glasses. He chewed on a pen the entire time, nearly gnawing it down to the ink cartridge. The man next to him was dressed in some version of Gateswear: loosely fitting pants and a few loosely fitting layered shirts in various pastels. The other two men seemed to be in a competition for cheaply made suits – one pilly and solid hospital green, the other in a yellow plaid which looked more fitting for a used car salesman from the seventies. Annie smiled slightly thinking about the state of the briefs beneath those outfits. There has to be holes everywhere, she thought, nodding in a horse-like manner, knowing somehow that she had the job.

These four males gawked at her legs and the hint of cleavage peeking out from under her tightly fitted dress. Annie was aware that this exposure was another form of 'cheating' as her sister would call it, but she knew that the company would be pleased with her after a few weeks, never mind the clothing. She was right. After Annie designed two sites which brought in a huge response, they raised her pay.

Annie did manage to make a friend there. While she was quietly teaching herself coding basics for making webpages, computer books began randomly appearing on her desk. They were always exactly what she needed to solve the problem at hand and Annie found the information so timely and dead on as to be unsettling. Someone there knew she had little more than the faintest idea about what she was doing. Yet, this person was helping, not snitching.

One day, she caught her guardian angel leaving several large books earmarked with sticky yellow notes.

'Hey, this is my cube,' she said, pleasantly, teasingly.

'I know,' replied an attractive Italian-looking man. 'I'm John.'

A line of Ayn Rand's came to her: 'Who is John Galt?' The creator of characters with dreams that they were the ghosts in the machine of the entire world. She didn't like that author.

Instead, Annie asked, 'Not John Cunha?' She had

heard through the grapevine there was a computer genius in their midst, someone who managed to make what baffled the rest of them seem mere child's play. Probably someone the author would have admired.

'That's me,' he giggled. 'And you're Annie. They say "Goddess of the webpages".' He giggled again. It wasn't sarcasm but some hint of a jest.

Annie did not know what to make of him. She was grateful for the help yet annoyed at the intrusion. She had been so good at pulling the wool over the other geeks' eyes. It was not good to be found out so soon.

'Well,' she said after a minute, 'thanks for your help.' She looked into his eyes. They weren't dilating with excitement for her. Nothing about John intimated the slightest hint that he might have an interest in her – hence an ulterior motive. Surprisingly, she wasn't disappointed. Something about him though looked vaguely familiar.

'No problem. Actually, if you didn't do this . . .' he went to her computer, sat down, hit something on the keyboard '. . . and did this . . .' he typed in another code at a billion fingers per hour '. . . you'd be finished by now.' John giggled, turning the monitor screen so dumbfounded Annie could view it.

Annie couldn't control herself and gave in to hugging him from behind, smashing her cheeks into his.

'Ouch,' she said, pulling away.

'Yeah, today's Wednesday. I don't shave until Thursday.' And with that comment, he left her cube, giggling.

Over the next year, she and John had many lunches together in her cubicle. He said he was too bored in his to hang out there. Stupid people who did not do their homework hounded him all day. He brought his lunch of Top Ramen, Annie her bowl of vegetables and brown rice. They sat together at her desk, with John manoeuvring Annie through all the facets of better web-page making.

Where his giggle made her giggle, his swiftness at the computer made her feel inadequate. But due to John's manner of assuring her that it really was very easy, the coding did become so for Annie.

John shared with her his methods of saving money. He brought his coupon filer with him, showed her the web-sites where she could save even more money, split bulk items with her, gave dead-on tips where and when to invest money, and generally gave Annie all the lessons a good Jewish family might have taught her – if she had had one. Annie's own family was prone to buying cheaply made products for the moment of necessity and not planning wisely for the long haul. Consequently, they illustrated the saying that a cheap man pays twice. Annie thought she had done a good job of breaking the McDermott model of thoughtless debt, but John showed her a way to wealth. She wasn't prepared always for the sacrifices he said it took to be a millionaire by the time you're thirty, but she did have to thank him for the growing amount in her portfolio.

It was not a one-sided exchange, though Annie felt it entirely uneven. She did help him with the style of a design, the way to lay out information so consumers would be teased into reading it and seduced into buying it. Yet John seemed more interested in her company, in the idea that they had a secret partnership. It was Annie and John against the rest of the idiots at Webmatter Inc. At her funeral, John appeared on a pedestal, rotating around the room saying, 'She was so talented, so quick. If only she had learnt how to save money better, this funeral might be more spectacular.'

From time to time, John obliquely referred to his friend Angelika. Would Annie like to meet her?

Annie did not know what to make of this. Angelika was, apparently, a performer at one of the clubs in the

Castro. And getting to be famous too. John mentioned that she was even going to be on TV.

Annie, impatient with this sort of guessing game, blurted out, 'Why don't you just marry her?'

John giggled and giggled. 'That might be difficult.'

Annie, for many reasons, all of them involving sex, never did get to the club and meet Angelika. They did meet, however, many years later. Not at a funeral.

Seeing her creativity for layout and design made Annie think that she was in the wrong line of work. The web asked for interesting access of information but it did not play enough with the enticement, the seduction. It was too easy to ask for information and get it. The mystery, the possibility one might never know, was how Annie began seeing the art of seduction. Seduction, indeed, was becoming more of a vital interest to Annie with each passing year. That is how she turned to advertising as her next career. She was already doing it for Webmatter Inc. But their material was so dull. Selling computer chips had a certain type of audience she could only work with for so long.

During all this time, Annie went to school – high school and then college. Her father insisted that she have a good education, but forgot to mention to either of his daughters how they were to pay for it. Once away in Florida, her parents seemed to have forgotten them completely. A lone postcard from Dad in Dade read 'Hey! Never believe this used to be a beach for blacks only! It's beautiful!' Nancy wanted to keep it but Annie insisted they throw it away. Their father had taken his prejudice with him to Florida, and he could keep it there.

Fortunately for Annie, she liked working. Annie was not enough of a stellar student to win any scholarships. Most of her high-school teachers hadn't noticed her in terms of academic performance. A few of the older female maths teachers had – delighting in awarding her

Fs on final exams. One male English teacher read a poem to her for her seventeenth birthday. He had blushed above his beard and Annie had wondered why the fuss. She remembered the first line, 'Come, my Celia, let us prove'. She thought it odd since her name was nowhere near close to anything sounding like 'Celia'.

Annie was surprised to discover, in college, that she loved literature, even though it often broke all of her rules. Literature felt like caulking, pushing thoughts into deep crevices and patching up chips. She discovered the author of 'her' poem was Ben Jonson. While in high school, the rhythm and melody of 'Celia' had impressed upon her that this was a wholly inappropriate poem to read to a seventeen-year-old girl in class; college showed her she hadn't seen the joke in it. No one in class had – that was the point. The bearded teacher had read the poem, laughing at the teenage eyes going blank over a few abbreviated words and strange syntax. Laughing, they didn't understand the seduction:

> Come, my Celia, let us prove
> While we can, the sports of love . . .
> 'Tis no sin love's fruits to steal
> But the sweet thefts to reveal . . .

Annie later thought that to seduce without mutual understanding was akin to rape. The poem's reader was another enactment of the poem – which was beautiful by itself and ugly through the mouth of her English teacher.

Rule 6. Do not laugh at people period. Unless they are Nancy.

Rule 7. Be wary of those who offer to help you – especially older men.

Rule 8. If you are going to seduce, be upfront about it.

At college, Annie took whatever courses suited her fancy, feeling obliged to no one since she was paying for her own schooling and living better than most students who didn't come from trust funds. At the end of three years, she realised that she had enough hours in English Literature to declare it as a major. Not that she thought it in the least useful, but that appealed to her as well. Annie didn't need to hold on to her degree to be respected in the workplace.

Literature coated the inside of her – not only with great quotes from Shakespeare but with a feeling of grandeur mingled with flippancy. Edgar Allen Poe encouraged her Gothic way of dressing while Wodehouse made her laugh harder than she ever had in her life. Joyce's ironic ego filled her with an inexplicable longing to do something grand, and Jane Austen drove her to have tea in the afternoon. In fact, she had tea at four in the afternoon three times a week at the Palace Hotel. Every so often, John Cunha would join her, remarking every other minute, 'This is so fancy, Annie. So fancy.' Then his giggle could be heard bouncing around the marble walls and mingling with the harp music.

Annie understood her readings intuitively, not intellectually. In class, she could turn in brilliant, unusual papers ('*Civilization and its Discontents* compared to *Civil Disobedience*') which received As with comments like, 'I wish you would share your ideas more in class.' Annie was capable of weaving all her readings together into a fragile tapestry which delighted some.

Not all. She received Fs for what one professor deemed, 'A left-field paper if ever I saw one' ('The Mythspelling in Camus' Sisiphuth'). Not so much tapestry as a messy spiderweb.

Carrying her readings into life, without deeply reflecting on any of the themes which had crossed her eyes, Annie somehow managed to tap into, if not 'the' then 'a' psyche of mankind. She never consciously thought about this, the knowledge bubbling in and out with her as an unobstructing conduit.

She worked, slept, never watched television, mail-ordered new clothes and special accessories, drank coffee to the Kronos Quartet, finished school, ended her affair with current beau Jeffrey, and moved to advertising at Nepravina Advertising. John had shamelessly tried to discourage her. 'But now everyone here is so boring. You have to stay.'

Her newest job devoured all spare creativity, often leaving Annie feeling drained at the end of the day, anxious to put something back inside. It was as if the coating from literature was being siphoned off with each day and bits of colour were draining out of her and being given to someone else. The loss and the ache was every-where in her, but most acutely in her cunt. This was where any of her hungers started – large or small. Look-ing for a new dress could start her cunt throbbing as could a juicy prime rib. Annie read literature with her cunt as well. It pulsed to Hamlet's love of Ophelia as well as throbbed when Dr Frankenstein's creature yearned for human contact. It pulsed the most when she was afraid, something she would discover later. It seemed everything, every feeling for her at some level involved sex and an undeniable rhythm between her legs.

Annie began to sense that men know a woman whose being is most at peace in sex. It's not push-up bras that attract as much as the intentions of their wearers. Perhaps that was why she was never without a lover. They came easily to her. Consciously, her blue eyes attracted them and her soft, smooth skin which made them want to stay. Unconsciously, they fed on her because it was her desire. If you lined up all of Annie's lovers (which one might want to do for they were quite gorgeous) and asked what drew them to her, they could not say. It was a yearning to be consumed, to have the irises in those eyes widen to an opening they could crawl through or crash through, depending. She lured, seemed to silently beg *Fill me up*. If they got lucky enough to move beyond admiring her from afar, Annie's utter abandon yet distance in bed enveloped the men in a desire to crack her code, to possess her, to own her. They had to be inside her, every ounce they could squeeze in being one drop short of reaching something they could not name. They never wanted to leave for Annie seemed vast. The Taiga, a virgin wilderness. Wildness.

Annie often wondered what would happen to her with her first rejection. She simply couldn't imagine it. She was the one who always slipped away, without confrontation, just merely disappearing to the bewilderment and sometimes grief of her lovers. Jeffrey had even stalked her and, though she wasn't truly afraid, she used him as an excuse to switch from Webmatter Inc. to Nepravina Advertising. John could understand that one, though they had spoken very little of Jeffrey. Discussion of private lives was not the nature of their relationship.

Annie was afraid of very little – perhaps because she acted first and was, consequently, rarely acted upon. She had hit upon the formula while in her high-school drama class. She had wanted to be an actress until she came upon the line, 'Acting is 10 per cent action and 90 per cent reaction'. She decided it was not the career for her, though she took from it a few credos. She remembered a student doing her best, in front of the class, to show how she was dealing with her mother. 'Stop it,' the drama teacher had yelled. 'Coping is so boring. Do some real acting.'

Annie could not stand people who coped with their lives instead of acting. She did not want to dwell in the intangibility of regrets and hopes. This made it difficult to form close relationships with the women at work because she did not know how to make 'girl talk'. Women would stand near the water cooler and complain about how their partner did this or that which was utterly devastating or depressing for the receiving end. The others would sympathise, offering condolences and good cheer. Annie tried a few times to enter into their conversations but her 'Why are you putting up with it?'s drew jagged looks from the other women. Annie wanted to solve their problems, not re-enact them over and over. She thought she was being helpful but a few glances around at the impatience or confusion on the others' faces told her that it was a game she need stay out of. Her only female friend was Nancy. Not exactly a friend but a sister is not a source to ignore or be ignored by easily.

However, her relationships with males at work were seldom fraught with confusion, being almost completely charged with sexual tension. Annie's way of holding a folder or pointing to a product storyboard seemed meant to entice. Even her gay co-workers smiled at her in appreciation of a well-made woman, which caused a stirring jealousy among their female work buddies. Her sharp new style of dressing, with black lace under a well-fitted business suit, or fishnet stockings with a conservative dress, always drew comments. Nice comments from men, screechy comments from the women behind her back. She was an appealing and popular candidate for presentations where the clientele were most certainly going to be male.

Annie disliked acting but, in front of an audience, she was quite charming. Given a platform, Annie could perform, though she disdained normal talk which seemed to her to consist of a retelling of past events, plans for the future, and, most importantly, where one was going to eat that evening. Perhaps it was the one-sidedness of presentations that brought out the best in her. She didn't crave conversational interaction, wanting to speak or listen – not both. She appreciated being able to speak without interruption, with male eyes looking up at her from a lower seating. Annie was never beneath being worshipped.

Though she appeared to be the kind of woman men need to have and to fill up, no one could accuse her of being overtly flirtatious. Annie seemed so utterly natural and unaffected that even her female colleagues sometimes forgot she was not a part of their group. It was often the women who recommended her for forums and conventions. They weren't particularly angry with her for presenting the 'hollow woman' archetype, and some went so far as to have feelings of admiration for her aloof sensuality. A few pleasant comments had made their way to her, including one she mused over from time to time when stuck on public transportation: 'Even if Annie McDermott were to weigh two hundred pounds, they'd still be beating down her door.'

Wisely, Annie made it a point of not mixing her social life with work. She did not go to lunch with her colleagues. Mostly she brought organic vegetables and fruit, perhaps some brown rice and herbal tea to drink while she continued working. She did not go out much at all. She ate to keep going, to keep her stamina.

Her work was nearly flawless and she gave no one any type of gossip they could sink their teeth into. At work, she worked; at home she fucked. Until Tom.

She couldn't say exactly why she and Tom worked out. On a rare pensive day, when she never quite got back to that white borderland time in the morning but woke instead to pre-formed thoughts she need only step into, Annie believed it was because he did not ask her to be either more or less than who she was. He was not afraid of her sexuality, as some men had been. He was neither jealous nor insecure, and asked very few questions. Most importantly, he didn't demand that she know *him*, in accordance with Rule 18: *To know someone is not always to love someone.* He spoke little and didn't go on about his work or his sexual prowess. That he skated over the standard agreements couples made to each other lured Annie to him and seduced her even after the many months they'd been together. Tom always found new ways to kiss her, seduce her, love her, and keep her wanting more.

He had been present at one of the forums. When she asked if there were any questions, his hand shot up first. 'Could you please brush through that titillating angle again?' Annie, seemingly unconscious she had done so, angled her body sideways so that her left breast could be glimpsed through her blouse. She briefly explained the needs of the market they were targeting while running her fingers up and down her water glass.

She went up to him afterwards and asked, 'Did I answer your question satisfactorily?' She saw the eyes dilate, lips moisten, fingers flex, and knew he wanted her. Instead of handing her a business card and asking for a lunch date, he said, 'Would you come with me?'

Annie hesitated for a minute but he had turned and begun walking. She followed him through a labyrinth of corridors and dimly lit hallways. Then they were outside, he was running down the stairs which connected the upper street to a lower one; she after him, watching his shoulders touched by moonlight and shadows.

Around another flight of stairs. A clattering of their shoes echoing off the street below then only her shoes hitting the old wood. Her heart was pounding. She continued walking down the stairs, feeling on her face the cold night air with a hint of salt from the ocean – something akin to tears.

The heat from her running rose up to her face. She felt it climbing through her hair, somehow making her sense of hearing particularly acute. She heard the far-off cry of the sea lions, the flutter of pigeon wings, an ambulance siren, breaking bottles and young men's voices carrying insults up into the night. Each step up erasing the loss of the chase.

When Tom grabbed her and pulled her under the stairs, she wasn't surprised, only pleased. He kissed her and kissed her and she kissed back, with only her lips touching his. Her arms hung at her side, jostled by Tom's fierce embrace. His mouth was salty and hot and she felt the heat rise up through his clothes as it had risen though hers. She kissed him very hard and pushed him with her mouth, forcing Tom to put his back up against a damp stone wall. He sighed and relaxed his grip on her. She kissed him again, her tongue running along his teeth. She kissed his face hard, even his eyes. He was panting and moved to kiss her again but she turned and ran. Up the stairs and back into the presentation room, where some of her colleagues stared at her incredulously.

'What happened to you?' asked Carol, the waif.

Annie put a hand to her hair to smooth it back into its bun, then shrugged her shoulders. She picked up her portfolio and made her way to her car.

A few days later, Tom called her at work.

'Do you know who this is?' His voice was not deep but it had a throaty quality to it that Annie immediately recognised.

'Hello. I'm sorry I didn't get your name the last time we met.'

'It's Tom. I love the way your tongue moves. You are very sensuous.'

'Thank you, Tom. What's the last name?' She tried to sound casual in case any of her co-workers were listening.

'It's Tom with Stiles Incorporated. I'm their accountant.'

'Thank you for the information. I'll get in touch with you.'

'I'd much prefer it if you'd touch me. I just don't do what I did with you the other night. We must see each other again. Or, I know *I* must see you again. I hope you'd like that too.'

'I'd like that very much. I'll touch you, I mean' – she heard her colleagues laughing – 'I'll get in touch with you.'

'Stiles Inc. Can I help you?'

'Yes, I'm with Nepravina Advertising. I need to locate an accountant who works for you by the name of Tom.'

'Well, that will be easy. We have three accountants and they are all named Tom. I don't suppose you have a last name?'

'No.'

'Well, could you describe him?'

'He went to our presentation last week. He meant to give me a business card but we got to talking and forgot.' Annie kept telling her mouth that too little information was much better than too much but she could not stop herself. 'He has broad shoulders, wavy brown hair, long fingers, beautiful lips . . .'

'Well,' said the secretary, 'you sure *did* get a good look at him. Now, you are describing two of our accountants here. How tall was he?'

Something about the use of the past tense startled Annie. She knew the woman knew this was not a business inquiry. But the voice on the other line sounded reassuring, even encouraging. And it was an older voice. Perhaps someone who would like to see Tom with a woman.

Annie tried to calculate Tom's height, half suspecting this was a test on the secretary's part to discover how intimate the two were already. Tom's chin came to the top of her forehead.

'About six feet.'

'That'd be Tom White,' she said, her voice warmer, amused. 'Nice guy but kind of quiet.' A hint of a sales pitch in the tone. Lilting a little. 'You said you didn't stop talking?'

'Well, maybe *I* didn't stop talking.' Annie laughed and

smiled to herself, knowing that it was always a pleasure to sleep with a nice man. *It is easier to make a nice man sexy than a sexy man nice*, Rule 11. 'What's the number?'

She hung up, let a few minutes pass, then rang up Tom. He invited her over to his office. A competitor's office, Annie reminded herself, making sure that she wouldn't blurt out any company secrets. It wasn't likely, for she did not plan on discussing business.

Annie spoke in a monotone voice as she moved towards the door. 'Carol, I'm going out. Tell Marty the Clarence account is on my desk. I'll be back by two.'

The waif Carol eyed her suspiciously and rolled her eyes over towards another female worker. They knew something was up simply by the way Annie clutched her purse tightly to her chest and walked hurriedly out of the building instead of her usual languorous stride with hands gracefully brushing objects as she went by. Annie saw the picture in her mind of the funeral now, eyes roaming the scene to discover the mysterious man she left her work for. The only one she ever had.

'Send her up,' came Tom's voice through the secretary's intercom.

'The elevator's around the corner,' smiled the secretary, a lovely-looking woman in her fifties with Asian features and a touch of grey in her black hair.

'Where's the stairs?'

Annie ran up three flights of stairs and burst into Tom's office, panting slightly. 'You needed to see me?' she asked.

'Yes. Would you close that door behind you?'

Annie turned and went to close the heavy mahogany door. When she turned around, Tom was standing an inch away. He kissed her left breast through her blouse.

'I loved the way you flashed that at me during the presentation.'

'Did I? I wasn't aware,' Annie said.

'How could you not be aware?' His breath smelled of orange juice and chocolate and Annie simply wanted to eat him. 'The entire audience watching you was producing so many pheromones that I thought I might need a gas mask.'

'The lady downstairs described you as quiet.' She emphasised *quiet*. 'And a nice guy.' Then Annie kissed him.

Tom smiled. He asked her to sit down.

'Where would you like me to sit down, Tom? Near you? Next to you? On you?' Annie flashed her eyes, now a deep blue.

'Actually, across from me would be fine.' He was still smiling, his teeth dazzlingly white and a bit fang-like.

He sat in a black leather chair and Annie sat in a similar one opposite him. They did not speak, simply looked at each other. Annie was amazed she didn't find it utterly boring, being such a violation of many of her rules. There was something so peaceful in Tom's gaze, something so trusting. She didn't feel as if he were trying to sum her up and see what he could get. He seemed to be taking her in – her body and her energy.

There was that heightened sense of hearing again. She heard the hum of his small refrigerator, the ticking of one of the clocks, the faint footsteps above. She detected the same radio station she listened to in the morning playing faintly in the background. She could swear she heard her back muscles relax and the blood thump between her thighs.

He wore a paisley tie knotted neatly near his neck but not tightly. Annie noted that the sperm shapes in the design were especially vivid. Tom's shoulders and arms gave his shirt a square look which was definitely appealing. He had a sexy, dark beauty mark near his lower lip. His brown eyes had flecks of gold in them and they were extremely dilated. His nostrils flared when he breathed and his chest rose discreetly with each breath. Annie sensed that he was smelling her. She liked it.

After nearly fifteen minutes, Tom pulled a book out and read: ' "She came to him to tame him. He came out of the wildness of the woods and she gave him the wildness of her forest beneath her belly." Is that you, Annie? You seem like a high priestess of sex and conquest.'

Annie still stared at him. She had gone into a stillness inside herself that she rarely experienced. It was too pleasurable to give up so she said nothing.

'Not talking? That's OK. I'll talk. I'm a simple person, Annie. I know what I like. I like you. You have a mystery about you that probably makes every man you know want to fuck you. Am I right?'

Annie smiled again, feeling a new kind of warmness spread over her cheeks. It felt like when her mother had kissed her when she was a child, but with an edge. It confused her, this peacefulness yet need to restrain herself.

'So, what I'm saying is, would you like to be lovers? Would you like to be my lover? I'm clean, I'm faithful, and I'll be good to you. All I ask is the same in return.' He said this gracefully, without a trace of confusion, as if he were asking her if she'd like chocolate or strawberry ice cream after dinner.

Annie's smile widened and then, as if replaying the words, started to shrink. 'Hmm. This is quite a proposition. Are we to commit to each other even before making love?'

Tom smiled ruefully. 'I love how you say that. Most women would be coy or ask for more specifics. Not Annie. Dear,' the gold in his eyes caught the light, giving him a panther-like quality, 'I thought we already made love. I'm talking about fucking the daylights out of each other.'

Annie got up and clutched her handbag. 'I'll think

about it, Tom. Really I will. How about a goodbye kiss for encouragement.'

Tom kissed her breasts again through her blouse and then pulled the left one out and kissed it. He kissed Annie softly on the mouth and said, 'I really hope this isn't a goodbye kiss. May I call you?'

'I'll call you.'

She walked to the elevator, her legs rubbery and her knickers soaked. She thought about his graceful hands lying on his lap. They had seemed to be caressing her without moving, much the same way his eyes stared straight into hers and yet she could feel them undressing her, holding her, ravishing her. It was as if she were midway through an addiction she hadn't found the name for yet. She remembered the hotness of that kiss and knew Tom would be a good lover. A great lover.

Why not? she thought, and turned around to go back to Tom's office. She didn't even have to knock. Tom opened the door and thus began the agreement.

Chapter Four

*A*nnie decided that she would never live with a man. They could sleep over but not often enough to leave toothbrushes and socks. With Tom, it wasn't any different, only he never came over: Annie went to his place or to a place Tom had arranged. She liked this. It felt as if they were having an affair, not a relationship. For all she knew, perhaps they were. She hated the word *boyfriend*. And it was freeing to have a man who didn't look in her closet for character clues or introduce himself at social functions with 'I'm Tom . . . Annie's *boyfriend*.'

Compared to her previous affair with Jeffrey, Tom felt like the epitome of a lover with an animal unreality.

Jeffrey, before he had taken to stalking her, left notes. Cute notes which did nothing for their recipient. Annie hated to admit that her main affection for the boy rested solely on his large cock. When Jeffrey pumped her full, Annie felt warmed from the inside out. She didn't need Jeffrey's hands on her body or his lips on her neck but she did need him inside of her pumping away for hours at a time.

Things would have gone on a lot longer had Jeffrey just kept on servicing Annie; however, he had really wanted to have a conventional relationship with her – eventually having kids, a house, maybe even getting married. He worked at wearing a groove into her, where he could rest his head and not move it again.

At first Jeffrey's notes were disgustingly sweet: 'Darling, you are the sun in my coffee, I'm sure now I'm thinking of you, You are the most beautiful woman on the planet, I see my unborn children in your eyes,' etc. But they later came to have an edge whose origin Annie could not quite pinpoint. It was like a Bach fugue that changed keys somewhere but one could never locate the precise measure.

Suddenly, things were in G Minor for Jeffrey. He wanted to see Annie more; he wanted to move in or find a place together; he wanted a promise or an offer of permanence. She never promised and he began writing: 'Why do you treat love like a game? Am I a Monopoly piece? You just play me. Where is this going? Don't I mean anything to you? I see our love as a precious gift that I want to tuck up into a gold box and put in my pocket.' At this rate, he would be tacking notes inside her coffin and proclaiming to the world that Annie and he were just about to make the leap.

The gold box in the pocket did it for Annie and she suggested they see other people for an indeterminate amount of time. He seemed insane for a while, leaving messages on her answering machine which took up an inconvenient amount of time. Annie was too busy to listen to Jeffrey's all the way through and usually erased them after a few minutes. It wasn't that she was being particularly cruel; she simply erased *any* message over a minute long, feeling that if one couldn't say what needed to be said in that time, it wasn't a message but a monologue. Plus, she had already told Jeffrey she didn't want to speak to him any more.

At that time, Annie could not sleep with someone if she felt he weren't a good speaker. Not a talker, but someone who showed imagination. A few words were always needed for the come-on. And they had to be original. Jeffrey's first words had been, 'I'd like to take the blueness of your eyes straight into my groin.' That had worked.

Annie responded, 'I'd like you to try and then I'll suck that blueness right back out again.'

If only he had been as poetic after that. And he never should have written anything down. *The way words lie on a page or on a lover's tongue settles everything*, Rule 19.

For a while things were fine, dazzling even, but Jeffrey began to hold her too close, to whisper he loved her too often (and she never replied), and to be uncontrollably jealous if she did not answer her phone or be at home when he decided to drop by. Annie was not the unfaithful kind in the traditional sense: she did not sleep with others once she had begun to regularly sleep with someone. But she did have her secret time, particularly that white morning time which seemed essential to her. This meant that she would get up at four in the morning and go home or, if they had made love in her place, she would ask the man to go home. Jeffrey never left when she requested so, after a few times, she decided to only sleep with him at his place. Then she would put on her clothes before the sunrise, leave, and make it back into her own bed for a few hours before beginning the day. Jeffrey said she did this because of another lover but how could she explain? So, she didn't.

After he showed up twice at her apartment, early in the morning and just after she had left his place, Annie decided that it was time to put a solid end to the relationship. If she allowed these problems to persist at age twenty-four, what would she permit later in life?

Unfortunately, her usual feat of slipping away was complicated by Jeffrey's unwillingness to believe that she simply had changed her mind and did not want to sleep with him any more.

'What did I do?' he pleaded nearly every day on the answering machine. 'Was I a bad lover? Was I mean to you? Did I change in some way? Did I say something wrong? What? Dammit, Annie. What did I do?'

How could she explain he did nothing except need her more than she wished to be needed? That he crowded her and ate at her sense of the proportion of things? So, she said nothing.

Then came Jeffrey to her door at all hours, throwing the same questions at her, hoping he'd find her Achilles heel and she would fold, saying, 'Come back, Jeffrey.' He was becoming like a drop of rain that wishes to make a hole in a steel wall.

But Annie was already finished with Jeffrey. He was a small circle in her very small concept of things gone by. Once, in a training seminar, the participants had been asked to draw three circles representing their view of the past, present and future. Annie's past and future circles were mere dots while her circle for the present was large and symmetrical.

Finally, not out of fear but out of annoyance, Anne got a restraining order against Jeffrey. He was not to come within one hundred metres of her or he would go to jail. He had seemed to comply yet Annie used the policeman showing up in the web-site office as an excuse to quit.

John was giggling, whispering into her ear, 'I told you *not* to touch that button, Annie. Wait until Angelika hears about this! Crime in our company! You really know how to make a scene!' He was beside himself with excitement.

Everyone at the computer place thought they understood her need to leave and offered her glowing recommendations to Nepravina Advertising, little knowing she had no intention of ever touching a web page again. Nor did she intend to move from her apartment. A change of locks kept Jeffrey at bay.

Chapter Five

'*H*ave you tried the Vietnamese restaurant?' asked Annie's design assistant and office waif, Carol. She was holding Annie's elbow and steering her towards a restaurant around the corner from Nepravina.

'No.' Annie answered quickly.

'Want to?'

'Sure.' Annie didn't sound sure, because she couldn't quite place what Vietnamese food might taste like and wondered if dog were allowed to be served in San Francisco. She also wondered if it were appropriate for an associate to have a hand on her elbow.

Carol failed to notice anything unusual, perhaps because she had already invested so much energy in making herself appear so.

They were seated in a small café with patched-up red vinyl chairs and Formica tables. Voices rang out in gong tones, crashing into each other, sounding musically angry – like all languages one doesn't understand. Annie could imagine they really were in Vietnam, except for the white people in business suits with closely cropped hair. Did the Vietnamese go to the beautiful people's restaurants or was this exchange one-sided?

Carol ordered for both of them. Fresh spring rolls with mint and two 'small' bowls, fit to feed an entire block, of noodle soup with five-spice chicken. Annie loved the spring rolls with their clear dipping sauce. She liked the taste of the soup but could not figure out how to eat the large pieces of chicken in it with her chopsticks. The slippery glass noodles and bean sprouts were giving her even more trouble.

'What do you normally eat for lunch?' Carol asked.

Annie thought for a minute. 'Do I eat lunch at all? – that's the question. I'm usually so busy.' She said this with a hint of pride.

'We can see how thin you are. Now, tell me what you eat.'

'I guess I just have a huge bowl of oatmeal for breakfast and then eat fruit all day.'

Carol looked annoyed and snorted with a full mouth of dripping noodles. 'No wonder you look like you do.'

Annie wondered if the real reason Carol invited her to lunch was to hit on her. It wouldn't have been the first time that a woman had made her attraction known.

But, as the lunch progressed, Annie felt sure Carol was not making any subtle advances, although she was certainly attempting to be subtle about something. Annie chose to ignore it and forced her mouth to engage in some form of conversation. She felt she was in the veil Blake wrote about which separated man from being able to perceive his true reality – what separates us all from each other. It was growing denser with each minute. Annie worried she might not be able to see Carol through the haze if this kept up.

Feeling uncomfortable sitting there making idle chit-chat, Annie thought to involve Carol in a topic which might lead somewhere or nowhere, either fine with its proposer. 'Carol, there are French speakers here, Spanish speakers here, beautiful people from the financial district here ... Do you know if any of the Vietnamese go to their restaurants?'

Carol's eyes glazed over a bit. 'I have no idea,' she said, not intending to get one any time soon.

So, in an attempt to find common ground, Carol and Annie talked about food – good meals, memorable tastes. Carol was executing a near soliloquy on the subject, so little did Annie contribute to the conversation. She could see Carol shocked to learn that Annie's favourite food was a boiled potato. As they were speaking, Annie realised it had been, with reluctance, that she had allowed Tom to take her to her first 'foreign' restaurant, right near her flat. Thai food – lemony, grassy, with basil, peanuts, peppers. Now when she went there – with or without Tom – she ordered nearly the same thing every time: chicken satay or chicken coconut soup, green papaya salad, and pad Thai.

Carol, midst waxing on the pleasures of eating a mango completely naked, interrupted herself and asked Annie what her plans were for dinner that night.

'I have plans,' replied Annie vaguely, sensing that this was the reason Carol invited her to lunch.

'With Tom?' countered Carol.

Annie felt as if a small pin had pierced the base of her neck. She could see the conversation was at last taking the turn Carol had planned on from the beginning of their meal.

'Have you and Tom met?' Annie asked, trying not to sound suspicious.

'Not exactly. But we all know of him. Come on, Annie. Spill the beans.'

But Annie didn't. She didn't tell any more than how tall Tom was and the nature of his job at Stiles. The latter was to make sure that Carol, if she were spying for Nepravina, wouldn't have a thing to show for it. And yes, Annie told Carol, she and Tom were eating Thai food that evening.

'So, are you in love?' bleated Carol in her nasal voice, loud enough to be heard over the slurping of soups.

Annie found this familiarity, this 'hide the ball' conversational tactic, irritating and unnerving.

Carol seemed to be enjoying watching Annie drop her chopsticks on to the table and avoid eye contact.

Not able to see beneath the table, Annie hadn't noticed her own patterned stockinged foot moving in and out of the deep burgundy velvet pump it had been placed in that morning.

Carol, on the other hand, had stopped all her extraneous movements such as her habitual finger-nail biting, lip-smacking and hair-twirling, and appeared to be very calm. She repeated her question, trying to paraphrase it in the manner therapists coach their clients to do: if you want an answer, keep working at asking the right question.

'So, I mean, is it serious?' she asked, a little more softly this time.

'Aren't all relationships serious?' quizzed Annie, unconsciously excluding the superficial ones she deftly maintained with all of her colleagues.

Carol tried again. 'Do you guys have long-term plans?'

Annie, tired of evading the annoying questions, turned the tables. 'Do you really *need* to know?'

Carol's cheeks suddenly matched her hair colour of the week. She stammered, 'No, no. I guess I don't.'

Annie leant forward and whispered in mock confidentiality, 'Can you keep a secret?'

Carol looked relieved. 'Sure.'

Annie grabbed her purse, stood up, and whispered in Carol's ear, 'So can I.'

After work, Annie walked the cliffs in the evening. It was summer and the days were growing longer – though with no guarantee of more sunshine or heat. Mark Twain had said that the coldest winter he ever spent was a summer in San Francisco. Fog rolled in and Annie wondered if her leather bomber jacket was going to be enough against the icy wind. She decided to walk very fast and let her body heat warm her.

In the distance, she could barely make out the top of the Golden Gate Bridge – it hovered like a phantom vapour.

Today, the wind had nothing to say to her since it was shouting at everything. Her skin was being exfoliated from the fine little pieces of grit being lashed around. The black halo of curls twisted up, trying frightfully to leave her skull.

Annie walked down the other side of the steps, to the flowering blackberry bushes and peeling eucalyptus bark. What had this place looked like, Annie pondered, when the Native Americans lived here? It was difficult to tell what was manufactured beauty and what was wild beauty. Surely the wild onions, with their tiny bell flowers, usually drooping, now thrashing, were not there on purpose. Nor the messy eucalyptus. Nor the strawberries, though Annie imagined they came from birds bringing the seeds from the huge manufactured farms to the south.

There were days when she saw the sunshine hit a certain patch of green that she wished she could melt into the landscape. She tried to breathe in the spirit of this nature and to let it embrace her. Watching the grass with its foxtails appearing to run in the wind, she hollowed herself out to the scene before her. The ocean roared and whistled through her and Annie imagined herself like Venus inside a large conch shell.

This is how Carol disappeared, work disappeared, and Tom disappeared. She would meet him in an hour or so but, in the meantime, she devoted herself completely to the cliffs and the wind.

* * *

At the Thai restaurant, Tom kissed Annie's eyes in greeting. He'd already ordered the satay and motioned the waiter to bring Annie a Thai beer.

It was easy for Annie to be with Tom. He wanted to know about her day ... or not know about it, depending on how she inclined the conversation.

She told him about Carol, questioning aloud why it was that women had to sink their teeth into other women's affairs. What was possibly exciting about that? Why not just get their own affairs?

'That's why they're so boring, darling. Not like you. You are concerned with much more enticing topics.'

Tom then reached under the white tablecloth and began brushing Annie's inner thighs, delighting in finding the tops of stockings and not the smooth line of pantyhose.

She said nothing, only stared intensely at him, the one eye seeming to look deep into him and the other to see something far away as well.

Tom adored those eyes but could not look into them for long. They had a strange ability to make him feel false. Her lower lip moved in a sign Tom knew meant Annie was fully excited. He pulled his hand out from under the table and fed Annie another piece of the satay.

'Darling Annie, you are a dream come true.'

For a fleeting moment, the gawky child reared its head and completed the taunt of her childhood: *a carpenter's dream – a flat board.* But it died away in an instant and Annie replied, 'I'll make it *come* true for you,' she teased. Later that night, she did, feeling sure that all those little boys who teased her were certainly not getting any of what she could offer now.

Annie felt Tom had a secret which he was close to sharing with her. It made her nervous, for she would've liked the exchange to be even but she could think of nothing confidential to give him.

His secret had also given her room to lie, something she did not wish to forsake.

For so lying, I do not lie. If Tom didn't know who she was, didn't know the gawky kid she'd been or the fantasies she was not quite ready to share – Annie could be anything, anybody at any moment. The freedom was profound and necessary to her. It filled her body with a kind of certainty and her mind with what she believed was clarity.

Chapter Six

The communication she had with Tom felt devilishly reckless. She used all modes her office offered. She faxed pictures of her breasts hidden within standard-looking documents. Tom, similarly, played a 'Where's Waldo' game by sending her fake ads with little cameos of Annie going down on him hidden in the leaves of a tree or the ice of a drink.

The telephone and the e-mail, however, were their favourite means.

'Annie, this is Tom.'

'Hello, Tom.'

'Could you please come over? I think my penis is broken. It's completely stiff and sticking out. Would you be a dear and rush over with some first-aid?'

Dear Annie – Here's an e-mail limerick for you. Made it myself. Don't forget to erase. Anyone could read. Annie, a lass of five and twenty / Gives head good and plenty / a penis to sip / with a stiff upper lip / try toothpaste next, dear, hot and minty.

* * *

Dear Tom, to you I reply / that your cock makes you quite a guy / I absolutely trust / how into me you do thrust / get over here and unzip your fly.

Annie with your velvety tongue / I say, it's my bell you have rung / while quoting the bards / don't forget to see cards / in Tarot deck, I'm the man who's well-hung.

Tom, how sweet are your aims / to get me to play some 'them' games / Tarot don't believe / however, see my sleeve / up there you'll find magic by other names.

Dear Annie, look up *merkin* in your OED. I got you one with jewels.

'Hello, Annie, how's work?'
　'It's fine, though I'm about to go to a meeting.'
　'What if I met you later, tore off your knickers and stuck a greased finger inside you?'
　'Well, that sounds very nice. Let's discuss it later.'
　'Did I make you wet?'
　'Yes you did. Very.'
　'Would you like to spread that wetness on my face? Kiss me with your cunt?'
　'Yes, that would be fine, though I'll have to get back to you.'
　'When would that be?'
　'I have some time available today around four. You can come to the office.'
　'May I also come in the office?'
　'Yes, that would be appropriate. See you at four.'

Dear Annie – another limerick. There was a woman with a mole / located on the other side of her hole / it took all my might / for me not to bite / while spearing her with my big pole.

* * *

Dear Tom – I am so happy for your meat / that it often gets such a treat / refrain from chewing / while in my hole you're spewing / and I promise you I will not beat.

My Dear, on the other hand / perhaps you would find it quite grand / to have a little spank / before I suck your wank / if you don't bite me, I won't hurt your gland.

The communication between them flowed freely and, at times, Annie could not work from the sheer sweet agony mounting up inside her. She found new ways to cross her legs in meetings, thinking of Tom and sending little shoots of excitement throughout her body by pressing her thighs together or wriggling just so in her leather chair. She knew it was not safe to use her company's e-mail and telephone for such delicious keep-in-touches, but couldn't resist.

'Annie, we need your perspective on this,' said Peter, a man who always wore a white shirt, reminding her of Nancy's Phil when he thought of becoming a minister. An unevenly handsome man, nose pug, jaw square, eyebrows wiry.

'You've got to target them at the core – we're not really selling oranges here but sunshine,' she rattled off without thinking. Annie often amazed herself at the dexterity her mouth had when she suspected there wasn't a single thought in her head, only the blood pulsing in her nether world.

'Thank you, Annie. I believe you are right that orange commercials about oranges are not what we are after. Any ideas we can sink our mouths around and touch?' Peter was playfully drumming on the conference table with his left hand while seeming to wink at her over the coffee cup in his other hand.

'I will have something juicy for you very soon, Peter. You know I'm good for it.'

'But, is it good for you?' he asked in a monotone voice

and the meeting suddenly got very quiet. Annie was certain they knew Tom had been in her office with her; that she had gone down on him while clients were waiting outside for their appointments. A few coughs from the men and one or two snickers from the women made Annie momentarily wince.

She knew that her job now had a terminal illness and this news, surprisingly, made her feel relieved. Annie could endure anything if she knew the end was in sight.

'Actually, most things are good for me,' she said, pulling her papers together and laughing in a way that sounded to her observant ears slightly unbalanced. Annie hoped no one noticed.

She went out of the office that day feeling like the Dostoevsky narrator of *White Nights* who senses all of St Petersburg architecturally.

Her office was downtown in the shadows but if she walked for two blocks, there was sun again. The pastel-coloured homes, so close together like false teeth, smiled at her. She sent thoughts to them as she walked. You're looking fine today with your smiling bay windows. Oh no! Who put green cement on your lawn? Why do you, Mr Whitehouse, have a facade upon your facade? Old Victorian, was the earthquake truly frightening and how did you survive?

Those homes acknowledged her, smiling back. Annie sensed it. That acute sense of hearing happened again and she thought, for one instant, she heard tittering; old lady tittering. No one. A crow dropped its shadow on the awning of an off-white building. Little baby foot-prints permanently sunk into one of the sidewalk squares rose in front of her and she stepped on them.

The air parted silently to allow her to pass and soon she would be back to her sunny upstairs flat. If she curled up in her big chair, she could just see the Golden Gate Bridge through her window.

She decided what she was going to do was what she was already doing: go home and forget about everything. Make up some new rules and keep going. What's done can't be undone – only redone. Or, she mused, done again and again. A wicked smile came over her face. It had been worth it.

A mouthful of Tom while she watched feet hurry about the one-inch space at the bottom of her office door. Muffled voices and the energy of confusion seeping under. 'Should we go in? Should we tell the clients? How long will it, uh, take?' And Tom thrusting so slightly, his back up against the door (too bad it was not padded) – grinning with his hands laced into her black locks. Such a stealthy lover, able to release himself with only a very slight gasp from his lips. Annie could never have had such restraint.

This image of Tom stayed with her a moment but became fuzzy. It faded to his full pubic hair and then to the sensation of what he tasted like before he came. She brushed even those glimpses aside and instead said a mental hello to the Thai restaurant with its Byzantine dome and pale pink exterior. She walked past the cheese shop owned by a handsome gay couple, past the teddy-bear and chocolate store, past her old coffee place with a line now out to the sidewalk ... six more shops, three more restaurants, and she'd be home.

Just keep walking, Annie. That is the main thing.

Chapter Seven

*I*t was Wednesday and Annie had taken the day off.
   'Open me anytime,' said the envelope. Inside Tom wrote:

My darling. The only thing I can think of is your smell and your incredible juices. You smell like the ocean. And the forest together. Our lovemaking last night changed my DNA. God, how I want your body. I want you all over my face, my beard. I want to see your breasts move when you sit on top of my dick. I want to see how your body sways and glistens to its own music. I want to see your white ass, perhaps a bit pink from where I held you too hard but you liked it. I want to give you pleasure. You know I can. You didn't come enough last time, sweet. Come to me for more pleasure.

Annie squealed, something she rarely did alone. She felt hot from reading the letter and reached over to the phone to call. She had just finished the last sentence when he answered.
   'This is Tom.'

'I want to suck you and lie on top of you and ride you until you come so hard inside of me that you think your head is going to explode.'

'That's very nice. I get off work at five today. Would you like to meet at my place?'

'I dream about your cock and how you thrust yourself inside of me. Your letter made me so wet. What should I do before I see you at five? Should I masturbate with one of our toys on your bed? I can leave my juices every-where, if you like.'

'Yea. That really sounds like a great idea.'

'Do you have a hard-on?'

'Yes, yes I do believe so.'

'Are you sitting or standing?'

'Yes I am.'

'Standing?'

'No.' Tom's colour was rising to his face and he worried the other Toms might notice.

'Sitting. Good. Imagine me sitting on your lap right now and your cock thrusting up into me until my tits are shaking.'

'That sounds good. But I have to go. We'll follow this up at my place, OK?'

'OK.'

She wondered at times if she and Tom simply worked out because he only lived four blocks away. Uphill to get there, downhill at four in the morning. Safe neighbour-hood. Easy and convenient location for quick sex and then home for a good night's sleep. Location, location, location.

Annie put on a strapless black dress and wore no pantyhose. She threw her toothbrush in her make-up bag and ran out of her flat. Soon she came to the brown-stoned apartment building and she let herself into the top-floor apartment.

Tom had some flowers sent over and the doorbell rang

a few minutes after she got there with his thoughtful gift. She tore off her clothes and some of the rose petals and put them on the bed, on the pillows and a few half up her ass. Then she opened some champagne, lay stomach down on the bed, with her bottom facing the door.

She heard Tom come in and she pretended she didn't. She made motions like she was playing with herself. Suddenly, he grabbed her ass with both his hands. Hard. Then he said in a low voice, 'You've been a very bad girl and I'm going to have to spank you.'

'OK. I have been really bad.'

He lifted her on to his lap, she never once turned around. Then he began spanking her gently and every once in a while not so gently. She climbed off his lap and positioned herself doggy-style on the bed. He spanked her more rhythmically and she turned around to watch.

It was not Tom! She pulled away and the man said, 'Don't worry. Tom sent me here to keep you busy until he arrived. How should I do that?'

'Hmm,' she sighed. She had known Tom a while. Was this true? She decided to wait. 'Let's drink champagne and wait until Tom gets home.'

'Well, Tom paid me to begin having sex with you so that he could walk in and join us.'

'He can still join us. Let's drink champagne first.'

'You have a fantastic ass. I love the rose petals you shoved up there. They made me want to fuck you immediately.'

'You will fuck me soon, I am sure. Do you have a nice cock?'

'Look,' he said and pulled down his pants. Out sprang a huge member and Annie looked at it greedily. It was long and fat and smooth as marble. She had never before seen quite a thing and thought that with a cock like that, who needs toys. Perhaps that was what Tom was thinking.

'It's really beautiful. Do you show it around much?'

'Only to clients. I am disease-free by the way, if you'd like to see my chart.'

'What does that mean? You could have fucked somebody on the way over here.'

'That's true, but I didn't. I had my last test two days ago and this is only my moonlighting job. Really, I'm an actor.'

'With a dick like that, I'm sure you could find some rich lonely lady to support you and your expensive career choice.'

'Been there, done that. You can see my movies later. Want to touch it?'

'Why not? It looks so inviting.'

'Have you been a good girl? Maybe I should spank you some more first. I think you like that.'

'God, I do love it. OK, but gentle. On the fat part of my ass. If I put my ass out like a dog, I can feel your spanks on my clit.'

'God, you make me hot. Tom is a lucky man.'

He began to spank her slowly. After five swats, he reached through her wetness and rubbed her clit. She moaned and he withdrew to spank her again. 'Don't forget to be a good girl,' he reminded her.

'I'm a good girl. Spank me.'

'Just for that, I'm going to rub your clit again and make your head spin.' He played slowly with her clit, feeling the right pressure she wanted by noticing her moans. He began pressing harder and Annie began moving like an animal. Her left leg began to shake and he pressed a little less. She relaxed and then he began again. 'You're to come only for Tom.'

She was breathing quickly and hoarsely – locomotive style – and didn't hear Tom's arrival. He motioned to the other man to say nothing and quickly threw off his clothes. Tom stood beside Annie and began massaging her breasts. She still couldn't see him. The other man continued playing with her clit and she began to cry with ecstasy. Tom licked his fingers and gently pulled out the rose petals from her ass. He licked his little finger and pushed it slowly up her hole. She flinched for a minute and then began breathing even harder. Her asshole tightened around his finger and he was afraid he wouldn't be able to pull it out. She was about to come.

The man stopped rubbing her and Tom entered Annie from behind and she began to come. He rode her hard and didn't stop when she was finished. A few minutes later he came and they fell exhausted on to the bed. Tom pulled out and the other man put his face into Annie's crotch and began eating.

'Ohmigod. Ohmigod.' She writhed some more and didn't seem to want any more pleasure but Tom asked if he could pin her arms down.

'Honey, I want to give you as much pleasure as I promised,' he murmured. 'I want you begging us to stop. Maybe after your tenth orgasm, we'll take a break.'

'Ohmigod. Ohmigod.' Annie looked up at Tom and smiled and then her face went blank as the man sucked her clit through his teeth. He rolled it back and forth and she melted. Her juices were everywhere and Tom looked on. He went to the bathroom to wash himself. When he returned, Tom stuck his dick into Annie's mouth. He held her arms down again and the man continued to suck on her while she still came. Her body was rigid with pleasure, almost pain.

'Suck harder, princess. I can feel you. Come on, sweet baby. That's right. You always do it right. You always suck the best way. Good baby.' Soon, Tom came in her mouth and Annie swallowed it.

All three of them lay back on the bed and looked at the mirror overhead. Annie saw that beautiful cock again and remembered that she hadn't been offered it. They both seemed to understand. Tom grabbed her and pulled her on top. 'You haven't tried his fantastic cock yet, have you?' She shook her head no.

The man climbed on behind and Tom held her and kissed her and caressed her breasts while the man from behind stuck his thick dick into her. Tom held her tight as she had another orgasm. The man quickly came and Tom said, 'I think we ought to drink to that,' and got up and got some champagne.

'To making me die from pleasure,' toasted Annie with her smooth voice. 'Thank you gentlemen for knowing how to please a woman.'

'Thank you for knowing how to please us. You know what you want. It's so freeing. My name is Brad.'

Annie eyed him and then looked at Tom. She began to wonder how they knew each other, but neither of the men volunteered any information. It was Annie's rule of life that you didn't give to people what you don't like to receive. She hated prying questions and so chose not to ask them of others. 'Brad, you have a beautiful cock, as I said before. And it feels glorious to have it inside me. Tom, you too. I'm a lucky woman.'

She got up and walked to the sink. The kitchen lights were not on and the lights from the city glistened off her back. Tom was in love again. He loved her so much and felt so sure of her love for him that he didn't mind sharing her. Annie really seemed pleased by his present.

'Hey, Annie,' Tom called out to the kitchen. 'How do you feel if we have another time like this?'

'With Brad? Do you want to, Brad?'

'You make me so hot. I just want to warn you guys up front that Annie is the kind of woman that I could so easily fall in love with. And that would make everything very messy. Let's just do this sometimes, OK?'

Tom looked a little uneasy but Annie didn't seem to notice. 'Yes. Prolonged pleasure, or the absence of it, makes the real pleasure so intense.' She tossed off those lines and felt a bit surprised at her poetic abilities after such a mindless romp.

'Annie! Now I'm turned on by your mind and just

want to throw you down on the bed and fuck you again,' panted Tom, eyes dilated so widely the gold flecks in them seemed to quiver.

'Well, what's stopping you?'

'OK. Brad, can we catch you next time? I'll call you. Feel free to use the shower or listen if you want. I think Annie would like to be heard. And I would like that she's heard.'

Tom began kissing Annie slowly and passionately. He moved down to her breasts and began to suck the nipples, tenderly and then sometimes harder. She put her hand underneath his body and began slowly rolling his balls back and forth. Tom began to tell her how good that made him feel and she felt another rush of heat go through her body. How she wanted him every time! Was it possible? Could you want somebody so much? He drove her wild.

Tom positioned himself on top of Annie and looked into her eyes. He slowly pulled her body lower and raised her legs. She remained passive, staring intently into his eyes. The very tip of his cock touched her soaking vagina. He moved it slowly inside until the last fourth was still outside her cunt.

Then he thrust it in. Annie cried out and he held her hands down and interlocked his fingers with hers. He could feel the heat rise in her body. Her lips grew red and the pupils in her eyes grew large. She looked at him with so much desire he thought he might cry.

He shoved more. He raised her ass and pushed himself deeper inside. Annie couldn't control herself, how she felt so filled up, worshipped, craved. At that very moment, she thought, 'loved'. She put her knees around his back and he seemed to grow even further inside of her.

She could feel the tension building, as his balls slapped her ass. They hit with a wet glee. Tom's cock stretched her and she felt as if she had taken a hit from a joint.

'Oh Tom. Ohmigod. Yes. Yes.'

'You like how I'm fucking you?'

'Yes. How you fuck me. How you make love to me.'

'Annie, I love you. Can you feel my love? I want to give you it now. I want to shoot into you. God, you are so tight I can't control myself.'

'Tom, you can come into me. Come to me. Tom, now is good. Tom, yes, yes,' she cried now. It sounded like she was in agony but Brad understood differently, as he closed the front door.

Was it love though? Annie touched her diary every morning, considering if new rules needed to be added or old rules touched up. It was part of what she considered every morning between snooze alarms: do I need to add or subtract? Forward or backward? An emotional accounting of how she had spent her energy.

After last night, though, doing took precedence over thinking. Something was needed to ease a mild haunting feeling in her. She wrote her first line, considering that today might be the day she would actually begin keeping a diary.

'Is this love?'

It felt foolish. She stopped writing. Did love even matter in the picture? She adored Tom, he adored her and gave her great pleasure. But, somehow after they parted, she rarely gave him much thought. He existed when they touched but did not have a permanent residence in her mind or heart.

He'd never been introduced to Nancy so Annie couldn't even discuss Tom with her sister. It might have made him more real but there wasn't any part of Annie's psyche which could permit him to be more than a lover she took, so to speak, in and out of the closet from time to glorious time.

Annie lived as the opposite of Nancy. But who was whose shadow? Annie felt sure that she didn't pick her path in life merely as a foil to Nancy's straight ways. Nancy would've contemplated this tenuous situation with Tom to the very bitter end, Annie felt. Turning it over and over again, seeking a kernel of truth in the lover. Nancy did so with Phil – despite how much Annie cut to the chase of her complaints. To Annie, it just looked like her sister came back in a muddle to point one.

Nancy's question: Why won't Phil take me out?

Nancy's answer: That's for God to know. Don't judge.

Nancy's question: Why won't Phil help me in the kitchen?

Nancy's answer: Phil doesn't help in the kitchen. He believes that part of the Bible, at least.

Annie wondered why she was even included in on the one-sided conversation. When the topic got to Phil's poor love-making skills, Annie drew the line very clearly for Nancy.

Annie asked, 'Why don't you just leave him then?'

'Thanks, Annie. I'll be sure to talk to you only about finance next time. I just needed to complain to someone.'

'Don't complain, *do*.'

It came to Nancy, yet again, that Annie just didn't get that things were not so easy. Or that by discussing, she *was* doing something. Nancy wondered if her sister wasn't missing some gene the rest of us have which makes us human. Her sister had always seemed to her either infinitely superior or infinitely inferior to her species.

Chapter Eight

*T*he next night, Annie was at Tom's. Her dream happened again. Annie would come to a large room with many men and women in it. She would smile but they wouldn't respond. She then would take off a piece of clothing; each time it was something different in the dream. Often it would be her pantyhose. An older man would stretch out the article and everyone would walk by to examine it. Some of the women would comment on the quality. Annie would then take off a second piece of clothing, usually her blouse. There would be a sigh in the crowd and then the black-haired man with the wolf eyes would come forward.

She loved his eyes. They bewitched her. He would say in a very low husky voice, 'I can't control myself. I have wanted you for ever. I'm going to have you now.'

She felt confused with all these people. Would they watch? Would they touch her? The man would say, 'I said I want you now. I am going to have you everywhere I want you. Come with me now.' And he would grab her wrists not so gently.

Suddenly she'd be on the street and the black-haired man was nowhere to be seen. She would be naked now in the street, worried where to go, knowing that the man had left her. Then a limousine would pull up and the back door would open. There would be the man, smiling and surrounded by young women. 'You too, now.' He commanded and she would get inside.

The leather of the seat felt cool while many other dainty hot things touched her. Annie wasn't able to make out from the bumping of the car who was touching her intentionally and who was not. The man thrust her legs open and pushed in a leather-gloved finger. Then he pushed in another. Then he pulled them out and stuck one very wet finger up her ass.

'She's hot and ready. Now, ladies.' The women hooked her wrists into some kind of silk-feeling straps and attached them to the sides of the car. Then they wrapped her knees with the same kind of material and attached her to each door handle, leaving her completely exposed and vulnerable.

'My dear, this limo is full of lesbians. We smelt on your clothing that you're one of us. You see, I'm a woman too. We are now going to fuck you silly and there is not a thing you can do about it. Heather, where's the gag? Thank you, dear. This is so our driver doesn't suspect that we are having a complete orgy back here. You are excited, aren't you? Of course you are. You are dripping all over this nice leather seat. Angel, clean her up, would you?'

An Asian woman smiled and got between Annie's legs and right up into her crotch. Annie tried to keep her away. She didn't want to be a lesbian! But she couldn't move the right way. When she tried to move at all, it seemed like she was intentionally grinding into Angel's face.

Cries went all around, giving Angel praise. 'That's how to lick. Good girl. Suck her clit. She writhing now. She wants you. Nice tongue work. Look at her. She's bucking like a horse.'

Annie's left leg began to twitch and then her right. Another woman was shoving her fingers in and out of her vagina, and the leather glove had been left behind in her asshole. Then she saw a dreadful thing. A video camera. The idea that she was acting shot a hot feeling of dread radiating out from her stomach. She could see them all licking her and fondling her. She wasn't a lesbian but she gave in. The pleasure was too intense. Women were kissing her breasts, drawing her nipples into their mouths. Someone had begun a hickey at the nape of her neck. Row after row of women seemed to be sucking and prodding her cunt until she was no longer sure there was anything there except her wetness. She felt so swollen and satiated and yet they still kept giving her head. She moaned through the gag to stop. She writhed from the pleasure. She felt she would pass out. She did pass out.

That is how the dream ended every time. She decided to tell the dream to Tom. She was feeling closer to him. Or wanting to be closer – she couldn't say. It seemed important that he know her dreams. She thought that perhaps, one night, she might even try to stay the whole night. Telling the dreams was a step towards that.

'Don't worry, my sweet. You're not a lesbian. You just love sex. What's wrong with that?'

'How would you feel if you dreamt that you were being fucked to death by a million men?'

'Well, what if I did have a dream like that? It doesn't mean that I'm a homosexual. It just means that I would like to experiment.'

'So you don't think my subconscious is trying to tell me something?'

'Only that you need to have as many orgasms as possible in this lifetime. Let's go for one now. Your dream turned me on. Can you see?' Tom pulled back the covers to reveal a huge hard-on.

'Oh lover! You always do the most wonderful things. Like always being hard. Tie me up and fuck me like a bunch of sex-starved women.'

'Can do. Which side of the bed?'

'Your side. Don't forget the key.'

Tom pulled out a pair of handcuffs and fastened one around Annie's left arm. Then he raised her arms above her head and pulled the handcuffs through the slats in their headboard. He fastened her other hand and then pulled each of the cuffs a little tighter.

'Are you comfortable?' he asked.

'Yes. For Godsakes, please slam the living daylights out of me.'

'I'm going to rub you first. I want your first orgasm to be manual.'

'Where did I find you? I love your digital work.'

Tom went to his pinewood armoire and pulled out a pair of black gloves. He slowly caressed Annie's body, pinching her nipples and pulling on her toes. His hands slid up her thighs.

'You are a good girl, aren't you? Because if not, I'm going to stick my hand up your ass.'

For a moment, Annie truly felt alarmed. She had never had anything larger than a finger up her ass. She wasn't sure she ever wanted more than that.

'Yes, I am a very, very good girl,' she replied with a little desperation in her voice.

'Because if you're not, I really am going to fuck the daylights out of your ass and you are not going to be able to do anything, tied up as you are.'

'But I am a really good girl. You can see. See how wet my cunt is, sir.'

'It's good when you call me sir. I won't stick my hand up your ass now, only one little finger. There. Oh, you are squirming a bit. Do you want more fingers?'

'No, sir. One is just great.'

Tom began moving his gloved middle finger inside

Annie's ass, making slow little circles. Then he shoved his thumb into her waiting cunt. He began moving both fingers so that it felt like he was massaging her insides. It made Annie cry out.

'Now, remember. No crying. You must be very quiet or I really am going to stick my whole hand up your ass. Now just lie there and relax. I'm finger-fucking both of your holes. I like how they meet. Ah. You like it too. You are so hot.'

Tom moved his fingers back and forth, shoving one in while pulling the other out. Annie felt filled up. Then Tom went down on her clit and she began to come, her body shaking so much that she bounced up and down on the bed.

'Now that's a very good girl. You are so open right now. That's right. Keep coming. Good princess. Good baby.'

Tom pulled his fingers out, twisted her arms, and turned her over. Annie was still moving to the post-pleasure waves soaring through her. She was compliant to anything. Tom then began putting Annie's juices on his cock. Annie kept calling out, 'That was fantastic,' but Tom said nothing.

Annie felt his hard cock press up against her ass. She lifted her ass a bit to allow him to get to her still throbbing vagina. Tom gently pushed her ass down again. Then Annie felt his cock pushing at her asshole. He unlocked the handcuffs.

'Relax, Annie. Let's try this. I've dreamt of it.'

'OK. But it means that I am no longer,' she said between pants, 'a good girl.'

Tom slowly put the tip of his cock into her ass. She was still very tight. Annie tried to relax, allowing Tom in an inch at a time. She decided she liked the sensation and tried to lie very still while Tom slowly fed himself inside.

Tom felt that her ass was even hotter than her cunt,

but he tried to control himself from just thrusting away like a madman. He really didn't want to harm her. She felt so good, like she was squeezing come from his dick. Annie seemed very still. Tom sighed as she reached her hand under herself and began rubbing her clit again.

Annie kept telling herself not to clench. It was hard. She was fighting the need to tighten and relax, tighten and relax, which had helped her so much to come. Now she tried only to relax.

Tom was almost all the way in now and Annie felt very excited but afraid to move.

'God, Annie, it feels so good. Are you OK?'

'It feels wonderful.'

Annie poked her rear out, allowing Tom completely free access. He was delighted.

'I'll just squeeze you until you come. I'm afraid a little now about you moving in and out. Next time, OK?' Annie said between pants.

'OK, but I'm going to spank you for that.'

'I wish you would.'

Tom began spanking her white ass and began thrusting, despite what she said. Annie was so wet it didn't matter. Tom was so turned on that he came quickly and Annie felt a new sensation of hot liquid inside her ass. She now understood why some people got off on enemas. It felt grand.

Yet when she returned home that early morning, she felt empty. Tom had touched her deeply physically but not fundamentally. She felt free around him, almost too free. There was no risk, except the possible loss of her job. No emotional risk and no powerful connection. She invested her energy in her sex with him but it seemed to come back to residing in her. Strangely, she felt sure that the energy, a feeling, would begin to grow.

Annie was hard pressed to say exactly where the disconnection was. Nothing in literature quite expressed it, nor had she hit upon anything while writing her 'rulebook'. How could such pleasure make her feel unreached?

Perhaps, she thought, I'm suffering the sadness after lovemaking, described in some of those poems I read. I've come so often that now I'm terribly sad.

Thinking on this, she was surprised to find tears on her face – hadn't realised she'd been crying.

The dusty light of morning pricked her. It was not the right hue. Instantly, she realised that she'd overslept.

To the closet to pull out three various pieces from the wardrobe. Annie's sense of uncluttered style had some-how made everything she owned interchangeable. She pulled on a short black leather skirt, a tight grey vest and a jewel green sweater. She pulled her curly black locks back into an unbrushed ponytail, brushed her teeth while washing her face.

On the bus, she realised that her life didn't allow time for a crisis. She wanted to have one. A little private crisis to understand the tears.

Later, she told herself, later.

Even thinking it, she knew she'd never spend the time to find out what was troubling her, if anything really was. She scoffed at those who went to therapy, spending thousands of dollars just to find out that there is no place to go. Annie's solution to anything was to greet it full on with maximum activity. Going to Tom's that night appeared the prescription to dry up the tears and to make sure she was doing something and not running away from something. Annie thought those were the two basic directions anyone took in life, at any moment: fight or flee. She fought with energy, though, not with words or fists.

Chapter Nine

'*A*nnie, this is Brad.'
　　'Brad, how did you find my work number?'
'I know where you work. I work across the street. That's how Tom and I met. At the bar on the corner. You know the dark dive? The one made for affairs?'
'Yes, I know it.'
'Tom and I had one there.'
'Had what there?'
'Annie, don't be so naive. Think about your lover. Think about his needs. Think about my needs. I need to shove my throbbing dick up you right now.'
'Brad, this is going to have to wait. Everything. The conversation, the invitation . . .' She smiled and looked down at the line of her co-workers. 'I really can't talk right now. I am swamped. Good luck.' Annie hung up the phone.
'What was that about?' asked Carol, now pink-haired and yellow-fingernailed; she was perpetually redesigning herself.
'Why are you asking?' Annie eyed her back. Carol moved away and Annie stared back down at the papers on her desk.

Carol and Peter exchanged a long look, which ended when Peter brought his oversized coffee cup up to his face, obstructing the view. Annie failed to notice that he seemed to be winking at Carol and that she was rolling up her eyes and, for a ghastly moment, looked like a reverse albino. The overhead light made strange squares on Peter's balding head.

How could this be? Annie pondered. Is it possible that the true love of my life is gay or bi or whatever you might call it? What about last night? My ass is still sore but ... what am I thinking? Honestly, the idea doesn't even bother me, though the deceit does. Nancy would say you are truly immoral, Annie. You are excited if anything. Brad and Tom together ... and you could watch. You could tell Tom right now that you want to watch. If it were Tom and another woman, that would ... well, bother me. But this. Thinking of the tryst made last night's tears move slowly to her groin.

She was so wet and the yearning between her legs so strong that she went into the restroom to masturbate. Yet she couldn't come quickly and felt uncomfortable that she was in there so long. She flushed the toilet and came back out to face the pile of papers and lose herself in work until five o'clock.

'Goodbye, Annie,' hailed the waif as Annie strode out the door. She waved back absently, already thinking of her possible encounter with Brad. She was planning to tell him to arrange for a surprise meeting with Tom like Tom had done with her. She thought of the three of them together and moisture began, once again, gathering between her thighs. So many hands everywhere, so many entrances ...

The bar on the outside had a black door, black windows and a black overhang. Inside, it was equally dark, smelling of ancient beer and musty wine. She sat in the darkest booth she could find, after ordering a tequila from the bartender. He brought it to her with a whole lime and a knife. Nice touch, she thought, if I were on a pirate ship.

She could barely decipher what was taking place inside. Her flesh was tingling with the chance of meeting Brad. Her clit was ringing the way it did whenever she was unable to locate something. Had since she was a little girl. She could never understand why *not* finding something could somehow make her excited. She told herself to calm down and to stay focused. This did not seem like a user-friendly bar. She could feel many eyes on her and was sure she was the only female there. No, over there was a big, leggy, buxom blonde. She was laughing and smoking a cigar. A big cigar. Annie supposed that women could do that. She had even read that some men find it sexy. Then she noticed the thick moustache on the woman.

She remembered when she went with Charles to the 'wholesome' sex exchange bar. There was nothing wholesome about the exchanges in this bar and she thought, 'OK Annie. You drink your tequila and leave. Either they smell how straight you are or they think you have great drag. Either way, you don't belong here.' She began to slide out of the booth when she saw Brad. He didn't see her and she didn't want to shout. So she sat back down again in the dark, and observed.

He was talking to one of the blonde's friends and it seemed as if the man was giving Brad money. Brad was smiling and shaking his hand. For some reason she didn't understand, they all looked in Annie's direction.

'Annie! I am so glad you came here. What a surprise!' Brad rushed over to greet her. 'Friends, this is Annie and is she ever great in bed.'

Amidst the accolades, Annie felt the temperature rise to her cheeks. She did not want to be remembered this way, in front of complete strangers. What a funeral that would be, Nancy standing up there in the front, holding her mother's hand, aghast at the rumours about her sister. Mother smiling, saying, 'Well now, we don't really know anything, do we?'

Brad must think that Annie was some kind of thrill seeker and he was helping her to the next level. But she was normal, sexually hungry Annie. Nothing else. Meat and potatoes, straight sex kind of person, except for that delicious trio last week.

'Hi, everybody. Sorry I have to leave.' She hurried past all of them and out the door.

Brad grabbed her arm in the street. 'I thought you went there for a special reason.'

'I went there because your phone call made me hot and I wanted to talk to you about Tom. I would like to give Tom a surprise, but not with someone who is a regular prostitute. Jesus, I now need to get an AIDS test.'

'Annie, I told you I was clean. I am getting tested all the time. Would you like to see?'

'Your track marks from needles? No, thank you. Stay away from me, Brad. I feel a little dangerous, after knowing our previous intercourse.'

He was walking briskly beside her and whispering, 'It was so beautiful, you know. You have the most perfect body of any woman I have ever been with.'

'Forget that we had that encounter. Don't call me, I'll call you.' Annie hurried down the street and Brad went back to his business at the bar.

'Honey, we really need to talk.'

'Oh no! Annie, you know what talking does to any relationship. It will be ruined in a matter of months.'

'Tom, I saw Brad today.'

'You did?' Tom's mouth appeared to twitch. 'Well, that was nice, I suppose?'

'He called me to tell me that he wanted to fuck me.' She tried not to stare too hard at Tom.

'Well, hmm. I told him not to contact you without me.'

'What else have you told him in your past life?'

'Why, Annie,' Tom laughed, 'if I didn't know better, I would say that you are accusing me of something.'

'Actually, I am. It doesn't bother me if it's true . . . Have you slept with Brad?'

'That sounds like an accusation to me.'

'Only if you think that sleeping with the same sex is bad.'

'You know how I feel about that.'

'You feel OK about it, right?'

'Well, if it doesn't hurt anyone . . .'

'Tom, your truth is not going to hurt me emotionally.' She breathed in, feeling punched by this. Why shouldn't it hurt her emotionally? How else could anything hurt her? What was her problem with word choice? Now, however, was not the time to be tentative. She needed to act. Keep moving.

'But do you know that Brad is a prostitute?' she continued.

'You really talked a long time today.'

'I met him at that bar across from my work.'

Tom sat down on the edge of the bed and ran his big hand up and down his face, as if brushing off a smirk or brushing in a frown. He laced together his long fingers and hung his head down. Annie did not go to him but stood, feeling rather detached, and observed his beautiful physique. His hair shone in the soft light, its darkness offsetting his chiselled marble-looking face. His new beard was neatly trimmed and Annie purred to herself when she thought of its softness. But Tom's fingers were his biggest asset. He had the hands of an artist. It didn't matter that he was merely a CPA; she knew when she saw him that he would touch her gently. She did not expect that he would be more than a great lover. Such a creative lover. Such a sensitive lover. He allowed Annie the distance she desired in their love-making and he always knew when to hold back or to go forward. It was easy though. Annie always wanted sex with him. His thick cock excited her and his eyes magnetised her being into a pleasant state of semi-consciousness.

Even now, sensing a strange new conflict between them, she wanted him. Wanted to pry open his arms, rip open his pants, and take his cock into her mouth. It would soothe him, to be sure. But she controlled herself. She saw him on the edge of the bed, looking sad and she knew exactly what she could do to make him, and her too, happy. She resisted pulling him to her and stroking his manhood.

'Tom, I am worried that we haven't been tested for anything recently.'

'Yeah.'

'Tom?'

'Annie, you know that I love you. Sometimes it's hard always to be so honest. My greatest honesty is when I make love with you.'

'Baby, I feel that. I am not upset if you slept with Brad. I worry that Brad has slept with a few others and could give us something awful.'

'All right.' He turned and his eyes weren't so sweet. Annie had not seen those eyes. She felt afraid. 'I will get a test. There. Are you happy? Jesus! You know, you make love like a gay man.'

'I didn't think I said something to make you so hateful.'

'What!'

'Hateful. You are looking at me with anger and hate.'

'Don't I have a right to be angry sometimes?'

'With me? Why would you be angry with me? We only have fantastic sex all the time. Gay, whatever. Who cares! What's to be angry about?!'

'Forget it!'

'Tom, forget what? I want to hear you. Forget what? Look, don't yell at me. What did I say to upset you? I said I don't care if you and Brad slept together . . .'

'Listen, you bitch. I care what you say!' Tom stood up and stormed out of the room.

Annie had never heard any but the sweetest words from Tom's mouth all ten months they had been together. She never wanted or expected to hear anything but sweet words. Maybe naughty, nasty words. Anything but hateful words. For what? The truth?

Annie didn't believe in second chances. She knew from watching her sister in failed relationships and a dull marriage that once a man makes a mistake, he makes it for ever. Like when a dog kills another pet. It has tasted the blood and will never go back to pretending the rabbit or rat was a friend and playmate.

Annie left Tom's place, thinking that she had found the end to an amazing time of glorious happiness and pleasure. Scratch the surface of any man, she thought, and you'll find a tyrant. Or a little boy. Or both.

She walked the cliffs of her old haunt – listening to that something which seemed just out of hearing. Were there really voices in the air?

She was at the place at the top of the worn wooden steps she'd shown Fred. The portal. The sun shone, exposing the salt on the tree leaves. Below, the ocean roared.

Waves crashing upon the extended arm of a long dead ship engine. Crazy surfers were paddling around the bend, daring the sleeper waves to not claim them, as the waves had done with hundreds of other lives. This Pacific Ocean here was anything but its name. Or did it *need* to be pacified? Annie recalled that the year before, three children simply playing around rocks at the ocean's edge, were snatched by a sudden big wave, never to be seen again. Her father would say they were 'Away' but she knew they were gone.

A foghorn blew, a long blast then two short ones, for

the large tanker which was approaching one of the other shipwrecks in the bay.

She had seen on Tom's TV a special about Russians who had come here. This very port below. They had established a fishing village and then vanished. Nobody knew what drove them away. Annie suspected it was not sleeper waves but a calling from the other side of the world. A sense of home Californians never could understand or possess.

Ridiculous, she knew. But the wind reminded her of that story. She stood still when the word 'fate' seemed caressed into her ear, stood still enough to revive good old Rule 15 to control the situation: *Stop the Ouija board. You control all the answers.*

Chapter Ten

Rule 9: *The illusion of love makes us weak; the wisdom of sex doesn't. Or, as Nietzsche said, that which doesn't destroy me only makes me stronger.*

It had been four months since she had left Tom. Annie walked less freely now. Being with him had made her feel a bit impervious to the world. But since their break-up, it was as if Tom were a painting removed from a wall which causes the room to suddenly appear naked.

Annie was worrying, too, that she really didn't want sex. Up to now, she thought, my life has been ninety per cent sex and ten per cent everything else. Now I still have that ten percent but what's filling in the void? When she tried to think further on her thoughts, a slippery veil clouded her mind. She didn't fight it but succumbed to the vacuity.

She remembered all the wonderful books she had read in college and how it was necessary for her to touch each of them to have their contents vividly spring back to life. As soon as she handled her Riverside Shakespeare, floods of lines and images crowded into her mind. The book became a conduit for her to the lives of its characters inside.

Perhaps sex is like that too, she thought, sighing wistfully. Tom's touch was fading from her physical memory. She knew she'd awake one day and have no idea what he did to make her so excited. Her body could not retain the information in its entirety.

Nor could her mind. It was true that she didn't have a great capacity for storing information for any significant length of time, something Nancy possessed. Her older sister could remember to the day every fight they ever had and who had hurt who when and where and why – according to Nancy. Annie was able to remember astonishing amounts of information related to projects or people; but her mind could only hold on to things for short periods of time. She had devised clever methodical ways to organise large amounts of information but if an account wasn't talked about for over six months, it was as good as non-existent. She had to go back to the files to revisit even a shred of the story, which was difficult for she had often already forgotten the file's name.

Annie could not recall most details of the nature of a transaction or the people involved. Fortunately, in her business she didn't have to. Carol relished finding files for Annie, and Annie, in turn, praised Carol no end for this deed. It made her design assistant appear efficient – which she really wasn't – and it gave Annie a feeling of being in control – in which she equally wasn't.

With sex, however, she could remember bits and pieces as if they were drilled into the core of her being. Into her bones. It was not whole people who filled her mind but a lip on an avocado, a thrust of a certain hip, the salty taste of Tom's mouth – those were images never to leave. Words like *gold box, bitch, the kind of woman I could fall in love with* haunted her as well. They lay tucked in some obscure sanctuary under her ribcage.

The design place she worked in was decorated with many colourful people who had felt they were geniuses since they were in grade school. Her colleagues had reinvented themselves so much that they ceased to have any foundation left. Peter was an ex-hippie who now liked to listen to Beethoven, and looked as if he washed his face in Mop-n-Glo. Carol, the waif, had now reversed her hair and nails so that her head was yellow and her nails pink. Marty, the chief around there, wore only black and kept his long hair greasy and in a ponytail. Every day, he was telling somebody about Vietnam but Annie one day caught a glimpse of his birthdate on his driver's licence and realised he could not have possibly served there. It seemed that, for a hobby, he was a self-proclaimed suffering, coping, angry victim. Sasha, the androgynous woman, came from East Texas and had worked so hard at losing her accent that now most people, if not convinced of her sex, were convinced that she came from Canada. Sasha's face looked as if she bleached it nightly; indeed, at the end of a long day, it would appear to gradually turn into a poor reproduction of itself, a sourceless shadow.

Annie sat at her drawing table and looked at the ad they wished her to mock up.

It was a woman with a car, of course. It was about sex, of course. She just couldn't get into it. Lately, her white mornings had been filled with diary contemplations, with no thoughts given to advertising tactics and designs.

Looking at the picture, she knew the idea had been hers months ago. Now she hated it. All of them assumed that people equated cars with sex. It was the American way. How many of her colleagues had lost their virginity in a backseat somewhere? But it seemed to Annie now that sex was for sex and cars were for cars. Cars were certainly not substitutes for sex, otherwise Phil, if Nancy were to be believed, would have a motor-home instead of the used Hyundai he drove.

Annie worried again that she seemed to have no energy or even desire to go out and get a new man. She didn't even masturbate now. At age twenty-five, Annie had never heard the word 'bitch' yelled accusingly at her. And she never wanted to again. She thought about how physically close she and Tom had been, and that when you get that close, you should know each other. But they didn't. Or *did* she know Tom and had he hated her for it? What on earth was wrong with the truth?

Something else yearned in her as well but she couldn't name it. Inside her, it felt soft and aching, like a rabbit out on a field during a very cold day. She felt that someone could just come into her life and trample it. So she stayed away. She barely remembered Tom's touch and wondered if everyone felt the same after a break-up. Only pretending to feel miserable but, in fact, all sensations being suspended in hibernation.

Annie felt something worse than depression, and better: she embraced the hollowness at the core of herself. She felt that someone could open her up, pour all of himself inside of her and yet she would be unmoved, still hungry.

Men seemed to sense this about her, this vastness and emptiness which begged to be cornered, planted, covered. She couldn't count all of the propositions she'd received since becoming a free woman. Yet she had felt more free before when she was attached to Tom. Now she lived like a caged panther, watching and cautious. The wildness Tom had so enthused about lay dormant, perhaps even withering. Annie didn't know it was possible to be so on fire with sexual energy one day and then to have a complete absence of it the next.

Her AIDS test had come back negative, which made her feel secure. About the only thing which did. Being alone . . . she craved it but no one gave it to her in the way she desired. Peter's winks were becoming more like a nervous tick – but with an angry bite to them. Marty sat a bit too close to her while explaining new proposals. Even Sasha had stopped by Annie's desk to give her a back rub, which Annie at first accepted but rejected after five minutes of hard horrid knuckles digging into the space between her shoulder blades.

Including Sasha's failed attempt, it just didn't feel good to be touched by anyone. It was too immediate and Annie's body felt to her like it was a long way off, floating in a crystallised state, waiting for someone to come back and give it definition and energy. Before, she had felt her self, her mind, off in a distance watching; now, the mind was close but her body away. The more untouchable she became, the more she was desired by others. It reminded her of high school – though this time she had grown used to the idea that she was beautiful.

Strangers approached her on the street, inside the bus, at the laundromat, in the produce section of her favourite store. Clerks at her store now seemed to leer at her and offer samples of new exotic star fruit or baby zucchini. The attention tightened her chest muscles and caused her to avert her eyes. Annie had never felt vulnerable before. Had Tom been a buffer while they were together? Perhaps so had Fred, Charles and Jeffrey. Just knowing she had a lover made Annie more ready to smile and laugh around others. Nothing seemed as serious then. A smile to a man wasn't an invitation, just an acknowledgement of his beauty and sexuality. Feeling sexy, walking suggestively, dressing provocatively never brought on the aggressive proposals she had to deal with now. Or if they had been there, she had shrugged them off. She had an excuse waiting for her.

The waif was eager to be in on the ground floor of Annie's change. Carol approached the subject several times, making references to her own break-ups and how painful they were. Annie never even offered the slightest glimmer of a possible shared confidence, usually walking away saying, 'Too bad, Carol.' This not knowing frustrated Carol who, having grown up in southern California, felt entitled to her friends' and colleagues' confessions. Carol was always happy to 'share' her feelings with others and thought Annie, being her immediate supervisor and not head of the company, should do likewise. Annie became adept at defending herself by holding a verbal mirror up to Carol, reminding the waif it was none of her business by repeating, 'Why are you asking?' back at every personal question.

This loss was Annie's alone and she wasn't about to cheapen it with discussion. A secret was something you owned. This attempt on the devaluation of her current privacy weighed on her. How she had felt a secret life with Tom and how no one had intruded, except Brad. Now, all eyes seemed ready to judge her every move as if it were an invitation to attack. She tried to wrap herself in some kind of cocoon but the ants were swarming. It was odd. In some way Annie thought this was how Nancy must have felt when she went to school knowing that taunts and shaving cream awaited her.

Annie's white mornings were gone for now. She tried very hard to remember nothing, to be nothing. She knew people would call this a depression but it felt more like an emptying. Her sensuous movements became less and slowly ceased, though the animal energy which enveloped her was not in the least extinguished. She merely bristled with sexuality instead of emitting it.

She went to that bar after work one day. Something compelled her to go. Annie was walking in the opposite direction when suddenly she turned around, her body leading her to a place her mind couldn't recognise. She was already inside when she began asking herself why she was there.

'Tequila, please.'

'Welcome back,' said the bartender, and the darkness of the room seemed to be coming from the very breath of his mouth.

'You remember me?'

'We don't get many beautiful *real* women in here. And Brad told us all about you.'

'Is he here?'

'Will be. I'll be back with your tequila.'

Why was she conversing with such a sour-smelling man? Asking about a prostitute! She did not want to see Brad because she felt something inside of her was falling out.

Tom. It was the memory of Tom. She suddenly remembered how he felt inside her, how it was wonderful and warm. How he made her feel filled up and satiated and how she was so hungry right now. Suddenly, she thought that she could rip off her skirt and do the smelly bartender right there on top of the bar. She would have him fill her hole up with soda afterwards and then each customer could drink. A fire spiderwebbed inside her and she could feel sex slithering back into her. Rule 14 came to mind: *All good sex starts with one-night stands.*

Colour rose up from her wetness and flushed her cheeks. She looked down, hoping no one could notice.

'Hi, here's your tequila.'

Annie looked up and saw Brad. He pulled her shot off the waiter's tray and slid into the booth with it. Annie instinctively put out her hand and Brad caressed her palm as he passed the tequila, the gesture so faint that Annie might not have noticed a few hours before. Now, she was burning up.

'Annie, you are all I have been thinking about.'

'And talking about.' Her dark blue eyes squinted, roaming over his face. An attractive face, although not perfect like Tom's. Brad's face looked like that of a gambler, as if he were always washing the dirt off it. His Adam's apple popped out of his shirt. But Annie remembered him without his clothes. She thought about his other generous attributes and began to smile.

'Annie, I can't stop myself. I want you so much. I am aching to be inside you.'

'We'll do a blood test now at the clinic. If you pay a lot of money, you can get the results in a few hours. Can you wait?' Brad nodded. Annie eyed him. 'Can you pay?'

'Let's go now, Annie. Down that shot.'

Inside the cab, Brad pulled up Annie's skirt and made a small hole in her pantyhose. He rubbed her clit and she tried not to make a sound, although the cab driver stared so much in his rear-view mirror that Annie knew he knew. It excited her more.

She began to pant as Brad kissed her breasts through her blouse. Then he thrust a thick middle finger up her and began finger-fucking her until she cried out in little whimpers. He kissed her eyes, which she had closed, giving in to the pleasure.

The pressure was mounting in her crotch when they pulled into the clinic. Annie almost fell out of the cab. They walked along the bright pavement. The day seemed quite surreal, with such a wet darkness living in her and the sunshine smiling as if to expose her very secret.

And she felt secretive. She glanced at Brad and he was grinning. He knows that he is clean, she thought, and she wanted his cock even more. Brad put his arm under her coat, grabbing her soaking ass. Annie moaned as they walked through the clinic doors.

'Harder, harder.'

'Say it louder. You want it, shout it!'

'Harder. Yes Brad, that's right. Yes.' Annie felt his big cock split her in half. Her legs were up and he was diving in as far as he could. She lost track of where they were, or when they started, or, sometimes, who they were. It seemed she was one big pulsing cave and Brad a pounding in there that bordered on pain but was so necessary. Her pressure was unbearable. She wanted to come. Suddenly the vision of a hundred cocks appeared to her and she imagined that each new cock was being thrust into her as Brad pounded.

'Annie, it's so good. It's so good.'

She was saying 'Yes, yes,' but it felt to her as if she were calling it from a million miles away. Her head spun and she thought she might pass out. Suddenly, a surge of heat raced to her clit and then she exploded, first feeling herself coming from somewhere deep inside. Brad kept thrusting and seemed to sense right when she began to come. He kept his rhythm steady so as to not disturb her. He felt her pussy tighten with spasms. After about ten seconds, he thrust himself in even deeper. Annie howled and began to cry. He stopped but she said, 'My God, no. Don't stop. Don't stop. Don't stop.' So he continued to thrust until he came in one large torrent.

Brad lay on top of Annie and watched the dusty twilight shine on her flushed skin. He had never been with such a beautiful woman before, nor one who could so completely give herself to him. His instincts were right about that first encounter at Tom's: this was the woman he could fall in love with.

He eased his half-limp cock out and rolled over to snuggle next to her. She murmured, 'Tom,' and Brad's heart sank. He began to speak to her but realised she was asleep in that very special kind of sleep following great love-making. He felt touched to his soul. Did she? After calling him a prostitute? After their time in the clinic? Maybe she missed Tom so much and just needed a good lay. Tom was one all right. Brad decided that all those days of money were over. He really had what he needed next to him. Her very wetness was enough for him, but then, how she moved, what she felt, how she could soar in their love-making. He started to get hard again, then thought he would rather wait. He lightly stroked her breasts. She turned and put her head against his chest.

* * *

Morning came harshly in through Brad's second storey window. The light shone brightly and seemed to echo off the unadorned walls. Brad forgot where he was. There was Annie ... he couldn't recall her precisely because she seemed to him the essence of all women. She was their strength and wetness. She stood for all their greatest secrets and openness. He felt her, not remembered her. He smelled her deep inside his being. It was too much for Brad. He saw that Annie was still sleeping, still so real. He couldn't place the sleeping woman with all the ecstasy he had. He lost the feeling of his own sex and wondered where he was. Nausea. Overwhelming, not sick in the stomach but like you might have slept with your own mother nausea. He wished the sun had never come to haunt him. Annie was too real now. She would wake up, say that she had been too horny, that she had made a mistake, that she loved Tom ...

'Annie, darling.'

'Mmm.'

'Darling. Annie. Annie, darling, are you awake?'

'Mmm hmm.'

'Do you want to eat?'

'You.'

'I want to eat.'

'And I want to eat you. Please give me your glorious cock.'

'Annie! You are my woman.'

'Yes. I think you might be right.'

She reached over to his cock and began massaging it. Brad stood very still. He wanted to be passive and see what Annie would do. He felt bewitched by her. Her fingers were lightly playing with his balls, heavy with his head, light, heavy. He closed his eyes. He felt a very hot, wet, smaller cave enclose upon him. He gasped. Annie moved her tongue around the very tip of his head, sucking him into her mouth and then blowing him back out. He moaned and she began to move a little faster, but not like all those women who made him feel like they were doing him a big favour. Annie sucked on him like he was the one helping her. She moved her hips and positioned herself closer.

Brad felt the tip of his cock touch the back of her throat. Then she pulled him out. In, out, in, out. Brad didn't move. He couldn't move. He opened his eyes and was frozen by the beauty of her shiny black hair and the magic of her tongue. Suddenly, he began to come. He hadn't even felt that he was ready and suddenly he was shooting hot sperm down her throat. She moaned and sucked him harder. She siphoned all his come out of him. Brad fell on the bed, feeling like the very last of his being had been stripped off. He was a quivering core of sexual feelings. He lost the capacity to think. His heart pounded and swelled, as if it were a throbbing member too.

'Brad, you taste wonderful. Like a fine wine.'

'Jesus. How did you do that? I feel lost now.'

'You didn't like it?'

'I liked it on the other side of liking it. You are magic.'

'Thank you. Now, let's eat.'

Brad bounded out of bed, even though five seconds before he was sure that he would never be able to walk again. But he could still walk and talk. And Annie was still there, with a black halo of curls shining around her. He guessed that she was 25 or 26, but she looked any age. She looked any nationality to him. Her body was round and taut, her eyes without a bottom. All woman, every woman, his woman.

Annie dressed in the fading morning light, feeling very open, warm and rested. It hadn't even occurred to her that this was the first time in her life she'd spent an entire night in someone else's bed.

They went to a perfect greasy spoon that served New Mexican cuisine. Two red chile plates came out and they ate them while sweat poured off their foreheads from the spiciness. Annie had never eaten this food before and she couldn't believe its sensuality. She rolled the meat in her mouth and let the chile burn all the way down her throat. She ordered another plate.

'This is the best food I have ever had. I hope you will excuse me. I want to eat until I have a big fat stomach.'

'You eat all you want to. I love that you have an appetite.'

'I can't believe how hungry I am. What are you doing to me, Brad?'

'Loving you.'

'You love me? Isn't that a bit early?'

Brad sat back a bit, stunned. So she really doesn't feel anything, he thought to himself.

'Brad? Brad, look at me.'

He looked off to the left but Annie saw in an instant that he was trying not to cry. She wanted to hold him, to caress him but something made her stop. Didn't he trust her? Believe her? Wasn't what they experienced cheapened by the word 'love'?

'Brad. I feel something more than love for you. Brad,' her voice became low and almost demonic, 'Brad, if it helps you, I will say I love you.'

'Can't you do something normal?' he said in an incredulous tone. 'Most women would fall over themselves if a man proclaimed love for them after a one-night stand.'

'Would they?'

'Well, I suppose you know better.'

'Probably not. I don't know a lot of women. I do know that we better get back to fucking because if we talk, we might have a lot of problems. I want to feel, feel, feel, Brad . . . not analyse. Let's do that when our body parts fall off, OK?'

Brad wanted to tell Annie that he was emerging into something he had sensed he could be yet had never found the right spark. Somehow the strength of her sex bolstered him with the courage to redefine himself. It had happened in an instant.

From the moment they had touched, even with Tom there, his internal workings had been fretfully rearranging themselves in an attempt to adjust to the essence of Annie. He thought, before, that he was an island unto himself. His work had just been going through the motions. Nothing ever entered him deeply – there had been women and men who had wanted him to be *theirs*. In that very desire lay the key to Brad not wanting it. It made his work so easy. Automatic. He wasn't really even there for it.

Yet Annie did not live like that. He loved her for it. She was so outside anything Brad had ever experienced. Powerful, soft, and when she fucked, she fucked. There was no playing at it. She was one with the act. Just like when she slept. Just fall down dead sleep. No rituals, no special reading material, just sleep. Like a fine-tuned machine. A very fine-tuned fucking machine or, he hoped, lovemaking machine. He loved her in the way he had heard people say they knew their mates on first sight: 'She's the one.' He had never believed it could happen until it happened to him and he felt weak before the knowledge that he was beneath Annie's feet, struggling not to be broken.

Chapter Eleven

A rule circled about, begging to be written down. Annie couldn't name it yet, but was certain when she opened her diary and began writing in the rule section, she'd understand the rule.

It surprised her to find that she wrote in her diary instead.

Love. Such a short word. Does it contain how anyone feels? I think that I am in love but I really could not say. Something feels very profound with Brad.

Is there ever any future? I thought I would be with Tom forever and then one horrid word and one cold, cold look and I was out of there faster than Nancy says, 'Jesus.' You know I gave Tom every feeling I had.

And Annie, what feelings were those? The darkness of you?

Brad into the darkness of me. He comes in freely. But he gets all the other feelings too. Or I want him to, anyway.

My morning time – I've lost it. It's difficult to go to work. I didn't know that I create while I'm not aware of creating. I keep thinking at work that I've run out of ideas. Really. It's difficult to explain but it's as if Brad has come to fill that morning time and I drift with him instead.

Brad and I don't have anything else but a close animalness. It's as if we're linked on an instinctive level that can never be fully explored.

My head is whirling with all the other lovers and all the things we couldn't explore . . .

Tom was a great lover. I have never really had a bad lover, to think of it. I have been blessed. My sister tells me that I am lying. She said there are no good lovers. But what would she know? Look at Phil. Nancy comes home, tired from work, cooks him a meal, tries to relax and go to sleep before she must get up again at the crack of dawn. The man could help her around the house, the idiot. Her I mean. Why does she do it? Anyway, if she accidentally touches him in the course of the night, his little penis is ready to stick into her, except he doesn't care if she is ready or not. If her dryness seems uncomfortable for him, he tries to find her clit to rub it, but he never wets his finger so she gets sore immediately. When she pushes his hand away from her crotch, he takes that as a sure sign that she is ready, and plunges in, if he can. If not, he tries the dry finger on the very sore clit again. Usually she then turns over, puts her ass to him and tries to masturbate. But, the other day, he told her that he thought the problem they were having with sex was because she masturbated!

See, I understand that I am lucky. I have love, my own freedom and such incredible pleasures that I worry I am addicted. But what a great vice if it is with the same man.

Oh, Brad has opened a Pandora's box in me and I love the dark secrets which keep spilling out. Is this love? Is it?

He makes me feel so much like a woman, and so mighty. Is that possible through a cock? I ask you. This worship from Brad, it's something primordial. Sometimes I feel like there is no man or woman when we are together. It just is. For once, I feel deeply, profoundly connected to another. But I feel it now. I cannot say it yet.

So, dear diary, is this love or am I sorely deluded? Or has this love thing been so handed down through the civilisations that we just don't get it? It's some pre-packaged product with guidelines we have been trained to follow if we think we're in love. You know, the planning, the overnight stays, then the living together, marriage, ad nauseum.

Work has gone to hell but somehow I am managing. It's quite risky work too, these weird ideas I'm presenting – going out on a limb with strange angles for things. It's like I am inspired by Mephistopheles. I remember when I read Milton and how interesting his Satan was. That is how Brad is. He doesn't care about conventions. He is not trying to break any because there are not any for him to break. I want to break things up too. I want to rearrange my inner being, to bring it out into the light. Maybe rearrange his too.

God, it feels good to write. Am I going to use this when I don't wish to act?

Annie, just let it be. You're old enough now to contemplate. Now get busy and start doing that!

Chapter Twelve

She rang him up at about ten o'clock at night.
      'Tom, this is Annie.'

A silence. Then, 'Oh, hello.'

'Listen,' she forged ahead immediately, 'I just can't believe we were so close once, so intimate, and now we don't even speak to each other.'

'That was your choice, Annie.'

She ignored the bait to argue. 'Tom, I would like that we start speaking again. Would you?'

'Yes . . . I would like that . . . and more.'

'I'm sorry,' Annie switched to the voice she used to speak to customers with complaints, 'speaking is the only option.'

So like her. Tom laughed at the single-mindedness of Annie. 'OK, I'll take speaking for five hundred.'

Annie didn't laugh.

'Oh!' said Tom. 'I forgot. You don't have a TV. That's from a game show.'

Annie ignored what she thought was the beginning of sarcasm in Tom's voice and asked, 'Thai?'

* * *

At their old hang-out, the waiter automatically brought satay to the celibate couple. He inquired why he hadn't seen them for such a long time. Tom looked at Annie to answer but she offered nothing. Tom shrugged his shoulders and the waiter hurried off, aware he'd encroached upon a painful subject. Painful for at least one member of the party.

Tom stared intensely at Annie, willing her to come to him, come back into his life. Sadly, her blue eyes betrayed nothing except mild curiosity. No excitement, no vivid blue of a stormy lake, no 'come hither' look she was so devilishly good at.

Annie shocked him by relaying her intimacy with Brad.

Tom found it increasingly hard to sit across the table from his strikingly gorgeous ex-lover and hear her talk about that other strikingly gorgeous ex-lover of his. And to hear that the two were currently striking and fulfilling a beautiful image of the beast with two backs nearly put him over the top.

He confided as much to Annie, realising that she was already lost to him so there was nothing to lose. Annie only listened, not even adding an 'Uh huh' every now and then to the parade of losses he spelt out and the jealousy he now had for both her and Brad. Tom still seemed honest, at least.

He ordered a pumpkin curry, extra spicy. He wanted to give Annie something to burn her throat. Instead, she ate it with much relish, praising the dish as one of the best she'd ever eaten.

'I love the potatoes and pumpkin mixed with those mushrooms. That red curry is to die for.'

'Annie, when did you start liking spicy food?' Tom felt he could not hide the anger in his voice much longer. He felt betrayed again. Wasn't he the one who had opened up her palate to the realms of other foods besides boiled brisket and white bread?

Annie didn't answer, her mouth full. At the same moment, she noticed with a little alarm that she felt as if she were betraying Brad. Having dinner with Tom ... She and Brad hadn't promised each other anything but still ...

The conversation nearly died. Annie felt responsible to keep it going, since she was the one who'd invited Tom. But what could she speak to Tom about? The past? That didn't concern her. The future? Nothing of it yet involved Tom, though she did have a notion of something that would; indeed, this topic was the impetus behind their meeting.

The present? That was where she was right then and it was growing more and more uncomfortable. Despite her set of rules, she began to regret having taken the initiative of inviting Tom to the restaurant. There was at least a half hour before the meal would end and now time moved backwards.

Tom reached across the table and touched her hand. 'Annie,' he said, 'I don't know where you are right now but this is going to take some time ... I mean, I've been spending half a year trying to forget you and I really can't. So, what I'm trying to say ... I'll take you in whatever form I get you.' Underneath this stumbling speech, Tom kept thinking: I'll get you for this, Brad.

Annie was touched and relieved. This was the Tom she knew. The balance was back and she grew certain that he would agree to her proposal. A flicker of worship still glowed in his eyes. She hoped that they might have a relationship like those cousins had in Henry James's *Portrait of a Lady*: passionate admiration on his part and deserving of respect and honour on hers – all making for a fine friendship full of benevolence for all. At her funeral, Tom would be the one standing up saying Annie was a wonderful person to know and love. That she had been the light of his life for a while but then she became the light for another. And that was just fine with him, because all he wanted, ever, was her happiness.

It never dawned on Annie to interpret James as a novel where all pure desires are thwarted.

The food which kept coming began a seduction on Annie's senses: spinach leaves with toasted coconut, sweet sauce, limes and dried salt fish; vegetable curry with so much basil it almost tasted like the wild fennel growing along the cliffs; a sweet dessert of tapioca and tea. Her stomach was begging to be freed from her waist. Annie undid the top of her front button skirt, sighing as she settled back into the high-backed booth.

She felt sated. Looking at their plates, she realised now that Tom had eaten very little. He must have been piling the food on her plate the entire time – stuffing her with each new taste. Annie wondered if it weren't some small act of sabotage. Could she go to Brad tonight, with this huge stomach – the consequence of tasting new food with her former lover?

Maybe the headiness of the meal, plus the third beer Annie was working on, made the table seem to move away from her. She sensed a hole opening behind her and a force pulling her backwards. Tom's face appeared darker, smaller, grimacing, and she put her hands on the table to steady herself. She knew it was ridiculous but she felt as if Tom's intense will pulling on her had an equally intense opposite reaction somewhere else. In the restaurant or in the universe. Somewhere was the anti-Tom or the negation of the magnetism he was throwing her way.

For she wasn't feeling attracted to him in any way, yet he was drawing her in nonetheless. Annie knew she needed to stop it. She felt like something outside herself wanted her to stop it too. A will of the universe? Too much beer.

'Tom, I don't feel well.'

'Do you want to come back to my place? You could lie down there, darling.'

'No.' She thought he looked stunned but her vision was too blurry to tell. 'Just hail me a cab.'

'That's silly, Annie. It's only four blocks to your house. I still remember the way. Let me walk you home.'

She allowed him to, sensing nothing other than his simple offer of concern.

Outside, the cold air jarred her back into clearer thinking. She had hoped it would. The nights in San Francisco were never without a hint of crispness about them.

Tom had his arm through hers but without a trace of sexual overture. Annie began to believe they really might be friends – more than they had been when they were together. At her door, she said as much and more. She hoped her proposal would not push Tom away, yet she vaguely also wished it would. It was a risk she felt sure Brad would approve of. She imagined she would enjoy it equally, understanding now all the premises. As for Tom . . .

He kissed her softly on the cheek and stepped back, staring at Annie wistfully.

'I'll think about your proposal and I'll probably agree to it,' he said at last, once he was an arm's length from her. 'As I said, I'll take you in whatever form I can get you.'

Annie took this as a yes. She watched Tom walk off into the foggy night, then she hurried inside to call Brad. She couldn't possibly see him tonight. He'd be sad but, as usual, understanding. She would spring this very special surprise on him later.

Chapter Thirteen

*T*his morning, the first of many mornings where Brad lay in her bed with his radiant back shining in the light, Annie realised they had been touching the entire night. It seemed significant to her and her cunt responded to the deep feeling by releasing juices on to Brad's leg.

Brad was still sleeping and Annie watched him in that special white light, wanting to know his secrets. She heard a voice from an indeterminate place inside her beckoning to go further – to let go and let Brad be with her, to understand him beyond understanding.

If she'd probed just a bit deeper within herself, she'd have known it was her own secret she was trying to find. Something at the core of her being was shifting and it made her uneasy.

With a finger, she traced on Brad's back L ... O ... V ... E ..., adding a very light question mark at the end, in case he could feel it in the dream world.

'Here's breakfast.' Annie slid the large tray on to the bed. Fresh apple-carrot juice, whole grain toast, a bowl of strawberries, fluffy scrambled eggs with dill, and a pot of coffee.

'Mmm. I didn't know you could cook.' Brad's eyes were still puffy with sleep.

'Really, I can't. You inspire me. Gotta do these things with love, or not at all.' She flinched at her unintentional mention of love and hoped Brad didn't notice. What was she afraid of?

She sat naked on the bed and poured them both a cup of coffee with heavy cream.

It was still very early. Brad's face looked surprisingly innocent. His dirty blond hair was a bird's nest, his slate green eyes not quite focused. Her cunt throbbed, looking at his unpretentious beauty.

It was silent in the flat – comfortably silent. They sipped their coffee, ate strawberries, and looked at each other intensely. Annie did not remember ever feeling, like she did in that instant, that she was looking into someone's eyes but seeing something in them far deeper. A simple message she should have been able to decode had she spent a few more minutes lying quietly in that purifying morning. Instead, she was fast into the action plan.

The phone rang. 'Hi, Sis ... thanks. I'm planning on spending the day with someone special ... No, not him ... You haven't met ... We'll celebrate later. You don't need to get me anything ... OK, thanks for the wishes. Bye.'

'Annie?' asked Brad. 'Is it your birthday?'

'Yes, and I'm reborn.' She smiled sideways, shoveling in a forkful of scrambled eggs.

They wandered the park, going from the Panhandle to the ocean. Tulips were blooming in Queen Wilhelmenia's Tulip Garden, baby ducks were swimming in Stow Lake, the nasturtium vines were beginning to burst with red and yellow flowers. Annie picked one and ate it, to Brad's wide grinning eyes. Indeed a day for rebirth.

At the beach, she showed Brad something Tom had taught her: the delight of smashing up broken sand dollars. Like chewing tortilla chips with one's feet, cracking and popping the external skeletons until the dollar became the sand it was made from. For Tom, the act had the satisfying crunch of a thing being finished, whereas, for Annie, breaking up the already broken life felt more like a sweet mercy granted to a voiceless being.

Brad kept searching for the other half of the creatures. He was mildly alarmed at Annie's thrill for destruction and told her so.

She laughed. 'There are millions of them here.'

'Not where I come from,' answered Brad.

She realised she had no idea where he came from but it felt strange to ask. Thankfully, Brad did not make her need to.

He began to tell her of his neighbourhood in Chicago. Annie interrupted him, violating one of her own codes, and asked, 'What did you do there?'

'Same as here,' he answered. 'Well, not quite. Not any more. Do you know why?'

Annie shook her head, failing to grasp that this was not a rhetorical question but one that Brad asked in all earnest.

A plane flew loudly overhead, the only sound to rival the waves. Brad looked up. He wondered if it was one of his instructors – he'd been taking flight lessons and was five flying hours away from becoming a pilot. Someday, he was going to take her flying and they would soar above the city and see just how close all of those lives were. Then they would go North, looking for dolphins or whales. Up to Alaska. Then cross the Bering Strait. In the summer. It would be light the entire time and they could land in a new continent.

He said to Annie, 'Makes me want to see the other side,' indicating the ocean.

She nodded. She had travelled little outside the sphere of San Francisco. 'Makes me wonder what would happen if you just let go ... just dropped everything and sailed away.'

Brad thought to tell Annie that this was what he was doing with her, but did not believe she was ready to hear it. Not the imagined plane trip but his heart.

Annie splashed Brad with water and said, 'I baptise you, in the name of somebody's father, the sun, and some holy toast.'

He splashed her back. 'And I baptise you. Period. For being born.'

There was a new restaurant in the old beach chalet. Seated at a table, they could watch the seagulls land atop cars parked at the beach. Surfers scurried across the highway, dressed in dark wetsuits. Signs indicating the danger of the surf, as usual, had not deterred them.

The ocean and foghorn were audible to Annie, whose hearing had grown even more acute since sleeping with Brad. She could swear she heard his thoughts forming, his desire pumping out towards her like a big Kodo drum.

The place had a microbrewery and they ordered sample after sample, comparing.

'This tastes like those strawberries but with a hint of you.'

'Thanks, Brad. I smell like yeast and hops?'

'No, more like a fine ocean on a winter's day.'

They bantered for a while, flirting, provoking. Suddenly, Brad got serious.

'Annie, am I really someone special?'

'Of course you are.'

'I mean, am I someone special to you?'

'You're here with me on my birthday. And ...' But Annie couldn't say anything else. She choked and thought for a moment that she might cry. She wasn't ready to do that in front of anybody. Had never done that, in fact. And she wouldn't today.

'And? Oh Annie, I can't help myself. I don't want to be a fling.'

'You're not.'

'But what am I then?'

'Brad, this is my birthday. Let's do stuff together. We can talk later – maybe in my birthday suit.'

She saw his face crumple then compose itself again. For a moment, she was a thousand feet away, watching. She forced herself to come back to her body – to be present.

Brad surprised her when he asked, 'Where'd you go?'

She wished she could tell him but she did not know the answer. She struggled to enlarge Brad. He had shrunk to a mere pinhole in her vision.

'Annie, are you ready?'

'Ready for you. Are you lying down?'

'I am doing everything exactly how you said. Jesus. Look at you.' Brad did not know how to open his eyes wide enough to take in her sudden beauty. She had just stepped out of the shower and the water still beaded on her breasts. Her cunt smelled to him rich and heady, like raw mushrooms. Annie's eyes were dilated and seemed to grow bigger with every glance she stole at him. He edged back on the bed and propped his head up a bit. For a minute, her smell, her sex – it frightened him. He could see that she was ready to consume him. Her hands looked tense and her thighs poised like a cat's. His heart began racing. He remembered that he promised her she could do whatever she wished to. It was her birthday night and he said that she was completely in charge; he didn't know why he had told her so. Thinking of it now, Brad felt it was the wrong decision because women love to feel the power from a man. They love to know he will be the one, in the end, so to speak. He couldn't say it exactly, but the darkness, the mustiness he felt when his male energy flooded a room . . . he could see that women (and a lot of men too) were attracted to it. He smelt like success or sex – he couldn't say which. He only knew the moment when he felt it and then he knew everyone succumbed. Just like Annie in the bar. She didn't even know why she went there, but he knew. He felt her weaker sex, waiting for a sign that she was the high holy priestess. She wanted to be fucked through worship or worshipped through fucking. Even Annie didn't understand it exactly. But Brad could feel how she was willing to do just about anything for him in bed. And he had many surprises. And he was sure she would like them all.

Now he lay back and wondered if Annie didn't have some surprises too. Like making him fall in love with her by how she didn't want him to fall in love with her. She was like her cunt, so delicious and so unfathomable as to how deep she really was. Brad decided she was a beautiful dark tunnel he perpetually wanted to penetrate. He wanted to penetrate her to the core and get at her mystery. Why did she wrap him up so much? Why was he obsessed about her? Now, he smelt her everywhere. Before they had fucked alone, he imagined he saw her everywhere; now he tasted her and smelt her in his coffee, on his tie, in his car, at the bar. She pulsed through his pores.

'Brad, you look very hungry. You are going to eat me now. I am going to tell you exactly what to do and you are going to do it. OK?'

'Yes, ma'am.'

'That's good. I like when you obey me. Did you shave? Let me feel.' She ran her smooth thigh along his cheek and then sat over him and rubbed both thighs along his face. 'Yes, you were very good. You are so nice and smooth. OK, you are going to kiss me very slowly and I'm going to kiss you back.'

Annie lowered herself on to Brad's mouth and moved her cunt muscles so as to kiss him. Brad kissed her cunt and then made her cunt kiss him back. Her juices were already flowing so much they engulfed Brad's face in a sweet sticky film.

'Tell me that you like my juices.'

In a muffled voice, Brad whispered, 'I love your juices. I want to suck up every drop. Annie, I want to suck.'

'Don't worry, you will. Now, take your tongue and very carefully make circles on my clit. Oh God. That's right, baby. You do just like I say. Mmm. Yes. Yes, that's good, lover. Put your hands back now.'

Annie got out a pair of handcuffs and, before Brad knew it, both his hands were handcuffed to the bed. He liked this feeling of submission with Annie. He kept licking her cunt.

'Brad, very very good. Now, push harder with your tongue and move my clit up and down. Lover, that's so great. My God.'

She tossed her head back and began moaning or chanting. Brad didn't know how he was going to keep from ripping off the cuffs and plunging into her. She sounded like an angel and the devil together in some old monastery. She chanted and sang half-formed words. The light outside grew dimmer and shadows began to appear on the wall. Brad could half see everything through the wild cunt hair around him. He felt tangled in seaweed, the smell beautiful but growing too rich now. Annie was still chanting and he couldn't stop circling her clit.

Suddenly, she got off of him. 'You are a bad boy. You tried to make me come. I don't want to come. And I don't want you to come. You are going to be begging for me to let you come before the night is over.'

'Please, ma'am, let me come now. Look at my poor hard-on. How can I live?'

'Oh, you'll live. You'll see.'

She went around the corner and came back with a plastic glove on one hand. The glove glistened in the twilight. Brad felt a little nervous.

'Did you ever have this, Brad? When you were out whoring around?' And she shoved her gloved middle finger, coated with Vaseline, up his ass. Brad sighed. 'Oh, I see that you like this.' She continued, 'Well, I am the man now and I am going to fuck you.'

She sat back on her hand and let Brad's cock ride between her two cunt lips. She heaved into him, and her finger went deep inside his ass. Then she pulled out as she also moved away with her body. Again she shoved. In and out. Brad moaned. He did love it. With her, it justified all the times he had done it without her. He felt ready now for a woman who was a man or a woman or God knows. She was Annie, the seductress, fucking him. He began to moan and she said, 'You really like this. I knew it. I'm leaving the glove in, but I'm pulling out. You need to eat me some more, for that wondrous pleasure. '

'Yes, ma'am. I will eat you and drink you.'

'Good, because I brought some sweet liqueur and I'm going to pour a little on my cunt. Then you better lick like a good boy. '

'I will lick, don't worry. God. Mmm.' Brad licked for dear life because Annie ground herself into his face, not allowing him room to breathe. The headiness of her forest and the sweet orange smell of the liqueur almost made him pass out. She was moaning this time, from some far-away space. He sucked her clit though his teeth. She moaned and moaned and, suddenly, Brad saw another shadow on the wall. He thought it looked like a man's, but he couldn't tell. It seemed to come from Annie, as if a dark shadow was leaving her soul. He tried to see through her hair but she ground into him.

Suddenly, she came on his face, gushing the liqueur and her own fluids down his throat and on to his neck. Then he was sure he saw it. Another man's hands on her breasts. He pulled on his cuffs. Annie didn't seem to mind the hands and he couldn't figure things out. His cock grew an inch but he couldn't tell if from rage or excitement. Annie dropped to his cock and began to suck it. That was when he saw the face: Tom.

Tom entered Annie from behind and she bumped up and down Brad's cock as Tom's rhythm permitted.

Brad pulled on his cuffs. He didn't want to see his woman fucked by another man – or did he? She sucked on him and he couldn't stand it. An angry helplessness came over him. He didn't want to be there suddenly, but his body was yearning with all its might to conceive something. He wanted to fuck and fight with the shadow that had now become a face with hands on his woman. Was she his woman? Did Annie give herself to him? They hadn't promised each other anything, but now he wished that those hands on her breasts knew that she was *his*. And how was it that Annie seemed to be sucking the rage right out of him?

Annie felt he was about to come and she stopped. 'Brad, remember, you said you would do whatever I wanted. I want Tom to fuck you. I know Tom wants it and I know you do too. I'm unlocking you now and chaining you around me. You are going to suck me silly while I watch Tom fuck you. Mm, that's right, Tom.'

Tom moved to Brad's ass and Annie watched Brad's eyes as Tom entered him. Both of them moaned and Tom began spanking Brad's ass. 'That's right, Brad. I know you like this,' Tom panted.

Brad bumped into Annie's soaking cunt, his cuffs cutting into her back. She moaned and then managed to slide underneath him. Suddenly, his cock was in her cunt and he felt so full. Tom's fucking somehow wouldn't let him come and Brad felt he was about to burst. He screamed, 'Come on, Tom. Come now. Come now,' and Tom heaved forward and Annie felt some of Tom's come on her hands.

Then she grabbed Brad and he began fucking her wildly.

'That's right. Fuck her, Brad,' called Tom and Brad lost all feelings of the moment around him and felt the cave sucking him in. He actually didn't even feel the first wave of his orgasm because it came from a primordial centre in his being he didn't know he had.

He roared and roared and begged Tom to undo the cuffs. Tom did and Brad grabbed Annie's ass and still kept fucking. It was like he came and didn't come. He couldn't understand it. He just wanted to fuck her until she passed out. Instead, he did.

For a moment, Brad felt those first cruel moments of morning the way he felt them when he was still working the streets. The emptiness grows unbearable if you stay in bed, sick with what you think you might have done. Once Brad got out of bed, he could face what he had done, and the sickness slithered away. Now, he turned to get out of bed, and recognised Annie's strong back glowing in the soft morning light. His heart lifted. She was there and everything would be fine. She was there.

He tiptoed around the bedroom, thinking that somehow, today, if he woke her, it would spoil the feeling that everything was fine. Let her lie there, radiant and white, her black hair fanning out on the sheets in small puddles of curls. He didn't wish to hear her voice, although it could be so musical. He didn't wish to see her eyes or any part of her animated. He remembered reading that Edgar Allen Poe thought that the most romantic thing in the world is a dying beautiful woman. Perhaps better if she *were* dying.

Something shimmered in that thought, and it must have reached Annie. She sat straight up. 'Why are you sneaking around?'

'I didn't want to wake you.'

'Why not? Let's fuck, Brad. Do you want to?'

'Actually, um, well, can we eat something? I feel sick.'

'Oh, poor lover. What's wrong?'

'Nothing really. We had quite a night last night.'

'Did you enjoy? It's so important to me that you enjoyed it. Tom enjoyed . . .'

'Oh God. It was Tom. What the fuck did you do that for? Those days are over. Damn it!' Brad walked in and out of the closet, moving groups of hangers and then reappearing as if he had something to say. 'Why did you choose that, Annie? Why that?'

'Why not? It seemed to me you were enjoying yourself.'

'Just because I have an orgasm that makes me fucking pass out does not mean I'm enjoying myself.'

'Can you hear what you're saying?'

'I hear that your pleasure is, apparently, all that matters.'

'What!' Annie pulled the sheets over her breasts and her focus narrowed to the spot on the back of Brad's head where his hair was beginning to thin. She couldn't fathom what he was saying. His pleasure mattered a lot to her – more than her own. Since he had no boundaries that she could sense, she thought she should have none either. It seemed fair. And the closure with Tom was so satisfying. Tom even kissed her and apologised that things had been so difficult for him, for taking things out on her. She had blithely imagined that perhaps they might even become quite a loving threesome.

'Annie, I think this is going to be a day where I need some time, OK?'

'Whatever you want, Brad. You know I love you.'

'Jesus Christ, why tell me now? For the first time, you tell me now you love me? I am feeling really fucked, in every sense of the word. Annie, I don't know if I can do this. I just don't get you.'

'Maybe there's nothing to get.'

'That, dear love, is truly what frightens me.'

Annie saw the tears drop on to her chest before she knew she was crying. 'What did I do wrong here, Brad?

I did your very wish. You love the exciting, the unusual. Jesus! He was your lover.'

'Don't ever use that word. We were not lovers in any way you understand that word. We were users. He used my body and I let him do it. It was an exchange of fluids. It was fucking. You and I make love. I never wanted those two worlds to cross.'

'Haven't they already?'

'When you were a client? OK, but I wasn't connected to you. We were users, not lovers. Can't you feel the difference? I give you my heart, Annie. Maybe we don't talk about it, but I give it to you. It comes with my sperm, but it's from my heart.'

'Can it be from somewhere else?' Annie sounded alarmed and unsure. She really didn't feel the difference he was describing. She felt her back grow cold as she could tell this conversation, if she didn't stop it, was going down a very hollow place.

'OK, Brad. You go back to your flat and you call me if you can.'

'Could you wait a minute? Oh, please keep the sheets around your body. I can't bear to see you naked right now.' He breathed in. 'Do you understand me?'

'Brad, truly, I understand nothing.'

She wrote:

I fear that I haven't a soul. I really never thought about it before, but how can a man with a history like Brad's be frightened of me? And he is frightened.

I love to fuck. Through this, I feel love. The more pleasure I feel through this process, the more it seems I love. Does that make sense?

Been thinking about my older sister. She is not only religious, but very moral. I mean, she keeps her word, she never does anything to make people ill at ease, she tries to adjust to her husband, love my sweet little niece, and serve in the community all the time. She's the perfect woman the way it seems to me our world describes. She is still beautiful, dyes her hair, wears the appropriate beiges to everything, is the kind of mother her children will be referring to as the great Mom.

I don't do any of these things. But I am missing something. I feel like this space on earth that I take up should be for something. If I relax, it worries me, this direction in my life. When I am alone, I masturbate constantly and live for the moment when I will fuck again. There's nothing else which really matters to me. What is there to this world except pleasure? What were we given these bodies for, if not to feel every moment? To experiment – to make mistakes.

I am not making any sense. I made a mistake. I don't know how, but I feel guilty over how I walked on Brad's territory. How did I do it? I wasn't thinking at all. I just wanted him to be in the most submissive position possible. Why, Annie?

That body! I can see it completely in my mind. I mean completely. Oh, how his muscle on his outer thigh waves in and out as he walks. How his sandy brown hair seems to be forever changing colour, reddish, blondish, brownish. His green eyes can at times seem yellow like a cat's or blue like a bird's. His voice is what got me even in the first moment. He is all man. Which even, I don't know why yet, justifies how he would fuck other men. It's like he is so much a man he understands them so well.

But something is wrong. Terribly wrong. I think he needs me.

Chapter Fourteen

'*B*rad?'
  'Hello, Annie. God, it's good to hear your voice. You haven't called in a long time.'

'You haven't called either.'

'I was afraid. Really. I don't know what to make of what happened.'

'You mean with Tom?'

'And my entire life before you. You do something to me that makes me feel I have never lived before. It's like a drug.'

'That's so sweet, Brad. Why don't you come to my place now and we can kiss and make up?'

'Again, Annie, I am really afraid of you. You consume me. I don't know.'

'What don't you know? You know how to suck my pussy. You know how to give me the greatest pleasure I have ever known. You know how to enjoy and receive pleasure. You know how to use your wonderful cock and to . . .'

'That's just it, Annie. You make me feel more. I'm not hollow any more. Your lovemaking touched my soul. Did it touch yours?'

'What do you mean?'

'Please tell me you understand me, Annie. I need you to understand me.'

'I am trying, Brad. Really. I want to see you, to hold you, to suck on you, to feel you come. The door's open and I am too.'

Annie hung up the phone. She took off her work clothes, leaving on only her black stockings and garter belt. Then she lay back on her bed. Her room always smelled of lilacs, grown on her balcony, and it was filled with deep-hued reds and purples. Lately, Annie had hung several mirrors behind faux curtains to make the room a mystery with odd angles. She loved to lie on her bed and fantasise about a different time when people had more time for lovemaking

She reached under her bed and pulled out her favourite toy. It was a leather-covered vibrator with a large mouth. Annie put it on her pussy and turned it on. The vibrator shook her clit and her vagina, giving a buzz to the entire pelvic area with little swirls on her clit and a half dildo which moved slowly in and out of her hole. It almost made her come instantly and Annie had to think of stories which would elongate the sensation. She loved the pre-orgasm feelings but once she came with the vibrator, she immediately turned it off. It made her sad afterwards.

She began to think of one of her favourite fantasies, where she was on an old Victorian train. She was travelling for the sole reason of seeing new places. Annie imagined herself dressed in the clothes of the time, with high buttoned shoes and tight-fitting bodices. A stylish hat with a long feather covered part of her face.

It was night and she was attempting to get into her compartment, but the door would not open. Try as she might, she couldn't get the door to move. The train lurched here and there and she was thrown back and forth between her door and the one on the other side of the narrow aisle.

Suddenly, she felt a firm hand grab her ass. She started to protest, but no one was around to hear her. The hand began to move her long skirt up and then it reached under the hem-line and moved up her thigh. She couldn't move and the hand dragged her back into the opposing compartment.

The train rocked wildly to and fro as a pair of skilled hands lifted her skirt all the way up and unfastened her underwear. Now she was only in her stockings, with her crotch exposed. The hands began to massage her clit and she was torn between leaving, as a proper Victorian woman ought to, and staying to receive such pleasures as she had never had. She sighed as the hands deftly found a source of pleasure inside her vagina. They shoved in and out of the vagina and she began to wail. It was so wonderful to wail because nobody could hear her on the train.

She felt a cold hard shape being shoved up her cunt. She protested a bit and then discovered she loved it. The hands began to shove this in and out of her, to the rhythm of the train. She felt the hard cock at her back.

Annie stopped her fantasising when she realised she must have heard the doorbell ring. She pulled on a red silk robe and opened the door. It was Brad.

'I am so hot, honey. Please join me.' Annie grabbed his hand and placed him in the gold velvet chair opposite her bed. She threw off her robe and pulled out her toy again.

'Please tell me that you like to watch,' she panted out.

'Annie, I love to watch.' His voice sounded like he wanted to say more, but Annie's throbbing sex-spot wouldn't permit her to hear him. She coyly rolled on the bed, pulling the bedspread between her legs and up over her face. Brad was sure she must have been the high temptress in another time. He could so clearly see her seducing men out of every moral they might possess. He could see her hanged for that, burned for that, but *never* sorry for that.

She covered her face and positioned the vibrator on her cunt. Annie felt Brad's sexual energy all over the room and she delighted that he couldn't see her wanting eyes, her red, waiting mouth. She let herself go with the pleasure she felt, pushing the vibrator in and out at her own pace. She slid her body up and down on the antique duvet.

'Lover, how you dance! You are so *animal*, so woman. What are you thinking of?'

'Sweetie, when I masturbate, I don't truly know how to talk. I just am fucking myself. I have a fantasy now, but ... oh, mmm, it will be ... so hard ... to explain ... now.'

'Don't explain. I adore watching you. You are every woman to me. Tempt me, sweet Victorian doll ...'

'That's my fantasy. You are hearing me.' Annie stopped moving the vibrator and pulled the cover off her face. 'Brad, come to me now. I need you. I need *you*, understand? I need to feel you everywhere, to smell your come.'

'Annie, this is so odd to tell you, but I'm not sure I can. I'm off. Maybe I can play with you and your vibrator?'

'It's all yours. Play with me or use it on yourself, I don't care. But could you at least be naked?'

Brad stripped quickly and, part shyly, part Michelangelo's David, stood in front of the temptress. He felt her eyes measuring him up and he gave in to this feeling of powerlessness. He wanted to be her slave, to move how she wished, to be degraded or demoralised if Annie so desired.

Annie stared at this demi-god and realised it had been weeks since she had had real sex – or any real physical contact for that matter. A few social hugs at the office did not constitute touching in her book. They were so

118

strange anyway, the way people hug and try to be sure that no 'special' body part is touching another.

Annie certainly was clear about how she wanted to be touched as she looked at Brad's sinewy body, soft, strong and so male. He moved like no animal ever could, with energy radiating from him and layers of emotions hovering over every limb. Annie knew she would love feeling him all over again. She passed him the toy.

He kissed it, looked at her eyes and leapt on top of her.

Brad's pent-up passion moved through him like wildfire. He was pumping and thrusting into Annie before he even noticed her. He felt rage and longing and grabbed her ass so hard she cried out. But he kept thrusting, savagely. Annie's voice came from a long-forgotten plain he used to roam, her bush ripe and full. He wanted to mark her, claim her. With each thrust, he felt a fire run up to his brain.

She became submissive, receiving his thrusts like unavoidable blows. She breathed in, not out, and tried hard not to do anything to disturb his fierce rhythm. She could feel that Brad was ready to crack. He had to possess her, own her.

When he came, she thought he was going to die. His eyes rolled into his head and his body shook. Brad's breathing and his sweat made Annie worry that he was having a fit of apoplexy. She lay even more still as he ploughed away, still thrusting after the initial ejaculation.

Her hands burnt on his back and Brad felt unsure whether he liked her touching him at this moment or not. He felt he had just exposed something so primal and vulnerable in himself that he couldn't look at her. Her smell bound painfully throughout his veins. Who was she? What did she do to make him act so wildly out of control?

Annie sensed confusion and this lack of clarity and couldn't help feeling angry. Either he wanted her or he did not. If he wanted her, cared for her, touching came

119

with the bargain. If not, he needed to get up and out of here immediately. Then a wave of something she could only describe as 'feminine' came over her and, with it, her pity and love for Brad grew.

'Brad, baby, are you OK?' she asked, trying to see into his eyes.

'OK?' came the spent voice. 'OK about what?'

Annie felt an edge creep into her voice, although she wasn't sure Brad could feel it. 'I mean in general OK.'

'Why don't you just ask me what you want to ask me?' Brad sounded angry.

'I don't want to ask anything. Not now, anyway.'

'Annie,' Brad pulled out of her, sat up and stared into her eyes, 'what do you feel? Do you feel touched by me?'

'This again? You're touching me all the time, big boy. What's not to feel?' For the first time in her life, Annie was truly sorry for the words which slipped from her mouth.

'I am not sure you will ever understand. You *changed* me.' He took her face in his hands. 'Did I change you?'

'Of course.' She paused. She was overwhelmed with feelings for Brad and couldn't articulate any of them. Instead, she said, 'People always change each other.' Damn, she was angry at her mouth.

'*How* did I change you?' The hands dropped and now nothing of Brad's was touching Annie.

'Now? You want answers now?' She ran her finger unconsciously through his chest hair. 'OK. I'll try. Umm, well, you are wild. You have no boundaries that I can discover.'

'What?'

'Do you want to hear this or did you already have an answer for me?' She felt anger rising her lips, though it never quite spilt over. She wouldn't let it. Annie never remembered feeling so misunderstood, yet that wasn't it exactly either. It was like Brad were cornering her in an arena she hadn't the faintest idea about. Annie's thought,

120

or veto of thought, swarmed her head in a motion much like a rat on a hamster wheel: frantic, out of place, dressed up but clearly nowhere to go. She should be saying something, but what?

'Go on ... No, wait. Annie, do you have a soul? I mean, a place in you which feel all things. An overwhelming place?'

Without hesitating, she replied, 'My cunt.'

Brad fell silent. He didn't know how to illicit the response he was looking for. He realised that he never would. Although he couldn't say that Annie was hollow, there was something so right and something so wrong about her. He suddenly felt that she had no core. That she didn't have a place which spoke to her more than her cunt. That as much as she had changed him, he would never change her. They wouldn't be born again together. It was a purely one-sided conjecture on Brad's part. This was the woman, after all, who brought Tom back to him. The same Tom who had known of Brad's desperate financial situation and begged him to turn one last trick, with a girlfriend, before bidding adieu to it all. But how could Tom know that the lingering thought of the trio had occupied all of Brad's nights? He had to make it his last trick because he could no longer separate himself from the bodies he entered and was entered by. Annie changed that. It had begun the night of the trio but was cemented with their first kiss alone.

And yet, there she was, the emptiest of them all. Was that the reason why Brad had an overwhelming need to connect with her? He didn't want it just to be sex, he needed something more.

'Annie, you cunt is beautiful. But I'm afraid it's not enough for me.'

'What do you mean? I just don't get this, Brad. Aren't I wrapped up enough in you?'

'No, sweetie. You really don't get it. That doesn't

matter. Maybe I don't either. I love you. From my soul, I love you.'

'But you barely know me.' She had wanted to say *I love you too*, but it seemed forced, rehearsed, clichéd.

Brad stood. 'Annie, I don't know what there is I should know that I don't. But that is not my fault. I want to be with you. I want to live with you and feel you each morning. We were made for each other. I mean, everything fits.' He paused, encouraged by her smile. Then he blurted out, 'Marry me!'

'Like that?' Annie began to laugh. She, in fact, fell off the bed laughing. 'This is pathetic.'

Brad's face seemed to spit out shadows, sucking in the light about him and vomiting it out. Annie wished she could unsay her last sentence but she knew that *Once said, never unsaid*, Rule 10.

'Brad, please don't put on your clothes. I'm sorry. Stay. Please.' How she wanted him. Not like that, not to marry, not now. Things were unravelling.

'Goodbye, Annie. You just broke my heart.' He shut the door softly, seeming to hope she would stop him. But Annie remained motionless. The events hadn't caught up to her yet.

A few minutes later, she realised she had just lost the love of her life. Or at least, it seemed that way.

She allowed herself to cry as she put her toy away and began to dress. Now, her body felt like nothing and she wished to hide it – even from herself. At the funeral, the lid to the coffin would be closed and Brad would be hiding in the wings. Her sister would be holding her mother's hand, looking around for anyone to speak on Annie's behalf. It would be silent, though she would be pounding on the coffin to be let out.

Chapter Fifteen

To live is so startling – it leaves little room for other occupation.'   Emily Dickenson

There are some moments which move in reverse, not only suspending time but masking it. Anyone in a car accident knows this. There are a hundred moments for visions and revisions before hitting that morning tree. Hours and minutes have no meaning when woven like cross-hairs in a pendulum – back, forth, tick, tock, in, out. Sex can be glorious in these times for the body seems suspended, each molecule its own time zone. That's if the sex is good; if it's bad or unwanted, there lies an infinite space between coming and leaving.

There are different moments which hover like a cart waiting for a plague victim to die: cold moments, icy moments, atomised moments. Sex at such moments can be over before you know it or can grow like cancer, watered by danger or love or both. Cells can split in terrifying ways, causing one to wonder if there really aren't black holes, not in the universe but within ourselves, which suck dry all things of substance. Sex at these moments offers the promise of unlocking secrets but, instead, merely hollows the parties out, leaving them aching and unsatisfied. This is the type of sex which can drive people to celibacy and keep them there. Why wives complain that all *they* want is sex.

The mere act of living took every ounce of energy Annie possessed and the austerity of her inner life was now slowly being reduced to particles. She could watch the mourning doves outside her window strut and coo without realising an entire day had passed. Lint in her electric heater, running day and night now because she couldn't seem to jolt her body into warmness, could arrest her entire attention for an hour. She would wonder how the lint got there and was the device sucking it in or creating it to spit out? Ants, which recent rain had sent scurrying into her bathroom, commanded hours of her observational time. Annie could not fathom the network of their society and how they communicated over such large areas of space.

At eight in the morning, she woke up, for a moment happy to see the day. Then a film of reality settled over her, sapping the very radiance out of her skin. A longing grew in her stomach. How she tried to eat! She couldn't find any food which could satisfy her saturnine hunger. She took to measuring her life out not in coffee spoons but in the time it took to make toast. It required an incredible effort to remember to take it out of the oven at the correct time or create more charcoal to throw out the window for the mourning doves.

Between each biteful of toast seemed a lifetime. She chewed on the right side and tried not to think of the various parts she knew of Tom. She chewed on the left side and tried to forget the wholeness of Brad. Each swallow of her coffee made her think of Brad's words of marriage and commitment, the swallows burning down her like hot semen on a sore throat.

The act of chewing seemed too sensual for the moment, dusting it with a powder sugar of grief. She often found herself standing in a daze in front of her wall of books, fingering bindings and pulling volumes out at random. She needed a book doctor, someone to prescribe what she needed to read right then to bolster her heart. There had to be an answer somewhere in this literature.

Annie wouldn't quite permit herself to compare her life events to a Shakespearean tragedy but, nevertheless, comparisons arose: misunderstood Ophelia, powerful Lady Macbeth, Juliet so stupidly in love, Lear's simple and honest youngest daughter.

Books tumbled upon the floor, Plato next to the *Bagvad Gita*, cookbooks next to *Gray's Anatomy*, Freud next to Melville. Poetry lay on top of self-help books, her Riverside Shakespeare under a science encyclopaedia. So much information, so many images which had been bound into their respective boundaries. Annie believed that was how any of us can understand – through the bindings.

Nancy, after coming to the apartment before her sister's funeral would, Annie imagined, stand up at the ceremony and say, 'I did not know my sister well but she did read a lot. A rather intelligent woman, I think, judging by the books.' Mother would be holding Nancy's hand and nodding. A small crowd would gasp, astonished to learn that Annie liked to read.

In Annie's very real apartment, dust had settled everywhere, even in her loins.

Dressing caused aches as the silk and lace caressed her body in an intruding way. Annie wished to forget she had a body.

She was trying to find her soul and was caught in the mind body chasm which has long confused the Western world, but had, until then, eluded Annie. The Plato she read was helping her separate her body, piece by piece, until she had no idea who was the ghost in the machine, the cave in the cave. A poor choice for the distraught mind. Like reading *The Cancer Ward* while waiting for biopsy results.

Brad's words scabbed over in her heart, etching a fulcrum of painful separateness. All her life she had sensed that her body and her mind were one, with her body taking the centre stage more often than not. An unarticulated understanding, but one which lay at the core of her self. She tried to find the thread to this feeling, but it floated out of her hands, like a loosened helium balloon on the wrist of a child.

To tell the truth, it made her as deeply sad as that child howling when his treasure suddenly escapes. Another balloon will not do when you were holding the one of your immediate happiness. Her happiness seemed to have been Brad, something she was only able to understand clearly in retrospect. It had not been enough to make her marry him or even live with him. There should have been another way around that. She, Annie, was a creative person. Why couldn't she find an unusual solution to her desire and Brad's?

Marriage was not the answer, she was sure. Couldn't two people be together without compromising each other and diminishing their mutual and private desires? But until she had an answer, she was not going to call Brad. Annie did not want to be just another confused couple going through some hard times neither understood. She wanted a solution but it evaded her.

But what was her desire anyway? She had been moving along in her life, living in the moment, not contemplating some deep soul connection. Did she need to? Wasn't it like something Kurt Vonnegut is thought to have said: 'I've come to the conclusion that life is meant to be nothing more than fucking around.' She had been happy, experiencing things as they came, tossing out the bad and keeping the good. Why couldn't Brad have done the same? Why do people have to take something good and then desire that it be more than that?

Annie realised that she, unlike the other heroines in romance novels, had no hopes or aspirations about her future with men. She built no castles in the sky, nor had she ever been prepared to live in them. She wondered if those stone buildings that others built for their futures somewhere near heaven were the soul? That undeniable longing which soars in people and which religion claims to have a right to – couldn't it be seen another way? Was she, Annie, conveniently living in a second dimension while all about her shouted the third? Whitman bolstered her for a time – 'I am vast and contain multitudes'. Annie should have remembered the first part of the poem: 'So what if I contradict myself?' She could have spared herself an enormous portion of torment and confusion.

She found herself plagued with finding unity: the world in a grain of sand, heaven in a wildflower, a person in a soundbite.

Was there a 'truth' to a person or did one merely evaporate after so many layers? It was really an oyster/onion problem. Annie peeled away at her outer flesh, hoping to find a pearl but dreading that she would find nothing. Only layers at the end. No truth, no soul, only layers of Annie. Layers which made their peelers cry: Brad, Nancy, perhaps Tom. And now, Annie herself. She peeled away, trying to strip herself to the bone to find her substance – and it made her weep.

Work, these weeks, was horrid for her. The mere contact with people seemed so beside the point. Annie moved in a bubble and everyone unconsciously stayed away. They always had, but now she noticed that too. She wondered if they had souls and, if so, where were these things. They certainly did not reside in the waif's yellow hair, or in the ponytail's Vietnam shit. Did these people even consider such things as souls and mind versus body problems?

Perhaps her colleagues simply fucked like roaches with one central nervous system and no esoteric brain waves. No. That more than likely had been Annie: one long thoughtless orgasm. She had lived her life certainly in the throes of something.

Were there other ways people connected that didn't entail later gossip with the girls at the water cooler? Love – written about, warned about, a promise, a dream ... Annie didn't know. She knew people fell into it and, for the most part, that it was very messy and unpleasant.

Annie worried that she never had had any greater feelings in her life than fucking. And the greatest of those feelings was fucking Brad.

Telling Brad her soul was in her cunt! How could words convey what she was feeling? Then or now.

And what was it? She couldn't name it. Each morning, as the cream swirled in her coffee, she tried to name it, like Kakfa's hungry artist, lips pursed in need of the word that would unlock her internal mystery. In the back of her mouth, it was there somewhere. Or on her body in a place she couldn't reach. It was there.

And this feeling that something was lurking on her skin, hovering about and waiting for her to weaken a bit so it could crawl inside, frightened her. She had been sleeping poorly, waking up in a sweat and for a fleeting moment, remembering what it was, and then falling down to sleep again. Sleep meant falling down. It swooped through a dark cavern with mouldy, mossy steps and hollow clangs.

There were dreams of sex but they were of beasts and ghosts and whispers.

She believed she would never be with Brad, or even someone like Tom ever again. They might want her but the chemistry in her body had gone awry. She didn't pulse internally, she didn't thrive. She had no longing to be penetrated.

Unconsciously, Annie was celibate. She yearned for some mystical knowledge that stretched beyond the tautness of sex. She ached to be filled, to be sated with ...

The hunger artist – she wished she could name the

food. The moments hovered, waiting for direction from their time master. But she couldn't lead her moments or her body any more. She waited to be led. She waited for some sign, perhaps a rash on her skin which would say, 'This way to your soul.'

She felt certain it was there, hovering in her mouth, swirling in her cream. She felt certain she could wait this out. She felt certain she would remember the nightmare that felt so horridly familiar. The smell in the back of her throat, familiar-unfamiliar, as if she had been visited in the night by a demon who owned her soul – whatever, wherever it was.

The radio bleated out a Broadway tune, 'It only takes a moment', and Annie grinned crookedly, like the hearts five-year-olds draw for their mothers.

A moment, she thought. I have been stringing my life together with moments. The only thing my life seems to have in common is that it's my life. That's all.

She wrote:

I have never been so unsure of myself before. My head aches, my heart aches. Read in the newspaper a quote by the woman poet Millay: 'Life is not one thing after another; it's the same damn thing over and over.'

What have I been playing over and over? I'm an emotional record player with a scratch I can't hear. Think, Annie, think!

Or feel. Do something!

I am churning inside. I have never had headaches like this before. What is happening to me?

What's it all about? Funny, the paper I tore to write Edna's quote on has a quote from some other poet – I guess it was poet's day at the newspaper – Shelley: 'Some say that gleams of a remoter world visit the soul in sleep.'

Dear God! Be so kind to give me that sleep. The sleep which brings with it a soul.

I feel like one of those figurines hidden in marble, waiting for a talented sculptor to set me free.

Annie! That is not going to happen. No one is going to set you free.

So what am I doing? There's a lesson here, a story here, a pearl here. I *will* find it.

OK Annie. Focus. If you write enough, do you think you'll find your soul or whatever is hollowing you out?

Is there something I simply won't remember? I feel this intangibility, this food which beckons to be named, is closer to my onion layer.

What happened to me? I was so happy, so full of sex. Goddamn those men taking my simple life and ruining it. Tom with his words and Brad with his love.

Love. Can conceive of it. Think I now know what it is. How to recognise it? Brad loves me. Tom loved me. Jeffrey thought he loved me, ditto Charles. Fred probably did . . . Annie, the serial monogamist!

It's late. Oh sweet sleep, come to me tonight. I am about to be fired if I don't produce better work. But how can I? I am a zombie. Why can't I just ignore this? Everything. I want to crawl in some hole until this horrid lost feeling disappears and I feel I am at home again.

Is this dangerous? This forced inner focusing? If I keep at it long enough, I'll become Nancy. Maybe she's got it right after all. Give your life to God and your body to beige.

No.

Chapter Sixteen

'Annie, could you come into my office?' The ponytail had summoned her and she knew the rest.

Intuition keenly aware, throbbing, Annie said, 'I get it, Marty. I'm fired, right?'

'Why don't you come into the office and we'll talk about it.'

'I don't want to go into your office, alone, with you. Jesus. Go in there and then what? You can fire me without anyone hearing you? Get some chutzpah, Marty. Do you think you can get me to do what you want just because you're in charge?'

Her co-workers stood around, gaping. They'd never seen her express any strong emotion before or heard such a high-pitched strain in Annie's voice. 'Jesus – all of you. Stop looking at me!' Annie grabbed her purse and ran out. She never went back.

Oh, the funeral she imagined then! Peter would try to preside over it, only Carol would be pushing him out of the way. 'I knew her better than anyone else here.' And Peter would say, 'But I wanted to know her better.' Marty would have his head hung low down because he had fired her. Sasha would stand as the shadow in the background, sad but not too sad. She had long coveted Annie's job.

Nancy would be standing up in front, holding Mother's hand and saying, 'Would anyone else care to say something about my dear dead sister?' Nancy would choke back a sob, the sky would darken, and all her co-workers at once would say, 'She was the best advertising designer ever!' And they'd mean it.

Annie had worked it all out in her mind so well that she was truly sorry she wasn't going to be there.

Finding a mere job after you've had a career is not an easy direction to move without bitterness, but Annie did it. She decided to learn bartending and then she decided, what the hell, I'll just bartend: what's there to learn?

With that decision made, she began feeling more like her old self.

Annie went to the place where she and Brad first met. The sour-smelling bartender was still there, the one who looked as if he had always used his hands more than his mouth, but to a great disadvantage. Apparently, he still remembered her because he smiled in a sleazy, knowing way that made Annie want to puke into his jar of maraschino cherries.

Instead, she stretched out her hand and said, 'I've been fired. How can I work in a bar?'

'You wanna work here?' The words came out the side of his mouth and Annie could swear she saw a bit of pickled egg accompany them.

'I hadn't considered that option. I was actually hoping you'd point me to a place which would be fool enough to take someone with zero experience.'

'I thought you had experience.' He grinned and looked her over. 'At least, an experience.'

'Yeah, well, that was then, this is now.' She could feel herself getting angry, wanting to push this bartender around a bit. It felt good, having a strong emotion, whatever it was – love, hate, anger. An atom of relaxation crept into her for she had begun to believe that her feelings were vanishing, one by one.

Still, having feelings and acting upon them were different things, though Annie was never sure why. In the past, she'd preferred to eliminate those feelings she was not going to act upon – ignoring all irrelevant emotions. Thankfully, she now managed to keep from leaping up and pounding in the bartender's face with happy-angry fists. She forced herself to look him squarely in the face. 'Do you know of a place?'

'Like this one I do. I don't think you can handle it. Whatcha need is one of them fern bars with banana drinks and stupid rich people.'

'So, give me a suggestion.' She was encouraged by his accurate, if harsh, observations.

'Jesus, woman. Didn't you ever go out? Surely you went places with your . . . colleagues.' The way he slithered over that last word made Annie very uncomfortable.

'Yeah, you're right. I'm going back to where I belong. Adios.' She smiled a soap commercial smile, showing herself to be squeaky clean and not in any way on the same level as he was, then hurried out the door. The bartender merely grunted goodbye, like a sea lion falling off a ship.

Outside, the sun seemed to mock her feelings of dirt and disgust. *What is going on with me* played the new mantra inside of her. She walked more quickly because she felt watched, almost by something, not someone. Almost like being watched by a dream, the way the whispers came to her on the cliffs. Something was shredding in her universe.

In a mild daze, she found herself wandering into one of the upscale bars in town. In a deeper trance, she applied for a job and was hired right then. The manager, a dark-haired woman with soft white skin, freckles and mischievous green eyes, congratulated Annie on her new career.

'I am sure that you'll find every one of your skills to work perfectly here. Especially your charm.' The manager smiled pearly-white, sharp-looking canine teeth. The neon sign behind her made her look like a fallen angel with a florescent pink halo.

Annie felt so relieved to know she had a job so soon, within days of leaving the other. 'Thank you so much for considering me. I will really learn how to do this well.'

'I have all the confidence that you will. Welcome.' The woman touched her hand in a way that sent warm tendrils throughout Annie.

The $1500 a month rent in Nob Hill would not work. She tried to imagine every way she could pinch her money so as to stay in the lovely light there. But she knew it was only a matter of time until she'd have nothing, so she decided to pack it up before the choice was no longer hers.

Nancy and Phil came to help her move. Tom came too.

Annie felt her sister sizing Tom up. Nancy would probably come to a conclusion that he was arrogant only because he was good-looking. And she'd feel cheated because Annie, once again, had not given her older sister Nancy any information regarding their relationship.

Tom and Annie hadn't seen each other since her birthday two months ago. Last week, he was beginning to worry about her, feelings he didn't know he was capable of regarding his former lover. So he called.

Knowing Brad as he did, Tom could only surmise that the birthday treat had been difficult for Annie's beau. But not so difficult as to cause the two lovebirds to break up shortly thereafter. He was intrigued.

To hear the news from Annie made him feel guilty but strangely satisfied. He was surprised to hear from her that she had also lost her job and was about to move. Not for completely unselfish reasons, he volunteered to help.

Up and down went boxes of books, pictures, chinaware. Annie's back was already aching and they'd only been at it for twenty minutes.

She found herself in a pattern of following behind Tom and being alone with him for minutes at a time while Nancy and Phil were completing the other half of the impromptu moving factory all four had unconsciously agreed to.

'I'm in another relationship now,' Tom said on the second flight of stairs, the third time down.

Carrying a large box, Annie couldn't see him. She felt like he was waiting for her approval, her anger, something. He was definitely waiting so she said, 'Well . . . that's great.' No more questions asked. Tom seemed disappointed.

'You know, Annie, there's no one like you. I still miss you.'

She set down the box, hesitant.

'Tom . . .' she began. She felt that sensation again of her hearing growing acute. A fly buzzed overhead and she heard the air move around it. For a moment, she felt keenly alive and in full possession of herself again.

'Annie.' He was looking hard at her and she felt her heart quicken. All their touches flooded her mind, especially how he made the fire race up in her. Tom looked embarrassed. 'I mean, I'm really in another relationship now. I just wanted you to know that I'm sorry we didn't work out.'

She knew she should say, 'Me too,' but couldn't and picked up the box again to cover up her lack of words. Nevertheless, what she took to be a roundabout rejection stunned her. Tom was trying to tell her that he was over her and there was no going back.

135

She didn't know how much she had wanted to hear that Tom still wanted her. Strange. If truth be told, she didn't want him, merely a more vivid memory of their relationship.

Annie McDermott was not one to look back. If she would have admitted her absolute terror of doing so, the fear that letting go would mean that regret might consume her – she could have rewritten her whole life in that moment. But, as luck would have it, most of Annie's rules were still in operation.

Anyway, it wasn't the situation with Tom she actually regretted.

Outside, Phil was moving a huge mattress into the truck. 'Family!' he cursed under his breath. Nancy touched Annie's arm.

'So ... you're movin'. What's up with that? Any reason?'

'I lost my job. I can't afford it here any longer.'

'Probably for the best. Snob hill, you know.' Nancy put her arm around Annie. 'It'll get better. Tom can help you.'

Annie pulled away.

'Or not help you ... Well, Annie, he looks like a nice guy,' Nancy said, faltering.

Annie was looking at the ground. 'You know, we've been finished for some time.'

Nancy brushed aside the passing notion that Annie was referring to their sisterhood. 'How would I know? I never get to meet any of these guys,' she said a bit dramatically. 'Well, why did he show up?'

'I don't know, Sis. I think to help.' Nancy thought Annie sounding tense, angry or confused. Perhaps even vulnerable.

Suddenly a red Miata convertible pulled around the corner. Annie recognised him by the shape of his head. She felt her arms go slack, then her legs. She sat down on the stone steps.

'Annie, hi. Tom said you were moving,' called a voice over the car's engine.

Nancy whispered excitedly, 'Who is that?'

Annie watched him approach inch by inch, his arms sturdy, his abdomen hugged in a little rib T-shirt.

He caused Nancy to blaspheme. 'Jesus, would you look at *that*?' she said more to the air than to Annie.

The closer he got, the more Annie inwardly retreated.

'Hi, Annie.' He looked at her a bit sadly. 'Hello.' He smiled at Nancy. 'I'm Brad. So you're helping with the move? Are you the sister?'

Nancy stuttered, 'Well, yes. Are you joining us?' Annie cringed hearing her sister giggle uncontrollably.

'I'd like to. Annie?' He looked hesitant, ready to kiss or fight.

'That's just so nice. I mean really nice. Don't you think so, Annie? Annie!' Nancy stared straight at her.

Annie remained sitting on the stoop, stupefied. Her heart was in her throat and she couldn't look at Brad. Was too surprised by how much she had missed him to be able to respond. Her last image of him was frozen in an awkward time and this present moving picture was in sharp contrast. She needed time to process it all.

Brad looked at her and then said, 'Well, it looks like you got enough people to help.' He waited for her to respond but saw that million-mile stare he found so disturbing. 'Well . . . I guess it's see ya, Annie. Sorry to have bothered you all.'

Nancy called after him, 'We really could use another pair of muscles . . . uh, arms.' But Brad was too far away, physically and emotionally, to hear.

He drove off and Annie still sat there. Nancy hit her on the shoulder.

'Hello? Who was *that*?' she demanded.

'The love of my life, I think,' replied Annie.

'Hello! What are you doing letting a fine-looking man like that go?'

'He wasn't mine to keep, Nancy.' Annie started crying, completely shocking her sister, who was unused to any display of overt emotion in her sibling. 'Oh Nancy, I'm lost. Really lost.'

Nancy put her arm around Annie and, this time, Annie didn't pull away. She sobbed and sobbed. Tom and Phil finished the move alone, while the two sisters sat on the stoop, crying together about things the men could only surmise. Both men, for different reasons, felt a flicker of joy at seeing Annie weep.

When Annie had helped Nancy and Phil move, there had been a barbecue on the other end and brewskies waiting in both refrigerators. True, they had more possessions than Annie – a lot more considering this was a couple who professed, 'You can't take it with you.'

Her move spun in an imbalance. Needless to say, the arrangement hadn't worked out quite how Annie had envisioned it would. In two hours, everything was loaded into the truck and she had only carried three boxes down a few flights of stairs. Microbrew beer was waiting in the ice chest to thank everyone for helping. Now Annie saw they were going home without drinking any.

Phil was beside himself, Annie could see when she finally looked around. Tom was amused. Nancy looked content to be a big sister again. Or for the first time. Nancy didn't know which. Seeing as this was the first time Annie had clearly assented to the younger sister role.

'Hey,' said Nancy to everyone, 'let's get a pizza in North Beach. My treat.'

Phil looked even more perturbed, given that Nancy didn't ask his permission. He was the one who treated people in the family since he was the one who decided where the money went. But having Tom around nullified his impulse to put the head of household foot down with a big 'no' stamped into the tread.

Annie liked the pizza idea. She needed the distraction and there was no place to sit in her old flat or her new place in Richmond.

It bothered her a bit that she was returning to the area she grew up in, far from the Madding Crowd of Nob Hill.

Rule 12: *It's OK to look back if you like your life to be really salty.*

What rot! What's done can't be undone. Brad was trying to undo it, to go back. She could see it now. Could it really be undone?

Chapter Seventeen

*T*he grey-white walls in the Richmond flat would not do, and there was no sense in painting them a uniform white. The fog would only make their lightness look dirty.

With a small sponge, Annie began to fashion the interior walls in the manner she imagined a house in Tuscany to resemble on the outside. The wall with the least exposure to light got a rusty lemon pattern made by the sponges and now it resembled an unfinished fresco. The opposite wall got a light rust colour and above the windows on the eastern side, a warm peach plaster look was established.

All the colours blended into each other and it would have been difficult to point to where any one colour ended and another began.

Annie had created an Escher colour composition and was pleased with the results. If she couldn't have the light of her purifying mornings, she would at least awake with a mind awash in colour. Bright cotton sail drapes of blue, green and yellow decorated each window, throwing up a cascading rainbow throughout the day. Annie's use of mirrors made the apartment appear three times its size.

Yet it was the Richmond area, so the wind blew bits of Ocean Beach up into all the homes. Dampness scuttled about the parameters of the flat, causing her hair to curl in a way resembling a Pre-Raphaelite woman – sensuous, not completely tidy, but large like an extension of the heart itself.

If she stepped outside her flat and looked west, a grateful ocean awaited her. In the late afternoon, the sunset colours, which had inspired her interior decorating, painted the sky in a way to make Annie's entire being fill with admiration and gratitude. Not a bad place, her new locale. Just smaller and adrift in fog for most of the summer.

The bar with the green-eyed manager was near Nob Hill and Annie was back to her commute of living in the fog and working in the sun. Well, not exactly – since her shift did not start until five o'clock in the evening.

It wasn't hard for Annie to learn how to make drinks: that was the easy part. Margaritas: one part tequila, one part orange liqueur, one part sweet and sour or lime juice. She knew all the recipes within a week: Haemorrhaging Brain – one part peppermint schnapps, one part Irish cream slowly poured in over a spoon until it coagulates, then a dash of grenadine; Crotchless Panties – two parts coffee liqueur, one part orange liqueur; The Harvey Wallbanger – one shot of a liquorice liqueur and a glass of orange juice; A Screaming Orgasm – equal parts vodka, coffee liqueur, Irish cream with a splash of hazelnut liqueur; Grasshopper – crème de menthe in scotch blended until quite cold; Sex on the Beach – whatever alcohol one felt like throwing together to make a layered sunset.

The real difficulty was to take care of everyone's needs. The man in the corner needed his drinks to come out rather fast, never with any ice because he liked to simply slam them down. On the other hand, the young couple at the far table liked to nurse every drink they ever got –

stretching time out in the bar with their melting ice. Some thought you were no more than a circus seal, ready to be tossed a fish in the name of a tip; others wanted so much that you be a person, it was difficult to do your job. Some people expected you to know they needed to talk to you; others wanted to be left alone. Annie had one gentleman say to her as she walked up, 'Here's fifty dollars; go away.' She took the money, smiled, and left him alone the entire evening.

Somehow, Annie managed everything. She felt the go-between for people and their needs. She began to like it. Part of the old Annie was back. She could match people up with their drinks and everyone asked her for advice when they were driven to try some new concoction. Annie sensed which drinks would best suit their tastes and appearances. She enjoyed that her interaction with people was large in the sense that she met many in one day; and small in the way that nobody seemed hard-pressed to get to know the bartender. No one really knew her. They flirted with her but it was a bit like high school: everyone assumed she was too pretty to be single. Annie was back in her safe bubble and had unconsciously returned to acting like she were not available. Plus, when her mind opened up to the slightest possibility of a romantic encounter, it immediately went to Brad. And her mood for bartending would be off for the whole evening. So she tried to stop thinking, period.

The bar resembled nothing like the one where she'd met Brad. It had a wholesomeness about it similar to how Las Vegas had become a family destination – a bit like Charles's sex exchange bar but without the visible sex. She watched everyone drink the sweet poison and do things they normally wouldn't. She realised that most people were hung up. She saw tight-lipped ladies come in and, after two martinis, be transformed into nympho-maniacs. Men became capable of getting up and singing love songs after nine or ten beers. Drinks were sent back and forth like business cards.

She couldn't quite put it all together. Before working there, she had never thought of the 'game' – the crazy things most people must go through before they have sex. Or just to enjoy themselves.

It wasn't only the older people – people her age seemed uncomfortable in general. Not until a few ounces of alcohol passed through their veins did the smiles on their faces become real and their hips start to dance.

There was one older couple who frequently came in and sat in a corner table. Annie liked them. They didn't talk much, but sat very close to one another, the proximity in lieu of speech. They drank only one scotch each, neat, with water on the side. They were playing courtship. Annie liked to believe they were a happily married older couple. She once shared this with one of her regulars. He said, 'Nope, I think that they are both on dates from the retirement home. Experiencing the carnal carnival.'

Yet, for all her observations, self-advice and hardearned knowledge, Annie felt that what she truly lacked in life was world experience. She hit upon this one day as she observed some women she had known in high school talk about their years in Europe. The furthest Annie had ever travelled was across one of the many bridges which connected San Francisco's peninsula tip to the rest of the area. And since people travelled from all over the world to San Francisco, the strong pull of wanderlust had not enveloped her as it had many others of her generation.

But watching and listening to her old high-school acquaintances made Annie realise that their travels had changed them and that they had outgrown the city of San Francisco. These women smelled of experience and depth, had grown richer inside.

When Annie met foreigners in the bar after that, she

143

went out of her way to speak to them. The cheesy chat-up lines she heard or the blatant sexist attitude some of these men displayed did not disturb her; in fact, she found them charming. It seemed so old-world and exotic. In the bay area, people weren't even allowed to think like that, much less say something to a bartender like, 'I love to have a beautiful woman serve me.' If this line was said with the right accent, Annie naively found it clever and bold. Most San Francisco men she encountered had had the come-on lines trained out of them and were too sensitive to show such blatant signs of lust.

Annie remembered thinking about a phrase of Freud's alluding to the idea that the older a civilisation is, the more repressed it is. And the more artifice there is, thought Annie. It was this element of complication, this longing to be an Isabelle Archer for a while and have another culture define and refine her, that made Annie very susceptible to the allure of an accent, not the intrigue of character. It was as if she had to be one step removed from a man, through his foreignness, to actually begin contemplating being attracted to him. For her simple, uncontrived heart was still Brad's.

She was longing for class in her life, an artifice which would make her seem infinitely puzzling. She did not understand that she was already so, just by being herself. Annie imagined a funeral with fourteen different languages, where each man got up with a translator to declare how he had loved her and what a terrible loss, for the world, was her death.

After a week, she learned that Angelika was coming in for her Saturday shift. Everyone in the bar stepped up a notch in drinking and conversation. The idea of Angelika infected them and boundaries began being cut loose – just by knowing that she would soon arrive. Annie was slamming out margaritas and martinis, wondering the whole time if this was *the* Angelika.

At eight o'clock, a whoop went through the crowd.

Some of the regulars, perched on their usual barstool roosts said, 'Oh, shit,' in a pleasant tone. Angelika was making her way through the crowd.

She had to be nearly six feet tall with huge gaudy blonde hair. Annie had never seen anyone wear so much make-up – though now she was understanding if not who Angelika was, at least what she was: a first-rate drag queen.

Under the tight dress, the breasts blinked out alternatively 'Love ya' and 'Mean it'. The crowd was shouting the same thing.

A sweet voice with a slight drawl said, 'Darling, I didn't imagine finding you here in a million years. What happened to that awful little advertising job you deserted me for?'

Annie heard the voice, which sounded like an affected Dolly Parton.

'Do I know you?' she asked.

Angelika giggled. 'Look harder, Annie darling.'

Annie peered into the face with the false high eyebrows, huge painted lips. Those eyes, that giggle. Could it be possible?

'John Cunha!' she shouted.

Angelika put her hand over Annie's mouth. 'Not in here, darling. I'm Angelika tonight, got it?' Annie nodded and Angelika giggled.

Annie asked, 'Are we working together?'

'You better believe it, girlfriend. Who do you think got you the Saturday shift? We're gonna have fun *and* make a lot of money. I'm so happy you changed professions. The other one was so boring. Plus, we get to drink for free here. Stay on budget! Didn't pay for a drink all last year.'

They fell to work, for the bar was extremely crowded. Annie loved how she and John/Angelika worked together. They'd call drinks to one another or set up glasses while the other poured. Annie reamed glass after

145

glass in salt or washed glass after glass in a vermouth rinse.

At eleven o'clock, the bar started clapping their hands and shouting rhythmically, 'An – gel – i – ka! An – gel – i – ka!' The background music was cut and Annie recognised the beginning strains of Dolly Parton coming over the sound system.

Angelika leapt up on to the bar, nearly tumbling over her own six-inch heels. Annie had not noticed her changing outfits but there was her friend, in a gold lamé evening gown with a zipper up the front and a red feather boa draped around the neck.

'I'll always love you,' mouthed Angelika, gesturing to Dolly's music. Her hand extended down to Annie and before she knew it, Annie was being hoisted on to the bar. She stood looking out at a sea of customers with lighters ablaze.

Suddenly, the music changed and started going very fast. 'Ain't nothin' dirty going on here,' belted out Dolly. Angelika hopped up and down a few times then ripped off her evening gown and threw it out to the crowd. Now clad in a corset with those blinking boobs 'Love ya' and 'Mean it', she twirled on the bar, pulled the red feather boa between her legs – and proceeded to jump out into an enthusiastic crowd that was willing to break her fall.

Annie laughed and laughed. The whole place seemed trained for Angelika. Five-dollar bills were being stuffed in every part of the corset while Angelika ran through the place, throwing glitter into the air, giggling and kissing people.

She slid back behind the bar. 'Darling Annie, could you pull these off me?' Annie counted out twenty-two five-dollar bills. She gave them to Angelika who said, 'Now, for the second act, we're gonna do what I promised. Let's make some money, girl.' She giggled.

Angelika strapped a bottle of tequila on to her left

breast, replacing the blinking light. She then strapped a bottle of gin on to the right breast, repeating the procedure.

'They love this. Like drinking mother's milk. Just keep the glasswork going, my little wet-nurse.'

Annie set up and rinsed, set up and rinsed, salted, vermouth rinsed, salted – surely over five hundred margarita and martini glasses. Angelika was indefatigable, squirting alcohol out the fake breasts to an equally inexhaustible crowd of drinkers. Annie did not know people could drink that fast or that anyone could make drinks that fast. Angelika was doing both and not showing any signs of the effect. Annie witnessed at least half a bottle of tequila going past Angelika's large ruby-red lips. Shot glasses rose, clinked, customers toasted Angelika with, 'Love ya,' slammed back the tequila, squished a lime in their mouths and finished by setting their glass loudly on the bar and saying, 'Mean it.' Angelika matched each group drink for drink.

At the end of the night, they split their tips. Each went home with five hundred. Angelika said to the green-eyed manager, 'Hey, not a bad night, Kerri. We sold over four thousand worth of booze.'

Kerri was delighted. 'Angelika, when would you like to work next? Anytime you need a shift . . . you are so good for business.'

Angelika looked at Annie. 'When do you work next?'

They arranged to work all Saturdays together and Annie was surprised she was able to earn nearly as much as she did in the advertising world. It just lacked a bit of certainty but was not lacking in seduction. She and John seduced everyone with their bar act and fast service. Three Saturdays into it, the customers had also begun to call out, 'Ann – ie! Ann – ie!' to her sheer delight.

A fourth Saturday, Annie was pushing through all the eager faces, following Angelika after she made her strip/leap scenario and worked the crowd for tips. They had decided that the best way to sell drinks while Angelika was away from the bar was simply to follow her. Annie then made nearly as much as Angelika. Money was shoved into every article of clothing which presented itself, and if those were full, dollar bills filled her hair. Both Annie's and Angelika's.

A pair of familiar hands shoved something deep into her cleavage. Annie looked about her but could not find the person. Then the gaiety of the evening thrust itself upon her again, and she forgot about it.

Back at the bar, she pulled out a red chile pepper.

Angelika was all ears as to who could shove a food item down her friend's chest that would make Annie smile.

'I don't know if it is him, but just thinking it is enough for me.'

'For godsakes, Annie darling, why don't you just call the man. You're acting just like a woman.'

Annie knew she was and it made her furious with herself. Yet, try as she might, she could not call him.

They rode home together after those shifts. It turned out John's house, which he miraculously owned at the age of twenty-six, was not too far from her flat.

On the bus, John, *sans* make-up and boobs, introduced her to his line-up of characters.

'There's the Skunk lady, the Chinese Roseanne, the Boy in the Red Pants, and Mrs Finklehopper who looks like my kindergarten teacher.'

Sure enough, every time they rode together, one of these characters would appear. The Skunk Lady was a short woman with a turned-up nose and a wide streak of white going through her black hair. The other characters were clear from the moment she saw them. None of them knew John by name. Probably referred to him as the Italian Man with Smudged Eyeliner and a Large Purse.

Annie and John took bets to see who they'd run into on the ride home and Annie won more often than not.

John said she had psychic abilities she wasn't using fully. 'It's the way to riches, Annie,' he giggled. 'Just plug in and you'll be on your way ... if you don't spend it all. Still buying *lattes* instead of making them?'

Angelika and Annie had become a regular feature on Saturdays. Single-handedly, they had managed to convert the yuppie crowd into a cross-section for all walks of San Francisco life. Gays, lesbians, blacks, Latinos, old, young, the pierced and the non-pierced came to drink and participate in the spectacle – which grew more outrageous with every show.

Annie sometimes showed up in her leather bustier and a whip to punish 'bad boys' while Angelika lip-synched, 'Who's sorry now?'

Angelika had trained the crowd to throw glitter and several of the Saturday Night regulars now wore shirts saying either 'Love ya' or 'Mean it!'

Annie had come up with an idea to have a strap-on bottle of her own. So she served chilled shots of vodka from a device which hung between her legs. Angelika would rush under her with a glass containing a bit of cream. Angelika would hold the glass up and say, 'Was it good for you?' before adding the Kahlua necessary to make a White Russian. The crowd loved the bawdiness, amazed a woman and a sort of woman could behave in such a way. They responded by drinking more and Annie and Angelika responded by serving more, and getting more and more risqué. At times, Kerri was so shocked she simply went back into the dining room and left the two to their own devices. Cops were called from time to time but when they saw Annie, they only stayed to watch.

Every once in a while, television crews would appear or a reporter would snap their picture. Since Annie had no TV, she had no idea how to gauge the celebrity. It didn't matter to her much anyway. She was enjoying the tips and had discovered a new and fun way to make a living.

Imagine the funeral then! It would be packed and all the regulars would show up with lighters ablaze chanting, 'Ann – ie! Ann – ie!' Nancy would be standing there, dumbfounded, at the sheer volume of friends her sister had accumulated. Father would be aghast at the type of friends she had acquired. Annie would be smiling to herself in her coffin, dressed in a special outfit assembled by Angelika.

And Brad would be wistfully holding up a single red chile pepper, sorry he let her get away. Perhaps better not to imagine the funeral. Annie needed to keep that part of herself closed up.

One night, while riding home from a particularly raucous Saturday shift, Angelika said to Annie, 'Hon, what I don't get is why you're not with a man. They all want you, girl – so ... what are you waiting for?' Angelika was still in full costume, though a five-o'clock shadow began to show through the foundation.

'Hmm. I guess I am just waiting. Had been hoping my life would put itself together without me. I've been the active agent in my life and look where it got me.'

'Annie, that ain't gonna happen. Some prince charming is not going to show his happy ass up in the bar and take you away from all this.'

'I know ... it's just ... I want some experience, you know?'

Angelika was giggling, not noticing Annie's sad, drooping eyes. 'That's all you ever have, girlfriend. It's one experience after another with you.'

Annie turned to face Angelika directly but found that she was more comfortable looking past her to the opposite wall of the bus which sported a few couplets of a poem sponsored by the Poetry in Public Places series. 'No, that's not what I mean, John. All my life, I've been bringing the world to me. I want off the island. I want to be somewhere where I'm not looking for the world, it's looking for me. I want to go to it.'

'It's Angelika, sweetheart. We've talked about this before! Now,' she fluffed her wig, 'it sounds to Angelika like you want to be more aggressive, not less.'

'No. I want someone to take me far from here. To infuse my life with class, to restrain my freedom a bit so I develop some depth. I don't have any depth. You know how those people who live in Europe and then come back to the States?'

Angelika did not look like she had any idea what Annie was speaking about. Annie continued, a bit annoyed that her friend seemed to make her words seem crazy, whereas they felt quite sane to the speaker.

'When those people come back, they are different. I've seen it. I want that. I want some sophistication.'

'Annie dear, it sounds like you want a facade, nothing more. Believe you me, I know something about that one.' Angelika looked away, red ruby lips in a pout.

Annie ignored the sudden mood change of her friend and began to speak more loudly, as if volume would make up for confusion and lack of conviction. 'I want to be seduced by someone exotic. To take me away from here and put me somewhere where I'll forget everything that happened to me before . . .'

She stopped.

Angelika, who was about to say, 'Callgon, take me away,' saw Annie's distraught face and put an arm around her. 'I'm assuming, dear, that you do not mean "before" we met or before you met John.'

Annie told about the nothingness she came to feel after having broken it off with Brad.

'What, darling? You wouldn't marry a prostitute? Why didn't you introduce me to him?'

Annie laughed and stood up. Her stop was next. She smiled at Angelika. 'Thanks, friend.'

'You talk to me anytime, Annie darling,' Angelika yelled out the window.

She had almost forgotten her soul search when one night, a few months later, a dark-haired man came in and changed everything.

'Hello. I'm Ilmar' he greeted her with the thickest of Slavic accents, one seeming to come from an era of aristocracy. Annie smiled, introduced herself and asked him to sit at the bar.

'You are truly one of the most beautiful Americans I have ever seen.'

Annie looked around to see if anyone had heard him. She saw that no one had and smiled. This man's wolf eyes had sperm in them, she could feel it crawling up her ankles to her crotch. Annie had thought those feelings were over, barely remembering there was a time when she lived from sexual escapade to escapade with life very meaningless in between. With the bartending, life felt not so hopeless and she relished being able to observe relationships unfold and fold back up again in the course of an evening. But there were no escapades. Yet.

'Ilmar,' she smiled again, 'What would you like to drink?'

'Could you bring me a bottle of Dom Perignon?'

'If it's in stock. I will find out right away.'

'Don't go. Send one of them to see.' He eyed the cocktail waitress.

'Cindi,' smiled Annie, 'could you check with Jim and see if we have any Dom Perignon in stock?'

'What? Dom Perrier?' Cindi shouted over the bar.

'Dom Perignon. It's champagne. Tell Jim it's *really* nice champagne. He should know.' Annie noticed that, by raising her voice, she had also managed to stick out her tits.

Ilmar followed Cindi with his eyes and then turned to

Annie. 'I can see that you have taste.' He purred this out, his voice smooth like Kahlua over ice.

'I taste good too,' Annie said and then immediately blushed. What was she doing? She didn't know this man. It was as if her pussy had taken over again. She could even smell herself wafting all over him. 'I mean, I have a good palate.'

'Don't worry, Annie; I know what you meant.' His eyes lingered over her slight bit of revealed cleavage. 'Some men can smell things the minute they are next to a sexual woman. It's the same as one can most assuredly tell the difference between Dom Perignon and some Californian sparkling wine.'

Annie blushed a shade of pink Zinfandel and then hurried to another customer at the bar who actually didn't need her attention.

When the champagne arrived, Annie beat Cindi away, who was trying to open it while it was still warm. Other customers at the bar ooed and ahed while Annie set up the ice bucket. One fat gentleman drawled, 'Come on, hon. Just let 'er rip.'

Another piped in, 'Yeah, make that popping sound. Whee, it's New Year's all over again!'

Annie smiled to them. 'Guys, get your own party. This man has just ordered something very nice.'

The drawl said, 'Can't be that nice if he's going to drink it alone.'

Ilmar simply smiled. 'I don't, gentlemen, intend to drink this alone.' He smiled at Annie and asked quietly, 'When will you finish here?'

She felt an ache in what could only be described as her loins. 'Pretty soon. Is an hour OK? Are you waiting for me?'

'Yes, I think I have been waiting for you for a long long time.'

The next hour in the bar was hell as Annie tried to make drinks and decided if she should go somewhere with a man she'd just met. She couldn't even ask around about him because he evidently wasn't from San Francisco or any other part of the US.

'Hon, table thirteen wants to order dinner,' the green-eyed manager said. She put her hand kindly on Annie's shoulder. 'Is that OK?'

'Well, if you could bring the food up with utensils, I'll cope.' The words choked in her throat and Annie felt an involuntary tear come to her eye.

'Are you all right, Ann? Annie?' The manager looked concerned more than the occasion required. Annie knew the manager was attracted to her – Annie was attracted a bit to the manager too – but Rule 16 came to mind: *Never sleep with someone simply because they seem concerned for your well-being.* Besides, she wasn't that interested in her own sex.

'No, I'm fine. Listen, I've got a few customers still waiting for their drinks. Don't worry,' she looked at her, 'I've got it. I'm fine.'

Annie found that as she was wiping up another table and cleaning up the spilt liquid and chewed-up cherry stems, the action seemed degrading. So did the bartending. Trapped behind the bar with a mostly male audience waiting to be serviced. With Angelika, it was all an enormous farce, a big wink at the universe of work. Now, with a gentleman in the wings who looked as if he had never in his life got his hands soiled, she could not find the humour in her work. It was drudgery. She was a serf who suddenly understood that aristocracy had been denied her. For a moment, she saw how her mother might have perceived her father all these years, for her mother had those refined features and demeanour – an aqualine nose and a quiet air that seemed to judge everything and often looked at her father as if from a very high plateau.

Ilmar sipped his glass of champagne and made small talk about real estate with the man on his left. Annie finished her shift, changed, and sat next to him. Jim, the closing bartender, put up a chilled glass for her. He slyly winked at her when it seemed Ilmar was looking the other direction. 'Good choice,' he mouthed.

'This is delicious champagne. Just look at those legs.' Ilmar pointed to the fine bubbles streaming up the glass as he put his right hand on Annie's silky covered knee. She moved ever so gently into his hand. He leant into her ear. 'I can smell you. I only wish I could taste you.'

Annie stood up, put a ten-dollar bill on the bar and began to walk out. Ilmar followed.

'Did I say something wrong, Annie? I am sorry if I did.' Ilmar followed her to the parking garage.

She kept walking quickly. When she reached the stair-well, she opened a sidedoor and said, 'Come in.'

Ilmar followed her into a small cement room and Annie managed to lock the door and kiss him at the very same time. His hands slid up her skirt, then they touched her face and caressed her hair. He kissed her eyes, her throat, her ear lobes. He mingled his tongue with hers, their teeth brushing, lips almost bruising each other. He gently sucked Annie's tongue into his mouth while moving his hand over her thigh.

She moaned and let herself go into the moment. She pushed herself into him and pressed her breasts up against his chest. Ilmar murmured, 'Is there somewhere we can go?'

Annie grabbed his hand and they went outside, to the bus stop, where they waited for a few brief moments before their bus arrived. Everything was quiet outside, the city a skeleton of itself.

'Ilmar, it's been a while since I've been with a man. But I must ask you something. Do you have any protection?'

'Why do we need protection?'

Annie paused. She began to speak and then paused again. Ilmar still seemed charming, from another time. His naivety about possibly transmitted sexual diseases bothered her but did not disgust her. In a strange way, it made him seem innocent, not arrogant. She could work with that . . . maybe.

Calmly, she asked, 'Ilmar, how long have you been in the States?'

'Not very long. Maybe a few months.'

'Your English is very good.'

He smiled at her and said that he did not believe it to be true. She guessed him to be about forty – older than her other lovers but not less handsome. His eyes twinkled while they spoke about the beauty of San Francisco. It reminded him of Istanbul, a city he loved. Just listening to him speak about the various cities he had been to made Annie feel taller. He seemed cultured and warm. He did not smile after everything he said, like most Californians did. Annie liked him.

Annie had got a hold on herself and did not invite Ilmar over. She needed to think how to address the condom issue – perhaps they did not even have the word in his language, whatever that was. She vaguely alluded to another visit but left it at that.

Ilmar got off first. Annie gave him a gentle kiss and asked him to give her a call.

Yet, with Ilmar out of sight, some of his charm was lost too. He wasn't one of those men who grow larger in your mind after meeting them. His very image was vanishing as Annie tried to conjure it up to help her decide.

Forget him, Annie, she urged herself, regretting that she had given him her number.

Yet that evening she had erotic bits and pieces of dreams all connected to him. His dark, swarthy presence, the way he had kissed her, had triggered something in her psyche. Her blood was churning and every time she tried to forget him, focus on Brad or nothing – Ilmar's voice came to her: *I smell you.*

Her dreams kept falling into one another. They began

at the time of the Inquisition. She was accused of betraying the faith when Ilmar stepped out, in a black cloak, and said, 'Let me speak to her alone.'

She was led into a chamber with stone walls and a huge, garish bed. He pulled back her hooded shawl and gently bit her on the neck. 'Do not confess, my dear. Just enjoy this.' And she was paralysed by the pleasure which sent goosebumps up her thighs and arms. She couldn't move as he gently bit again. Each bite seemed to remove a part of her clothing, until she was standing nude in front of him.

'You have nothing to confess, my dear. I know it. It is I who will confess to it all. Just lie there, darling.' And he leapt on the bed and mounted her, his cape falling over the two of them.

Then Ilmar became king of some small country and she was being brought there as a potential queen. He was going to examine her and see if she were worthy of the task. Annie was dressed in virginal garb, white and flowing. He seized her and held her so tight she could not move. 'Would you want to be my queen?'

She lowered her eyes and said, 'If it pleases you.'

'Forget about what pleases me. Does the idea please you? You are so beautiful. So white. So nubile. I want you to be examined.' He rang a bell and in came two attendants.

'Disrobe her and tell me if she's really a virgin.' Annie was led into another room where the attendants gently took off her clothes and laid her down on millions of small soft pillows. One attendant held open her legs while the other attendant went between them, first smelling, then licking. Annie felt excited and embarrassed by the whole affair.

'Oh, you're a virgin all right. And ripe for the picking. Tasty. So very tasty.'

They brought her into the room where Ilmar was. 'She

is as pure as snow, my lord.' Ilmar smiled and the next thing she knew, a ceremony was taking place.

But then something horrible was happening to her and Ilmar kept saying, 'This is what happens to whores. Just be still.' He had tied her up, leaving her with no mobility in her arms or legs. She was completely stretched out and the handle of his sword kept disappearing in and out of her. Others paraded in front of her to watch the bad woman be cleansed, Ilmar saying, 'This will kill everything.'

Again she was falling. It felt like the morning light she loved but in reverse. She was becoming unpurified by the sun.

She was in a very old field and conscious that it was shameful to be there alone. Fear, red and dark, dripped through her thoughts and the very sky. She knew he was coming and there was nothing to do, nowhere to hide. The trees were so far away.

The hooves came closer and sounded like the distant thunder, bellowing and groaning, and the horse's eyes were red. A man, no, it was Ilmar, the king, jumped off the horse and walked towards her. It was a different Ilmar. He was not comely, he was not handsome. Thank God he was not fat but his face seemed twisted and mean. She saw that he only wanted to do harm.

'I have rights with you as I do with all the princess's companions.'

Annie felt enormous fear. It paralysed her but made her sex throb. He slapped her. 'You will not be afraid of your king. I command you not to be afraid.' Then he ripped down her gown so that her breasts stood revealed. 'You will thank me for sucking on your nipples.'

'Your Highness, why me? I am a virgin. I am soon to be married. My husband . . .'

'You speak about your husband while the king is kissing your breasts?' And he slapped her again and suddenly there were a hundred men in the field. They formed a circle and cheered as the king slapped her and then put one of her tits in his mouth.

'Thank me now, or you will surely die,' he whispered, spitting into her ear.

'I will die then.'

'And so will your beloved.'

In the loudest voice she could muster, 'Oh, your Highness. Thank you for licking my nipples. Thank you for sucking them with such greed. Thank you for defiling me in public. Thank you for baring my breasts to these awful men. Thank you...' He hit her hard and then grabbed a sword. He ripped open her gown and nicked her skin in the process.

'Dear woman, I am going to put my weapon in you and then I am going to put my weapon in you and I will decide the order.' Shrieks of laughter from the crowd.

Instead of a usual rape, she dropped to her knees and began to suck on him. She herself pulled off his tights and began to lick up his shaft. The crowd went wild, shouting, 'Suck him, lass,' 'Eat the royal salami,' 'Lick like a nobleman'.

Ilmar, the king, went limp and could not stand when he ejaculated. Annie whispered to him, kissing him first with a mouthful of semen, 'I love to do this. Tomorrow?'

Ilmar smiled and Annie gathered her clothes about her, feeling enormous shame. She had betrayed her true love.

The problem with the last part of the nightmare-filled night was that it was dawn, and she had slept past that special morning light to purify her, to erase what happened in the dream world. The dreams seemed too vivid for her imagination to conjure. She smelt the mustiness of King Ilmar, felt the inquisitor Ilmar's hands upon her. Not a dream, thought Annie. The portal is ripping.

Chapter Eighteen

*I*lmar called.
    'My dear sweet Annie. How are you today? Any troubles?'
    'No. Why do you ask?'
    'You had something prevent you from an experience with me. I felt sure you wanted it. You are such a beautiful, sexual creature. I never saw anyone like you before, Annie. Come away with me.'
    'To your place?'
    'No. It's my crazy idea that you come with me to Latvia. I must go back to my country soon. It would be my great pleasure if you chose to accompany me.'
    Annie thought Ilmar's comments about her sexuality charming. She had not had enough experience with other cultures to understand that lines translated into English which sound original are, perhaps, the oldest pick-up lines that exist in their native language. Instead, Annie swooned thinking about the excitement of going away with a new man to a strange land.
    Annie's instincts, and her rule *Don't let everything open you*, told her this was not safe. They attempted to influence her decision capabilities. Annie always played it

safe, in her manipulated and odd way. Outside her specified rules she rarely ventured. It was insane to consider leaving with Ilmar. She could see herself wrestling with reason. Yet who would turn down an adventure to such an exotic place? The danger was seducing her. The possibility of a wildly different experience filled something deep within her – some need she could never name but was always present. She simply had to go, forget the rulebook.

'Annie, hello. Are you there?'

'Yes.' She paused enough to trick herself into thinking this was not an impulsive gesture. 'Ilmar, what do I have to do?'

'You want to do something? I only want you to come away with me. I'll do everything for you, Annie. Don't worry about anything. That is all.'

Annie felt herself yielding to this delicious desire to escape. Her mind tried again to register a warning: Don't go! Danger! It is not easy to untrain a forty-year-old man. You haven't resolved the condom issue.

Her mouth moved before she had gathered her thoughts. 'OK, Ilmar. How much time do I have?'

'If you want to come with me, you must say "yes" now. I need to do the paperwork.'

'Yes.'

'Good.' And with that, he hung up.

Nothing to worry about, she told herself. There was still time to change her mind. Yet, as Annie sat back in her chair and felt panic creep up from her stomach to her heart. She called her sister to tell her what she was doing.

'Annie, what about Brad?' Nancy sounded oddly hopeful.

Annie had no answers.

'And what about Ilmar? You don't know him. At all, really.' Nancy persisted.

'I know . . . please talk me out of it. You know, I really want to go, Sis.'

'Wait a minute. You're Annie, remember. You just do things, not ponder them. What's happening? You're not coming to church too?'

'No . . . it's hard to explain, Sis. I just want to get away from everything. You know, Brad, my job, everything.' Annie's voice sounded fuzzy.

'But I thought you liked your job. You said you loved to work with Angelika, though you forbade me from watching you on Saturday night.'

'You don't drink. It'd be conspicuous.'

They spoke awhile but Annie felt herself moving out of her body again and closed the conversation. This time, the first time in her life, she could admit what that taste was she had felt swirling around her those many months since she lost Brad: fear. Annie was actually deeply afraid of leaving San Francisco and that made her want to go all the more. It posed a challenge she had not met.

Had she given herself just even a few days to ponder her desire to flee, she would have discovered that it wasn't so much the artifice that such an experience might give her as the chance to once again not accept what she was really afraid of: loving.

She had loved Brad for no other reason than she loved him. Yet Latvia called and she wasn't going out of love or any well-thought-out plan, that was very clear. She was going because the idea of going made her afraid and she did not want to be afraid.

Annie would give herself until morning to consider it – then she would tell Ilmar yes or no.

At three in the morning, Annie heard a knock at her door. For a moment, she was still in that other world, her dream world, which felt increasingly more real to her than the one she woke to. She jumped out of the wrong side of the bed, hitting her entire left side. She tasted blood in her mouth and went to the door swearing under her breath.

'Sissy?'

'Darling, it's Ilmar. Would you be so kind as to open up?'

'How did you find out where I live?'

'I saw you walk to your place after you got off the bus. Could I come in?'

Too sleepy and in pain to be apprehensive, she opened the door.

In he leapt. It seemed to her that his face had changed and looked threatening. She shrunk back a bit and he seemed to sense it, grabbing her arm.

'Sweet Annie. Do not be afraid. I only want to take you. Really take you.' He drew out a pair of scarves and bound her hands behind her back before she realised what was happening. He put his arm on her belly, pulled off her robe and not so gently threw her on the bed, rump high in the air. Annie's left side hurt even more.

'You trust me?' he asked.

'Ilmar, I can't trust you until we discuss the condom issue. Untie me.'

He slowly pulled the scarves off of her, caressing her body where each scarf had lain.

'Annie, I understand condoms. Is that what you meant by "protection"?'

She nodded and smiled. After a minute of looking at each other, Ilmar said, 'Let's kiss again, Annie. It was so captivating.'

They kissed and Annie felt wetness swell up in her. Ilmar's kisses were intoxicating and he seemed to know it. A small part of her wanted to flee but she was caught up in the web of his charm and sexuality.

'Annie,' he pulled away, 'have you ever been spanked?'

She decided to be truthful and told him, 'Yes.'

'Did you like it?'

'Yes.'

'If I promise to use a condom, would you care to try something very new?'

Annie liked the idea of 'something new' and agreed.

He tied her up again with the scarves into a position she could easily get out of it she did not approve. She heard him undress. Then she heard nothing.

Ten minutes of nothing. Twenty minutes of nothing. She felt time move backwards. Her side ached but her cunt ached more, positioned to be speared. She felt the beauty and danger of being so exposed. Her mind started travelling to the spot of hollow clangs and dark whispers. She felt as if she were on the verge of remembering something. The taste was back. Faint and pleasant.

Smack. It came hard and swift on her backside. Annie could not tell what made such a sting. It was not a hand. Then another smack. It really hurt. She was about to speak when she felt something being wrapped around her.

Her ass was being covered in something which felt like rubber. To be more precise, it felt like a condom encasing her genital area.

She felt a soft rubber tube slide up her ass and then another go into her pussy. She felt like seaweed, tangled and rubbery. Annie did not mind that Ilmar was violating all of her orifices. It occurred to her that this was more like a remembering than sex – not something new at all but more like an out-of-control homecoming.

Then he climbed in. He stuck something hard and thin up the tube in her ass so that hole wouldn't close. Then he put his dick in her. He slammed it in and held on to Annie's ass.

Annie felt so helpless because she could not support his weight without the use of her hands. She started to ask him to untie her but, instead, he brought another scarf over her mouth. Annie didn't protest, although his thrusts were becoming violent.

'How does it feel to wear a device, Annie?'

The words made Annie angry and she began moaning through the scarf.

'That's right. You like my ... member?' He said this outdated word with such a Slavic accent it was almost evil, like a voice from a vampire movie. Annie did like the feel of him inside of her. She hadn't realised how much she missed being filled up. Her body relaxed now and the object in her ass made her cunt muscles ache to contract the way they normally did for her to achieve an orgasm. She understood that, in this position, she could not.

She thrust into Ilmar's thrusts the best she could; for pleasure and to keep from sliding off the bed. He savagely flailed away. Annie felt a pulse begin deep within her which she knew led to orgasm. She tried to stay with the fever that began coursing through her sex and up through her belly. The fire raged. It flew with abandon and yet she still could not come. There was not enough friction for her. Not only was she inactive but the rubber device had diminished her sensations. She cried from frustration, ready to take Ilmar in any form he offered.

He didn't offer. On and on went his thrusts until Annie became almost nauseous with anticipation. At last he pulled out and spurted come over her back.

After a few minutes, he undid her gag and her wrist restraints. He pulled off the rubber device and it made an obscene slurping sound. Annie was unsure if she were happy, afraid or both. It annoyed her that she could not pinpoint her pleasure or her fear. These emotions blurred around Ilmar.

After some minutes, she smiled.

He sat across the room on her Victorian chair, his penis limp. This was the first time she saw his naked body. It was white, taut and muscular. She liked it. He didn't smile back at her approval.

'So, you like my body. That is nice. Are appearance and being safe all that matter to you?' He said this playfully but she looked at him for some way to respond that would not displease him. She so needed to be filled right then. He made her afraid and that made her sex tingle more.

Annie was indeed afraid . . . and awed. His eyes paralysed her, the way they blazed across the room. She was afraid to break the mood with anything so trite as a word.

It occurred to her that she always got what she wanted in bed. Always. Ilmar's denying her an orgasm seduced her more than if they had simply fallen into bed together with him happy to do her bidding. This was more like the artifice she had pondered. Not straight-forward-have-a-few-orgasms-go-to-bed sex: it involved a busting up of herself, a restraint.

'Tell me about our travel plans,' Annie said.

Ilmar didn't answer her. They were sitting in Mishka the Bear, a restaurant around the corner from her new flat. Annie felt comfortable hearing the foreign language around her. She often heard Russian in the produce shops she frequented. When Ilmar spoke Russian, his upper lip never moved. She marvelled at the beautiful angel fingerprint above it.

'Please, Ilmar,' she tried again, with more urgency. 'Tell me where I'm going.'

He flashed his dazzlingly white teeth and said, 'Only if you say "Ludzu".'

'OK. "Ludzu".'

'Now say, "Ilmar, ludzu".'

'Ilmar, ludzu.'

'Cry a bit on the word. It means "Please".'

'Russian or Latvian?'

'Latvian. It is my first language. Russian was a forced second language. Far inferior, don't you think? "Polzhaluista" is their word for "Please". How can you beg on that kind of a word?'

166

Annie shrugged her shoulders. Something about Ilmar's Adam's apple reminded her of Brad. She felt a sharp stab of pain. This time with Ilmar – was it self-punishment for her ruining her relationship with Brad? Most likely. There was no going back in Annie's book. She knew right now that she didn't care what happened to her. Period.

Ilmar was reaching under the table. Maybe she cared about that. It was an action, after all. Caressing her knee, moving his hand up her thigh. Delicious.

The caviar burst in her mouth, many salty volcanoes. Annie traced their roundness with her tongue and eagerly dived in for more.

'I see you like Latvian food.'

'I thought this was a Russian restaurant.'

'Fish eggs, Annutchka, are Baltic – Russians just incorporated them. Lovely, aren't they?' Ilmar moved his hand up her thigh even more. She put her legs wider apart just in case he wanted more access. She was ready to come any moment.

Ilmar seemed to sense her desire. He whispered tauntingly, 'If you want it, say "Ludzu".'

'Ludzu, ludzu, ludzu.'

'Sorry. Not here. I lied.' He smiled now and Annie felt a terribly unsatisfied burning inside. She wondered how long she would last. Was her face beginning to show that perpetual European pout she saw in the magazines?

She needed an orgasm. The tension in her loins was unbelievable. She began to understand how frustrated men started wars. She was hot and beginning to get angry.

'Annie, sorry I can't give you what you want. You'll have to trust me.'

'Ilmar . . . I don't.'

The hand on her thigh grabbed her now and it hurt a bit. 'That could prove a problem.' But then borscht was served and Ilmar put both hands on the table, urging

Annie to do the same and forego the American way of keeping one's left hand under the table at all times. He laughed again and Annie believed she was getting used to his black sense of humour. He liked to tease her a bit with the possibility of danger or pain, but then he always retreated.

The rich, red beet juice slid down her throat, making her think of the earth's blood.

Salt fish came next. Very salty and wonderful. Annie drank shot after shot of vodka, noticing that this action seemed to agitate Ilmar.

'Latvian ladies don't drink so much.'

'I'm a bartender,' she had wanted to say. Instead, out came, 'I'm not Latvian.'

Ilmar shook his head, showing a disbelief and amusement. Did he know something about her?

Next came meat in a creamy walnut sauce. Then cakes and tea.

'At last.' Ilmar, looking suddenly jovial handed Annie a small cordial glass.

She looked at the black liquor in front of her, wanting to ask what it was but deciding it was best just to taste it first.

'Drink it, Annutchka. It's Rigas balsams – sweet and dangerous.'

A berry taste she could not name warmed her inside. Sweet, almost too sweet. All the exaggerated flavours of this meal felt familiar to her: the very salty, the very sweet, the very pungent. Nothing resembling the boiled meat and potatoes she grew up on, but comforting nonetheless.

Her bones were melting when the cab came. Ilmar's arm was proving to be the surest point of guidance she could find. The world was moving backwards.

Drunk. Annie was drunk. She'd never been drunk before. Tipsy yes, but that rolled out once she rolled into bed – usually not alone.

But this was close to falling down drunk. How reckless, she scolded herself. Annie lay in the throes of a physical insanity she couldn't stop.

They went to Ilmar's hotel room. A crackling sound could be heard when she threw herself upon the bed, squishing the chocolates on the pillow.

'Now, Annutchka. You're lying on my bed with your clothes on. Not good manners.'

She laughed but Ilmar looked stern.

'Come over here to the couch . . . ludzu. I will tell you where we are going tomorrow.'

Did she hear the word? *Tomorrow*? Her head was spinning.

Ilmar pulled her on to his lap and passed her another portion of that black drink. It almost had the overtones of a funeral parlour in its aroma . . . but the sweetness satisfied a great need within her.

Ilmar gave her yet another glass – Annie couldn't refuse. Her sex was melting, melting into him. Praying for a completion.

'We will be going to Sigulda in Latvia. I am sure you don't know it. Most Americans don't. Perhaps you've heard its tale? No?' He was stroking her hair, putting her into a trance. 'A very long time ago, a beautiful woman died in the cave there. That is my little hometown. That is our famous story.'

He told her they were flying to Moscow and then taking the train over to Riga. Someone would then take them to Sigulda.

The name of the city enchanted her before she was even there. Annie couldn't shake the idea that she had heard it whispered in the wind at those cliffs. Ridiculous, she knew. Just a thread to hold on to as Ilmar was turning her life inside out. She was trying to keep a narrative going. A simple story that connected events in her life together.

Rule 20: *Once a tapestry begins its weaving, the pattern is difficult to find with misplaced threads.*

She must have fallen asleep. Four in the morning came and she went to retrieve her clothes. It was time to go home and figure out this cloudiness she'd been living in. Time for reading the old rules and writing some new ones.

Moving softly, slowly, so as not to wake Ilmar, she groped around but came up with nothing. Giving up on her stealth, she turned on the bathroom light. A horrible bluish white light blinded her. It made her feel exposed. A hospital X-ray.

No, her clothes were gone. She could see now.

Ilmar's open eyes startled her. 'I didn't want to kill the old man but his evil eye' came to mind. Annie thought she heard Ilmar's heart beating.

'I didn't think you were awake,' she stammered.

'With such a beautiful woman like you near me, I should be afraid to sleep.'

She managed to ask, 'Where are my clothes?'

Ilmar said nonchalantly, 'Oh. I threw them away. I am not much for leather, you know.'

She looked at Ilmar and he burst into a grin. 'I can give them to you, Annie, but,' he paused, 'wouldn't it be more enjoyable to wear the clothes of the country you are visiting?'

Annie did like that idea, though she was reluctant to part with her leather pants which had been a staple of her wardrobe and part of all her relationships – Fred, Charles, Jeffrey, Tom . . . Brad.

Brad. What was he doing here in her mind now? It made her heart weep but she pulled herself out of that. She realised that Ilmar was offering her a clean break with past clothes, memories, views, the works.

'OK, Ilmar. But I do want them back when I return.'

'If you'll ever want to return, I'll give them back to you. Is it OK?'

She nodded.

'Good,' he replied, 'you're free of another possession. Besides, they will not do you much good in Latvia.'

Annie started, her head jerked back. She was completely present now. They were leaving for Latvia *today*. While it was still an idea, she was entranced by it, but now that the reality/imagination gap had been closed, she felt an unmistakable sense of dread.

'Yes, Annuchtka. You seem surprised. You didn't forget what we agreed to last night? You're coming with me, my American beauty. Latvia needs good blood like yours.'

Annie went to the door but Ilmar was faster. He stood in front of it. Annie was motionless. A frozen pendulum, an immobile planchette. This was just like one of those games in the books she had read.

He bit into her neck gently, paralysing her and causing goosebumps to run down her spine.

She meant to say, 'Get out of my way' but out came, 'Do it again.'

He pushed her, face down on the bed, nibbling her ears and biting gently on her neck.

When she began to moan, Ilmar stopped. 'I brought clothes for you. The car will be here in two hours.'

She agreed. It seemed inevitable. The Ouija board was moving and she had to see through to the other side.

When she called Nancy and asked that everything be put into storage, Nancy said, 'No. I can't help you do something I don't understand.'

'I don't understand it either, Sis. I just have to do it.'

'Can't help you, Annie. I don't want to be part of something which'll harm you.'

'OK, please call the movers or John. I'll send a cheque.'

'Have you thought about this?' Her sister's voice sounded worried on the phone. A tone of worry Annie rest, it just kept appearing on the kitchen table, tempting her with a glimpse into her sister's inner life. She often had wondered if there was indeed such a thing with Annie.

Nancy wrestled with herself for another half hour or so, but gave in, saying accusingly to the ceiling, 'Why do You give me such tests to fail?'

No moving got done that day, as Nancy poured over Annie's rules and journal entries. She smiled now and then at her sibling's crystal clear observations of Phil. It made Nancy want to leave Phil all over again – a feeling she woke with nearly every morning but then talked herself out of. She would never leave him. They had been joined together in the eyes of God – let no man (or sister) put asunder. Phil was her cross to bear. He did have qualities a person like Annie could not possibly appreciate. He was loyal to Nancy, knew how to massage her feet – although that was normally a ruse towards sex, went with her to church, took care of major financial items, and was very good to their daughter, Ryan. The way Phil cooed at their little girl tugged at Nancy's heartstrings and erased practically every other boorish thing he did. She had long ago given up on the power struggles Annie noted witnessing. If Phil wanted to play a power game, Nancy simply let him win. In her mind, she was always saying, I don't know what game you're playing, honey, but you win. All the other moms in her support group at church did the same. They said it was easier to concede because, as one woman put it, 'My husband might wear the pants in the family but I tell him when to put them on and when to take them off.' Nancy felt she had the ultimate power and it was her supreme sacrifice to God not to use it.

The lack of comments about their parents gave Nancy the idea that Annie believed herself to have popped out of their father's head, fully developed. Nancy couldn't remember the myth that concerned but was sure Annie had filed it away somewhere in her tidy brain.

Yet did Annie really dismiss their parents just like that? Nancy remembered a time, not so nice, when her father attempted to torment his younger girl with spiders and snakes. Annie did not even flinch when her father put a tarantula on her arm. Now, upon reflection, Nancy felt certain that the only reason her father did that was to see if his little girl was capable of crying or being afraid. Annie did not look afraid and she had never cried in her father's presence. With the tarantula on her arm, she had engaged her odd ability to look through her father. The look that made everyone, internally, run.

When Nancy began reading about Annie's sex life with Brad, her heart began pounding and she found, to her astonishment, that she was utterly wet between her legs. She really *should* stop reading now but Nancy could not stop herself. Gorgeous Brad with the work of art body. She had not been able even to glance at Phil for a few days after that encounter on Annie's stoop. Phil was made of infinitely inferior material – though he didn't know it. If nothing else, she had to admire him for his blessed ignorance. If only she could have seen herself that way on that long ago day, they would never have married.

God, did her sister really experience these pleasures? Did people truly speak to one another that way? To say 'fuck' and 'suck' to each other, not in embarrassment but in encouragement? To celebrate the body with abandon and to be so consumed that not any other thought was present, just the fucking, the touching, the presence of another tormenting one's limbs and infusing one's blood with an overriding need and purpose. To have someone own you, grab your breasts, your ass, and press you and cup you and love you until you thought you would die from the pleasure of having every inch of your body loved. To have two men do that. Oh Annie, you wicked girl.

How she wished she could, if even for a moment, go against the grain of her beliefs and just be *bad*. Invite Sodom and Gomorrah into her life – for a moment. Nancy did not want that kind of hedonism for ever but – oh, how she ached to have an overwhelming passion tempt her beyond all reason and push her over the brink of ecstasy. To be plunged, speared by the arrows of an overriding temptation. Not to resist but to fall in with the serpent and let him seep through her pores, her loins, her blood. Have the serpent enter her, climb up into her and fill the aching hole she felt needed to be filled. Imagined could be but had never been. Imagined there was a man somewhere who would step into her life and, if not act out her fantasies, at least give her some to imagine. To hope for.

Her hand reached under her dress and found the soft spot of flesh she knew made her body quiver. To be touched there and everywhere, she thought, touching herself harder and making those circles she had learnt long ago to make, by herself, which sent rings of pleasure throughout her spine. She wished someone else were doing this to her, were touching her in a better way so that her mind exploded and stayed suspended over her body while these glorious rings rippled through and through without end. Wished someone had his mouth on that spot and was kissing and kissing without end, his hands on his ass, on her breasts, kissing and kissing without end. Thrusting into her and driving away at her inner sanctuary, piercing her and thrusting without end until the tip of her spine met his tongue, his thrusting, and created a world. A wet world going on for ever, pounding and kissing and thrusting. A world without end, Amen.

The doorbell rang and gave her such a jolt that she fell off the hard wooden chair she'd angled herself on, just so. Annie's journal/rulebook fell open on to the dirty floor, leaving skid marks on those pages. Nancy prayed her sister wouldn't notice the stains and thanked God for the intrusion. She had been so exposed, so exposed. It was dangerous ground on all accounts. She had to stop walking it this instant.

Nancy thanked God differently for the intrusion she found when she opened the door. There stood Brad in a ribbed T-shirt tight over his perfect abdomen, a leather jacket slung over his shoulders. Her wetness, was it showing on the dress?

'Hey. You are Annie's sister, right?'

Nancy nodded her head. She opened the door wider and whacked herself in the face while doing so. She giggled and giggled.

'Are you OK?' asked Brad. 'That looked like it hurt.'

'I'm fine,' she shot back, grateful for the convention of automatic language. The next little bite out of her mouth said, 'Nice weather, huh?'

'It's great. So, uh, is Annie home?' He was still standing outside, looking a bit worried.

Nancy regained her composure and let him in. For some reason she could not justify, she sensed Brad knew she'd been masturbating. Maybe even sensed she'd been thinking of him. She felt so exposed and he looked increasingly uncomfortable. Could he smell her? Had he seen the wetness? Her hand travelled unconsciously to check for wetness on the backside of her dress.

'Sit down,' Nancy said, indicating a chair in the middle of boxes. She hastily put Annie's black book on top of a crate of books on the other side of the room. Getting the evidence out of their line of vision.

'What's going on?' he asked. He had guessed! He knew what had happened. Then he said, to Nancy's relief and disappointment, 'Is Annie moving?' His Adam's apple bobbed up and down, making him look very nervous.

'Um, well, she moved.' There. Nancy had delivered the

bad news. Was it bad news, though? For whom? Here was Brad, she alone with him.

Stop thinking that Nancy! screamed her inner gatekeeper. Stop it this instant!

Brad's face seemed to drop, letting gravity pull it into its natural disposition, perhaps all our dispositions when the animation leaves the face: sadness. His spirit and spark were gone and suddenly he didn't look so appealing to Nancy. She silently thanked God for the first tangible miracle of her life. She'd be good to Phil from now on.

When Brad asked, 'Where did she go?' Nancy did not know if she should offer the information, sketchy as it was. It would hurt Brad and it would hurt Nancy in Brad's eyes. Nobody likes to be the one to tell one lover about another lover. She was angry with her sister for leaving her in this position.

Then it came to her. Brad could have another way – not to find Annie but to feel as if he had. And he would thank her for it, oh yes he would. A safe thank-you.

She told him her idea and the light went back into Brad's face and Nancy beamed too. She wouldn't mind keeping an eye on him until her sissy returned. If she did return.

Chapter Twenty

They boarded the plane and Annie felt a flood of fear wash over her. It was akin to an orgasm but did not seem to have the same depth or thrill accompanyng it. Ilmar passed by a burly woman and Annie did a double-take as it seemed that Ilmar dropped a small package on to the woman's lap. Annie wondered for the briefest moment about the occupation of this lover she was travelling to the ends of the earth with. Drugs, icon trade, illegal money trading? She certainly did not know him well enough for this. She reassured herself by checking to see tht her credit card and extra cash were in her purse. Though she did not care what happened to her at present, she had the good sense to be prepared for a time when she might.

Their plane ride was laborious; Annie was not sure she would ever get there, and more importantly, if she would ever get back. In keeping with her other relationships, she and Ilmar didn't speak about the future.

'Come to the lavatory on the right in five minutes.' He got up and smiled at her. Annie waited, wondering what they could possibly do in there. She felt in her purse for a condom.

When she arrived, the bathroom door said 'Occupied'. She knocked. No answer. She whispered, 'Ilmar?' No answer.

She pushed her way into the unlit cramped room. Still she could not feel anyone in there with her. The voice came from above.

'Annie, take off your clothes.'

Annie obeyed and sat there shivering in the cold air above the stratosphere. 'I'm going to examine you.'

Again, she thought, Ilmar's theme for my 'paranoia'.

A small white moving light focused on her stomach. Its beam was so intense that she still could not see its holder or its source. The light travelled slowly across her belly and down towards her crotch.

'Open your legs.' Annie tried but she could not stretch them any further. 'Open them I said.' And then she felt a hard slap across her face.

Annie closed up her legs and said, 'This scenario is over. What is it with you? Take this stupid condom too.' She threw the condom in the direction of the light, dressed and moved quickly out of the lavatory, back towards her seat.

She froze. There was Ilmar sitting, calmly reading a book. Annie had never felt terror before but she could feel it rising now. What was this game? Who was that? A fleeting thought even posed Ilmar as some enchanted (or disenchanted) being.

'Hello, Ilmar.'

'Annie, we didn't expect you back so soon.' Then she saw the darkened face, menacing. He turned towards her so that she could see a tiny head-set. He smiled, as if at a child. 'Annie, I heard everything. I suppose you think that you are a very, very good girl.'

'I will not be hit by anyone.'

'Oh, we make demands now, do we? But you already have been.' He leant over and whispered into her ear, 'You enjoy the pain at your backside. You enjoy it in any form. I can see that. You fantasise about it. Just as you fantasise about being with many women. That was a woman in there. I was just,' and he sat back again, 'trying to take care of your very voracious needs.'

'Looks to me like you were taking care of *your* needs.'

'Annie, is this the time to fight, hmm? On a plane? All I want to do is give you pleasure. Are you still cold?'

Annie nodded her head reluctantly and Ilmar put a blanket over her lap. She was furious and intrigued – how Ilmar guessed her fantasies and how far removed she was from acting them out. Therein lies the gap.

He began caressing her hair and kissing her closed eyes. Annie found this hypnotic and began to drift off. She suddenly felt as if she were in the arms of a demigod, here to connect her to the other kingdom. She let her mind go and began enjoying Ilmar's touch, which was what she had precisely hoped to avoid a few minutes ago.

His hand kept stroking her hair while another hand travelled up her thigh. Yes, she had forgotten her underwear in the bathroom and Ilmar found a surprisingly wet pussy.

He began to stroke her little button while timing the strokes to her hair petting. Looking at her, one could not tell where Annie was, but it seemed as if she were on another plane, another planet. Her face an unearthly white, a rococo angel.

Annie felt immense warmth envelop her. It was dark and smooth and she let herself go into it. Someone knew things about her he shouldn't. But this aroused her. The mystery tugged at her heart. She was consumed by the odd passion of all of it. They hadn't even begun to make love in the conventional sense of the word.

She saw herself at a waterfall, but the water was very, very warm. It was gushing out of her somehow. And with such pleasure. Everyone came to drink. The warmth pulsed through her whole body. She forgot about her stinging cheek but now, when she could feel it, it felt warm too. Hot. She felt hot.

Then she understood that Ilmar was fingering her under the blanket. She moved her leg a little more to allow him better access. Now she ached. Her sex muscles opened and closed, like a child's mouth at a sweet shop. Yes, that was the feel. The taste she thought about but forgot. The surprise, the illicit part of a public display. The use of her body almost, really almost, against her will.

She tried not to make a sound as the stewardess went by. Of course, what could they do? Throw her off the plane? Yet the possibility of an unknown Russian or Latvian sex law kept her quiet.

Ilmar stuck his middle finger into her sex, his pinkie up her ass, and moved his thumb on her clit. Annie couldn't believe the sensation. She would be writhing even if she didn't want this man. She remembered Fred touching her virginal body in a similar way, playing with the thin wall separating the two, not yet 'deflowered', entrances. She hadn't been sure she wanted to yield but it was so delicious, she caved in to Fred's fingers. As she was doing now with Ilmar's, subtly gyrating her hips, arching her back.

Ilmar whispered, 'You move so beautifully, my darling. Don't worry. I'll never have someone strike you like that again.'

Annie wished later that she had paid attention to the words, 'like that' but, at the time they were uttered, she was climaxing. A great amount of pent-up goo gushed over the seat.

Ilmar began something like a fishing expedition. He put his fingers in and then into his mouth, apparently in order to clean her up. Unfortunately, the motion only made Annie wetter. She was literally a waterfall he was drinking from.

She came again and then yet again. Soon, she leant over to beg Ilmar to stop.

'But my dear,' he whispered, almost hissing, 'we haven't even begun.'

Chapter Twenty-One

*T*heir plane landed in Moscow. Annie was puzzled by how long they were waiting to disembark until an announcement in Russian and then in English made it clear: 'We cannot open door to plane because man on grounds forget our key. Please forgive our apology.'

Hands to heads, fists in the air, words shouted towards the cockpit. A general feeling of inevitability. A whole planeload of 'copers'. Annie was worried that this might be an indication of the rest of the trip. Perhaps of the rest of the country, for no one was really doing anything except complaining. She should not stay here long. Even the pilot felt resigned to step out into the general cabin, light a cigarette and shrug. People everywhere mumbled under their breath. She thought how those beautiful people in Nob Hill would have handled this situation. Kicked the door open and slid out on those inflatable ladders.

Eventually, the door was opened and a wave of people ran past the man who opened it. They were waving angry fists and Annie would have given anything to understand what they were saying. Ilmar said she understood enough already.

Outside, the air was cool and it was still light, though it had to be ten o'clock at night. Was Annie going to experience one of those 'White Nights' which Dostoevsky had burnt into her psyche? Before she had a chance to learn the character and characters of the Sherimetova Airport, Ilmar whisked her out through a side door.

She watched money change hands when the person Annie assumed was a customs official asked, 'Americanka?' and Ilmar answered, 'Da.'

A black Mercedes was waiting for them outside the airport, with its driver fiendishly filling up the inner compartment of the vehicle with unfiltered cigarette smoke. Annie, used to smoke-free California, nearly died from the lack of clean air.

Thankfully, the car ride only lasted a half hour – but with enough time for her to see the Kremlin from the bridge. St Basil's Cathedral rose up, a kaleidoscope of beet, carrot, blood-orange colours with onions on top. Then it disappeared and Annie saw the nondescript grey buildings everywhere. They looked like her false-toothed friends of Nob Hill except these teeth were dirty and chipped. Cranes surrounded them and Annie was curious whether they were just constructed or just about to be torn down. She was too exhausted to ask Ilmar and he was too engaged in smoking to answer her.

In half an hour, they were at the train station. She desperately craved to breathe clean air but coal and diesel fumes invaded her lungs.

Again, money was exchanged with uniformed men. Ilmar, it seemed, was not made to wait in line. He led Annie on to a train which looked ready to depart.

The cabin was charming, though Annie couldn't imagine how she and Ilmar would stay in there for the thirty-two hours he told her it took to get to Latvia. They'd have to be close, very close.

The compartment possessed two red-leather padded benches. There was a window with white lace curtains and a small table next to it. A tiny closet was near the entrance. Annie was wondering where they would sleep but then noticed the hooks above the benches, indicating that the back cushion could be pulled out and up. Then she wondered how they would sleep *together*. No doubt Ilmar had already thought of that.

The train started slowly, with a small crowd chasing it. A few members of the crowd with lighter luggage made it on board. Then the train descended past hundreds of other trains, some appearing permanently disabled, others ready to head out again. Everything was covered in black soot.

Old women peered out of the train windows, heads covered in scarves. They looked, with heads turned back, at where the train was departing from. On the platform, dirty-haired young men in leather jackets stood together in groups smoking insolently – appearing more like caricatures of hoods than of being any serious threat. Their eyes were riveted on the train's engine.

'Hooligans,' Ilmar spat out, as he noticed Annie watching them.

She thought she detected a hint of mockery in his voice, something she had observed with people in Nob Hill who were newly rich and quick to assert their changed social status by pointing out others who were not in it.

Ilmar pulled the scanty curtain closed and asked Annie if she'd like some tea. She said that yes, tea would be lovely. Ilmar disappeared and returned with a very hot pot containing a brew which smelled delightfully of vanilla and bergamot. He pulled out a wrapped bundle from his bag and prepared a small meal of sausages, bread, cheese and pickled tomatoes.

They ate listening to the rhythm of the train: *come to me come to me come to me come*. Annie wanted to see the countryside but Ilmar said there was nothing to see until tomorrow anyway. The curtain remained closed.

He showed her where to wash in a communal lavatory around the corner from the compartment. It wasn't a cheerful place to dawdle – apparently the collapse of communism left workers feeling they were not the ones for bathroom duty. With diminishing wages, the name of the game was to find a scam, certainly one not involving latrine duty.

While she waited for her turn to go inside a place whose odour was apparent in the entire carriage, she watched an old man reading a book. He licked his fingers after reading a page and then, instead of turning the page, he pulled it out and let it fall to the ground or handed it to the next to enter the lavatory.

When she came back to the compartment, Ilmar told her to take off her clothes.

She did and sat naked upon the lower bunk which had been made up in her absence. The train rocked and her pussy involuntarily began riding up and down the rough white sheets.

Ilmar turned off the overhead light and lit several candles which emitted a church smell and flickered demonically to the train's rhythm. He took off his clothes next and laid Annie down, beginning to kiss her lips, throat, eyes, breasts.

Come to me come to me come to me come.

She sighed. At last, they were going to engage in some traditional lovemaking. Not that she was opposed to the experimentation but now she needed a familiarity in this unknown landscape.

Ilmar gently bit her neck and she felt the tingling paralysis set in. She was unable to move while he put himself in her. Then Ilmar raised her knees to her chest and slammed himself in very deep. Annie looked up and saw the bottom of the top bunk shadowing Ilmar – making it seem like the two of them were inside of a red leather coffin. The candlelight swayed and swelled while Ilmar humped away.

Her legs were beginning to ache – he must have been at it for an hour. Annie had come long ago, though she didn't feel that was a concern of Ilmar's this time.

He finally spent himself, letting out what sounded like a shriek. In a few minutes, he opened his eyes and looked embarrassed, perhaps for losing control like that. He pulled out, tucked Annie into her bed, and then went over to his bunk, on the other wall. They weren't going to sleep together after all. Annie didn't know if she was saddened or relieved.

Morning was incredible on the train. Annie was covered in a white silk kimono Ilmar had bought for her, drank tea he'd made for her, and looked outside at the first kiss of the sun upon the passing countryside. Green, it was so green – a ripeness for the whole world.

Now and then, a small wooden house appeared. Some had brightly painted shutters or ones with carved holes resembling elaborate wooden doilies. Clothes lines fluttered with white sheets and brightly floral patterned clothing. She saw many chickens roaming freely, and one goat with a red cowbell around its neck.

Every few hours, the countryside would become ugly again, polluted with cinderblock buildings, unfinished or falling down. All those towns seemed to have people who only dressed in brown inhabiting them. A factory's smoke would brown the vegetation for miles around and the wooden houses along the tracks looked as if they were on the inside of a tobacco chewer's mouth.

Flies hovered over piles of rot, dogs with scabs ran along after the train, men boarded who smelt like they'd been dipped in acetone, and old women with no teeth came out to offer homemade brown liquid whose colour loomed as a crystallisation of the filth.

Ilmar bought some.

'It's Kvass, Annutchka. Good for your strength,' he said.

'But *what* is it? Animal, vegetable or mineral – or alcohol?'

'Not alcohol but some alcohol. It is like bread. Drink.'

He put it to her lips and she drank, fighting back the initial urge to vomit. Yet it was good: cool and a bit like drinking fermented bread.

Ilmar handed the glass back to the old woman, who wiped it out with a dirty rag and then proceeded to pour another serving of the same brew into the same cup for another customer. Annie hoped it really did help her strength – she needed that now in order to fight off the germs she surely ingested.

Annie was grateful Ilmar did not disturb her while she looked out of the window as the train continued its journey. In fact, Annie spent the entire day at the window, trying to breathe in countryside and fathom it from images through a dirty train window – apparently another worker task demolished after Perestroika. Don't do toilets or windows either.

After one more night of 'traditional' lovemaking, Annie woke to see a spectacular sunrise amidst a thunderstorm. She woke Ilmar to see. He grudgingly got out of bed and stood naked near the window. His perfect shoulders blocked the entire upper half of the window, letting light in only around his waist.

'It's June,' he remarked groggily. 'Month for thunderstorms.'

'Oh, but, Ilmar! Look at the sun wrestling with it!' exclaimed Annie.

He absently brushed her hair in a moment of unexpected tenderness. Gently, he turned Annie towards him and lightly kissed her full pouty lower lip.

'Annutchka, what is your blood?' he asked.

She told him she thought it was B negative.

'No, Annutchka, you did not understand me, although . . . perhaps that is good to know.' He paused. 'Who are your parents?'

She understood now and explained the confusion in her family background, no one knowing where anyone else came from.

Playfully, she added, 'One thing is for sure: my blood is not pure.'

Ilmar frowned.

Annie imagined her mother, at the funeral, saying that the blood indeed was pure. Annie had extremely pure blood from two fine races. That, at last, her mother was proud of her heritage and sorry her daughter died before she could tell her.

At about noon, she saw a skyline distinctly different from the ones they'd previously passed through. Three steeples rose up, Teutonic-looking. Surely they were at last entering the land of Ilmar – medieval, imposing and beautiful.

Off the train, into a private car which deposited them at a nondescript low slung wooden house. Three knocks and a little bald head covered with spots thrust itself out. Words and money exchanged, then the door closed.

Ilmar looked at Annie, whose brow was thoroughly knit. 'Don't worry,' he laughed.

In a moment, a fat man with thick black curls and a large moustache, which reminded Annie of Ilmar's pubic hair, opened the heavy door. He and Ilmar kissed and Annie wondered if she were about to repeat something she'd done with Tom and Brad, sort of.

No. They were led to a large room bustling with happy waiters and large laughing customers, who kissed each other upon arriving or departing. Annie understood now the greeting.

'Welcome to Riga,' said the fat host to Annie.

She looked around, noticing she was the only female in sight. She sensed that her tightly fitting skirt and blouse were somehow inappropriate; sadly, they were the only outfit Ilmar had purchased for her that she truly liked. All the others seemed repressive, modest or too basic. Annie was used to having flair.

Smoked sprats, tomatoes with dill and a garlicky carrot salad were set own. She fell to eating without waiting for Ilmar's cue.

Annie was famished. They had not eaten much during the journey and now even the sprats were enjoyable. In general, Annie hated anything which was overtly fishy.

Wine from Georgia came with the meat dish: beef medallions in a sour cream sauce with noodles. The beef had obviously been pounded until all the rebellion left it. Now, the meat melted on Annie's tongue and she was thankful for its submission to the mallet.

Tea and chocolates were served. Annie could have stayed in the restaurant all day, with its rustic booths and lily-white tablecloths which had evidently been ironed dry. But off she was whisked to another car with another smoking driver.

Thunder rumbled in the distance and Annie's hair, charged with electricity, shocked her when she ran her hand through it.

When they approached a very green stretch of space with hills rolling about it like ocean swells, Ilmar announced, 'We are here!'

As if on cue, a lightning bolt shot down a few kilometres away.

Annie thought to herself, But we are nowhere.

Chapter Twenty-Two

*I*lmar's 'small' house was 90,000 square feet, nestled deep in the woods. There were little huts sprinkled around but, for the most part, it was completely isolated.

Annie felt strangely at home there. Each beautiful or austere room did not fill her with the sense of awe Ilmar had seemed to hope for. She tried to show him she was impressed but, in truth, she already knew every room. It seemed like she was walking down a familiar dark tunnel which she must get through: on to the other side or perish.

As Ilmar continued to show her more and more elaborate rooms and Annie would nonchalantly say, 'Wow', 'Great', or some other American expression she thought fitting for the occasion. Ilmar was visibly upset and Annie could tell this was not the path to walk towards harmony. She tried to look really impressed.

'Annie, why do you lie to me?' asked Ilmar.

For lying so in the train, I do not lie, she thought. Aloud she said, 'I haven't said anything.'

'Your face says everything. This is nothing to you by American lifestyles? What do you feel here, Annie?'

The word 'Omen' came to mind, but she kept it to

herself. 'It seems austere and haunted. And like no one belongs here.'

Ilmar considered that for a moment, then said, 'But you belong here. You belong here with me. I want you to be by my side.'

Ilmar took three large steps in order to move closer to Annie. Until then, she hadn't realised how far away she was standing.

The late afternoon sun poured in through the upper windows, in filtered columns. She could swear she saw something move in the light.

Ilmar put his hand on her shoulder. It was gentle and she began to relax. He turned her and kissed her.

Such a kiss! It was as if her very self were being sucked out and then given back to her again. She felt dizzy, elated and weak.

'Yes, sweet Annuchtka. That's your name. My little Anna. It goes with you. So, you like my kisses?' Annie nodded. 'You need my kisses?' Annie nodded even harder. 'Annie, kiss me as I kiss you.'

Annie pulled his lower lip into her mouth. She began to take his tongue with hers but then pushed it back into his mouth. She nibbled his lip, then gently bit it. She drew both lips in, then out, then into her mouth and washed them with her tongue. Their teeth grazed each others'. The fire began inside, her head spinning. She swallowed his saliva, him, and felt she were a cannibal at a feast. Her brain suddenly went limp, as if too long in a hot shower.

Ilmar began kissing back, with passion and fury. He bit her lip and Annie tasted the blood. She pulled away confused, then scared, then furious. 'That hurt me, Ilmar.'

'I know.'

'I don't want to be hurt.'

'No?'

'Ilmar, I don't want to.' She was ashamed at the slight pleading she heard in her voice.

Ilmar looked at her outstretched neck. 'As you wish, Princess Annuchtka. The independent American one.' The way he said 'independent' made her understand it to be something he felt loathful.

Annie was thoroughly afraid for the first time in her life. Not with a fear of the unknown, but surely delicious, future; just with a fear that made her unable to think. It angered her, this fear. She felt muddled and not at all like the Annie who made rules and stuck to them. What was she doing there? Did she really care so little about what happened to her? Even Brad was not worth this agony. Ilmar was not a nice guy – how could she have missed that? *It's easier to make a nice man sexy than a sexy man nice.*

The general tone of everything in the house, the countryside, the entire nation of Latvia, spoke reminiscently of her dreams but, in waking, she found the tone present something worse and more subtle. Fighting against a foreboding sense of inevitability, her entire being screamed, Get out!

Yet she would need to travel deeper into her own darkness before she could listen.

Annie's current bedroom had only one very small window, the room brightened solely by the gold and silver leafing around the paintings on the walls. Ilmar had filled the room with those perfumed candles and Annie felt as if she were in a cathedral, ready to take some very serious step towards conversion.

Annie had never, for even a millisecond in her life, believed in God, or a god, for that matter. She thought that life ended when the body died, like salmon poached and steaming on a plate: cooked just enough to be done and finished for ever. No after-life spawning, no upriver suicides to meet destiny . . . just cooked. The 'mysteries of life' to her seemed constructed by some very hard-up men who could not justify why they didn't get any booty in this world. And the priestesses who were celibate not by choice. Once she went to a Catholic Mass with Nancy, who at the time was on a quest to understand all religions in order to proclaim hers the best. Looking at the crucifix, Annie had been tempted to scream, 'There's a dead guy on the wall.' She had had an evil urge to go up to the altar and rip the loin cloth right off.

Nancy was extremely upset to hear Annie wax on about how she suspected that this god Jesus was well-endowed. Otherwise, how could any self-respecting god come to earth with a little penis? And what did Nancy think about all those flowers with their pistils ready to spurt pollen into a willing receptacle? All churches were famous for their flowers, those organs of the flora world, God's bounty ready to pollinate. Who had come up with that idiotic notion of celibacy and restraint? God, surly or surely, was interested in sex.

Some people even gave their lives to this passion of God's. Gave their souls away to the Almighty. They swooned thinking of the coming rapture, proclaimed that the Holy Spirit flows through them like hot oil and honey. Bernini's *Ecstasy of St Theresa* being shot through by a well-built angel with arrows of God's love looked more like an orgasm to Annie than a rapture. Looking around any church, she never saw quite that passion of St Theresa's on any of the convert's faces, or she might have become a believer. Still, there had to be few who felt God's passion this way.

No, what other people believed with a passion, Annie could only understand in bed.

Brad's question still plagued her. His eyes drilling into hers, trying to fathom her. He had made her feel naked inside. *Do you have a soul?*

She heard that the eyes were the windows to the soul and shuddered at little, thinking she had not once looked directly into Ilmar's eyes. She had felt it too dangerous.

She didn't want to see into him – if indeed there was something to see.

Annie let her eyes drift over the walls of her room. Eyes in paintings seemed to look at her from all angles. Eyes of a mother holding a child. Eyes of a lover caught in his lover's arms. Eyes of angels and cherubs and little devils. Eyes of lambs and goats.

She decided her bedroom was probably Ilmar's favourite place in the house – she hadn't seen much else though. Something decadent, French rococo with a twist of nineteenth-century Pre-Raphaelite thrown in for charm. Innocence and evil intertwined everywhere.

What was the style of Ilmar? If she had to sketch him for an advertisement, he'd be 'good champagne and a little pain'. Annie felt the panic rise to her throat. She needed time away from Ilmar. He was intoxicating her and it was going to get worse.

'I must sleep. I must sleep,' she murmured, lying down on the huge bed. The mahogany posters reached up to the ceiling. Painted up there was a face. It was a woman. She was naked and fading into the background. Annie looked closer: she was tied to something. Her arms were painfully outstretched as were her legs. The face in the painting smiled wryly, painfully, and her eyes seemed to look directly down upon the bed.

Annie pulled the covers over her face and went to sleep, exhausted and close to madness. The days of travelling were affecting her eyes. That woman above her bore an uncanny resemblance to her own.

Annie woke to the rhythm, of her heart beating and a sense of terror left from her sleep – she had dreamed of the king again. Then she felt the rhythm stronger, another heartbeat. Where was she?

Then she understood that Ilmar was fucking her from behind. He had curled himself around her and was simply and urgently fucking her. His knee bit into her calf and his elbow pulled some of her hair.

He whispered, 'Yes, my princess. Yes. I am in you here at last. Yes, sweet princess.'

The rational part of her mind did not want him but a physical insanity had taken over and in her body fire raced and moisture flowed. It would be hard to tell Ilmar she did not want this when her nipples were quite erect and moans escaped her lips.

Succumbing to the thrusts, allowing herself back into the dream in the field ... millions were watching. She heard from far away, 'You have our blood. Our new blood.' She fell sleep again.

Morning came in sickly through the top windows. It mocked the sun. It illuminated only the ceiling and Annie's flying double.

For the first time in her life, Annie did not know which was better: waking or sleeping. In her other life, the one that now seemed a million miles away, she had spent a portion of most days wallowing in the luxury of that pre-day light, always leaning towards the waking end of its tunnel. Days held promise then.

The dream. How she felt morally sickened by it. Did she also dream Ilmar and his intrusion? Her crotch pulsed.

She pulled the condom off the floor and brought it to her lips. Semen. Sperm. She tasted again. It tasted like strong sperm. Thank God she was on birth control, just in case. It did ease her mind to know that Ilmar was using protection – even if it felt that he did it with a certain contempt and mockery. Or was that just Annie's interpretation of his Slavic demeanour?

She looked carefully at the flying figure. She saw that the woman was tied to the places where the mahogany posts met the ceiling. Very clever, thought Annie. She even wished she had a camera so she could sell the photos to some interior design magazine. She could probably start a career with this. People loved erotica and bondage, especially in their very richly embroidered bedrooms.

Annie saw that the woman's wrists were red. Blood was on them. She had bruises on her knees but a radiant smile. It was almost an idiotic smile. She was too happy for the situation at hand. As if she were showing her lover something she should not have, or pretending to enjoy something which in fact was horrific. A look Annie had seen from time to time on the faces of clerks in department store cosmetic counters.

'This is my dream,' said Annie to the room. Her voice startled her, coming back mimicked like the echo of herself on this wall.

She placed her feet on the cold parquet, pulled the sheet off the bed and wrapped it around herself, then shuffled to the door. It was locked. Annie couldn't believe it. She tried again. Locked.

She went to the door on the other side. Locked. She crawled back into bed, praying the need to pee would subside.

Ilmar came in a half hour later with a big steaming bowl of cabbage soup. It smelled delicious and Annie found that she was ravenous. He sat at the edge of the bed, first giving her cheek a peck.

She said truthfully, simply, 'Ilmar, this soup is delicious. Did you make it?'

'No. I have servants. And people who can deliver anything you wish into my little home. Like America, no?' He spoke slowly, not really looking at her.

Her bladder was desperate now. 'Where is the bath-room?' it forced her to ask. She glanced at Ilmar's side profile to read a reaction. Nothing. She saw only an aristocratic thin nose, full lips, long eyelashes.

'Oh, I'll take you there shortly. You are going to be at

my side all day, Annuchtka. You are my very special love.' He spoke to the ceiling.

After breakfast, he handed Annie another white silk robe and took her hand. He didn't use a key to open the door. Annie understood that it was unlocked now. She was afraid when it would be locked again but stopped herself from asking for the key. He already knows he can lock me in any time, so why would he give me a key? she said to herself.

Annie tried very hard not to kick herself at every turn she had taken to get herself in this situation. It was sex. It had led her here. A royal temptress gets tested. She had failed – not that there had been anything specific she was trying to resist. All of it was surreal – on a chariot with the horses going over the cliff. Going too fast to jump off.

Brad kept appearing to her, his words, 'Where's your soul?' wrapped painfully around her heart. She used his image now as protection. She couldn't stop her body from responding to Ilmar, but perhaps she could let her mind live somewhere else. Teach herself to resist his maddening touch. Break away from the sense that all of this was inevitable.

She still could not explain why the entire place had a déjà vu feeling. Had her mother been Latvian? Was this one of those horrible tales where she sleeps with her long-lost brother?

The lime green woods outside felt like home and nothing inside was unfamiliar – except Ilmar's controlling manner. But even that seemed predestined – a battle she had fought long ago. Had she won it then? Maybe she knew him from a previous life. Though Annie liked to say, 'I didn't believe in reincarnation in my previous life, why start now?', she could make a case for being reborn now. There was no way she could know all of this so clearly.

The bathroom was made of unpolished white quartz bricks. It looked cold but not sterile. Almost alive. A porcelain tub sat among the stones. There was no distinction in the white from the floor to the ceiling. Rather like a photographer's blank background. Malevich's white on white.

Ilmar pointed to the hole in the floor. 'That is the woman's place.'

Annie looked and could not believe it. If it hadn't been so long, she would have waited. Now she could not.

'Ilmar, I am so sorry. I must go now.'

He turned furiously on her. 'You are not going anywhere.'

'I mean to the bathroom. Could I go to the bathroom alone?'

'Oh,' he condescended, 'I'll turn my back.'

Annie understood that this was as much as she would get for now, so she accepted it. She stood over the hole and willed herself to pee. She thought she heard Ilmar murmur, 'Beautiful sound,' but had hoped she heard wrong.

'OK, Annuchtka, now come to the tub.'

She obeyed. What was it in his voice which made her so willingly do so?

The tub was full of warm water and Annie sighed as she slid in. Four days of travelling without a shower. Four days of strange lovemaking without a shower.

Ilmar bathed her, washing her hair, lathering her back. His hands moved lovingly over her body and Annie relaxed more and more. She found it hard to believe she had wanted to resist this.

His hands reached under the water and began caressing her sex. She felt him insert something up it and then felt a warm jet of water penetrate her. Ilmar soothingly said, 'My dear, I want you to be clean everywhere.'

He took her out of the tub and meticulously dried her

off with a fluffy white towel. He stuck his finger into her again and Annie greedily swallowed it up.

'Your vagina has a big appetite,' he hummed into her ear.

He pulled Annie over to a chair. He sat down and put her across his lap, arse up. Annie tensed for a moment, expecting to be spanked. Instead, she felt a tube being inserted into her ass.

Warm water began flowing into her. She couldn't believe the sensation and Ilmar helped by finger-fucking her until she was ready to explode. The pressure was intense.

He put her down on the chair and began to eat her. Annie felt sure she could not stand the throbbing on the ass and pussy. It was incredible but she could feel the shit about to erupt. What was she to do?

'Ilmar, I . . .'

'Annuchtka, don't worry. Do whatever you need.'

She got up and went to the hole and squatted. The contents of her bowels roared out of her.

'Annuchtka, that's very good. Now I will finish my cleaning.'

Annie felt very worried and a little ashamed. Ilmar led her back to the tub and positioned her on her knees in the now empty space. He backed her up and then turned the water on. It was warm and Annie felt the spray on her back.

Ilmar held the nozzle and washed Annie carefully, as if she were some kind of rare dish. He turned the pressure up and Annie felt the water begin to shoot up her ass. She squirmed but began to like it. Ilmar held her cheeks apart and let the water pour in. In a few minutes, it poured out of Annie again.

'OK, just one more time. You will then be really clean.' This time Ilmar inserted a nozzle up her ass and Annie felt the pressure increase. He turned the water on high.

Her ass clenched around the nozzle until her bowels and what little was left in them expelled the nozzle.

Ilmar patted her ass, turned her backside his way and stuck his tongue up it. He began sucking and, although Annie was half repulsed, she found the sensation overwhelming. He then stuck his finger up her ass and put his cock in her hole.

Trapped by the tub, Annie could not move. His cock inside of her cunt made her feel blissfully soiled, betrayed, ashamed. And orgasmic. Annie wrestled with the two feelings. Instead of mind over body, it was Brain versus Cunt. And Cunt was winning.

She was fucking before she had ever started feeling. A true physical insanity – body leading, mind trailing far, far behind.

Surrounded by blinding whiteness, images of come filled her, seducing her visually while Ilmar ravished her orifices. The entire bathroom was come-coloured. She was the receptacle in the valley of come – a replica of her morning whiteness unpurified.

Ilmar started moving very slowly in and out of her, pushing himself in and pulling his finger out and then reversing the process. Too slowly for Annie to come but not too slowly for her to feel waves of pleasure. She moaned and it echoed off the bare walls. She moaned into her moans and heard Ilmar's moans as well. They were seductive and animal-like. Low, in his throat, almost menacing. Almost loving.

I *will* get out of here after this, she promised herself and tried to tighten on his dick.

'That's a good Annuchtka. Don't give up on me. That's right, princess. Soon I will let you come to me. So very soon.' And Ilmar pulled out.

Annie's body began to heave in disappointed ecstasy. She thought she would cry. Ilmar dried her off and began to lightly kiss her pubic area. Annie's muscles clenched in longing for him to put his tongue on her clit. But she felt afraid to ask because then surely he would not. She stood frozen while he kissed her mound.

Suddenly, Ilmar brought out something very shiny. 'Annuchtka, you get too wet. I am afraid you will attract someone just from your fragrance. You do,' he added, 'smell like the Taiga and the wild hills.'

He had the shiny thing behind her and then it was around her and between her legs. Cool metal and leather against her warm skin. She heard a click.

'We have a long connection, Annuchtka. Sigulda is an ancient city. I'd like to think of you as my lady in waiting and this, your chastity belt.'

Annie's heart thudded and began to race. It moved like hot chocolate through her veins. She put her hand on the belt. It wouldn't move. She had allowed herself to be harnessed. 'Ilmar,' she said in the most real voice she had ever spoken to him, 'I do not want this.'

'And, dear Annie,' he replied, 'I do.' With that, he put the key on a chain around his neck.

Chapter Twenty-Three

When they walked around the centre of Sigulda, Annie heard whispers, mainly from old women. Ilmar, when he deemed it necessary, had the power to silence the gawkers with a mean glare in their direction.

She didn't care about the whispers and the finger-pointing. Annie had experienced something like that all her life.

Siguldian people were beautiful. The men had broad shoulders and curly hair, and the younger women had cartoonish hourglass figures. Every one of them.

But the older women looked much older than their American counterparts. Their ankles hung around their feet and lines dissected their faces into canvases upon which was painted a very hard life. Seeing this gave Annie a tremendous foreboding and a desire to leave. The older men did not look so haggard. In fact, with a few exceptions, they looked better than their American counterparts: red-cheeked, lean, few wrinkles, full head of black or grey hair. Only their uneven breathing portrayed a life of, perhaps, too much leisure. At least, too much smoking.

Ilmar had dressed her in a long floral dress cinched

tightly at the waist. Her beautiful curls were hidden under a scarf. The mixture of reds, blues, greens framing her face made Annie's dark-blue eyes shimmer. Her sex was throbbing from the excitement and hindrance. The chastity belt was still beneath her.

Ilmar's choice of clothing had made her an anachronism. Women her age were dressed in jeans or short skirts – no scarves. Only the older women covered their heads and wore brightly floral-patterned dresses resembling hers. An image of Tess flashed before her – beautiful plain simple maid. Did Annie look like that to the others here?

Many of the elderly had the face of her mother – broad, sharp-chinned, full-lipped. Her mother's face if she had had a life waiting in lines, fighting various enemies, losing loved ones in war. Not the life her mother surely enjoyed now: smoking and playing bridge. Or watching alligators romp in the Keys.

Annie's flat shoes slid easily over the stone streets. Yellow brick buildings, enveloped with brilliant blue and red flowers, reminded her of Shostakovich's music. So close and richly constricted. Everything too much. Dizzying colours, patterns thrust next to one another. Fantastic carpets on floors, criss-crosses of parquet, walls in different hues hung with tapestries, wood-cut shutters on windows with red frames. The art in the artifice and facade. Sarcasm from excess and a gulag waiting in the wings.

The smell of the flowers. Did flowers smell in San Francisco? None of the flora here posed as mere decoration. Its life was short and so very sweet.

Annie knew the old Annie would react to this like a postcard she had climbed into – a backdrop. But now that so much had been taken away from her, the vividness of what she saw and felt rushed through her heart. She could taste the deep purple of the flowers embracing the wall of a church. She smelt the eyes of the older women – saw their thoughts. She could hear the voices of all the inhabitants of the buildings she passed. Murmurings which reminded her of the sounds she heard walking those cliffs. Was it possible that was only a few weeks ago?

Past a church with chanting. Liturgy sung in parallel fifths and octaves – so pure no overtones were present. Just a brilliant drone of old women's voices, a smell of incense, a flicker of candles. Then the slightly open wooden door disappeared as Ilmar grabbed Annie's elbow to keep up the pace.

Young couples roamed about carrying flowering fern branches. Annie saw couples picnicking everywhere and caught a glimpse of at least one feast of red caviar on white bread and large pieces of roasted meat. Everyone everywhere was drinking what Annie now knew was Rigas balsams.

'Why are they carrying those flowers?' she dared to ask Ilmar.

He surprised her by answering softly, 'Oh, Annuchtka. It is so their love may bloom and be as beautiful as the flowers.'

She liked the tenderness in his voice, although she worried about letting her guard down. Perhaps, just perhaps, this would all work out once Ilmar understood her better and vice versa. Not that she wanted anything to *work*. It worked out if the diversion was larger than her feelings for Brad. So far, the confusion, the travels, the dominating sex had pushed Brad into a far corner of her heart.

Ilmar led her to a white wooden home. Inside, an old woman took her by the arm and led her into a small kitchen.

'Vat your name iz?'

'Annie . . . Annuchtka.'

The old woman laughed until tears streamed down her wide face. 'Annuchtka. Annuchtka.' The old woman did a half-jig, her bug eyes opened far enough to see the milky blue which surrounded the outer eyeball.

Annie felt colour rising to her cheeks. She did not see Ilmar anywhere, so she took off the scarf. Had Ilmar given her a ridiculous name? Did it mean 'slut' or 'stupid'?

Annie rose to go but the woman pulled her down again. 'Yeshte'. She put a plate of steaming potatoes in front of her.

Annie ate. She was ravenous. The potatoes were earthy, salty – dense. Not the potatoes of America but from a place where they didn't give their life up so easily.

Another plate of potatoes was set before her. Then some tea. Having finished, Annie replaced her scarf.

Ilmar came in. 'Hello, Annie. Now we are going to my assistant's house to really eat.'

Fairly sure that is what she'd already done, Annie hesitated, then moved, realising to her astonishment that she was still quite hungry.

Past an official pale yellow building, around a creek, through a thick group of trees, and she and Ilmar arrived at another house, also white and bathed in the scent of fir and pine trees.

Inside, they moved through a kitchen decorated in bright red, similar to the colour of a Monopoly playing piece. Out to a table in the living room, a place where computers lined the walls in lieu of books.

This time, Ilmar sat with her, on her left. Two other men were at the table and a woman, Annie guessed her to be not much older than herself, was setting down dish after dish of cold things. She gathered that this woman was Ilmar's assistant, but he did not introduce her at all. Assistant to what, Annie wondered.

Annie ate everything, as if she had not just eaten two steaming plates of potatoes. In America, she was in control of her lack of an eating schedule but now she didn't know when Ilmar would feed her next and it mattered to her like it never had in San Francisco. Perhaps that is why food tasted like it had a life of its own here. Cucumbers you could smell from the street, tomatoes dripping bloody flesh, garlic strong enough to keep vampires away for centuries.

The salt cod, the cucumber salad, the carrot salad teaming with garlic and mayonnaise, sprats, grey peas, onions and smoked fat, pomedorie with dill. She wanted to drink the vodka the men were drinking. No one offered it to her, though she desperately desired it. She saw how it would prove a divine thread through the meal, maybe through all of her experiences here.

A lovely soup was set down. The woman said, 'Maizes zupa,' with extra pride. Annie ascertained that its main composition was cornbread, currants and cream.

Then came pork with garlic. Hot and rich, with fragrant red peppers. She ate piece after piece of it upon white bread, thinking in flashes that she was taking communion with the man who had brought her the red chile in the bar.

The men kept talking, looking over in her direction from time to time. When the woman came to set tea in front of Annie, she whispered, 'I'm Anya. Let me help you.'

Just then, Ilmar cast a glance in Annie's direction. Anya went around the corner and returned with dessert.

Anya's cake, puffed up with egg whites and flavoured with berries which reminded Annie of that black liquor, nearly burst Annie's stomach. Never had she eaten so much in a single sitting. Unbelievably, Annie thought she might enjoy eating a little more.

Annie rose with her empty plate, as she had been trained to do by her mother.

Ilmar put his arm on hers and pushed her back into her seat. 'Now that's a good girl. But she doesn't need your help.' He smiled when he said it but Annie knew there was another message there she couldn't fathom.

208

'Yes,' chimed Anya, coming out of the kitchen. 'I take it.'

She took Annie's plate, imperceptibly dropping a folded piece of paper on to Annie's lap. Annie nimbly pushed the paper under the long sleeve of her blouse.

Out to the car, not even a goodbye to the hostess. One man stayed behind, his arm circling Anya's waist. Ilmar sat with her in the back of the black Volga as the other man drove. Ilmar and he exchanged knowing glances, laughed sometimes in a sinister way. Annie wondered if Ilmar were one of the new mobsters to come out of that part of the world, the Former Soviet Union. Was that why he was in the States in the first place? She hadn't seen him work. Of course not. How could she have? The four or five days she'd been there, she'd rarely seen him at all. And then it was in fragments: a mouth here, a penis there, a hand somewhere else.

She was thinking about how she might roam the house alone, perhaps uncover something she had unknowingly but instinctively come for. Craziness. She didn't know what it could be.

Ilmar pressed his hand firmly upon her stomach as the car made its way from the shiny street of town back to the damp, vivid green of the woods.

'Oh, Annuchtka. You are so ripe.'

The man up front laughed and then said a few words, to which they laughed again.

Annie was sure they were speaking about her and she was sure it was not pleasant. But then Ilmar's hand moved slowly downwards and she forgot everything.

How could he do that? With a few fingers he hypnotised her entire being. Annie told herself not to give in to the pleasure but she couldn't resist. There it was. Ilmar's fingers pushing on her clit through her clothing. Ilmar kissing then biting her neck.

* * *

Annie lay in a modern bedroom, apparently Ilmar's. The space was very dark, austere, inhabited by a sensual musty smell of old books and a very faint odour of brandy.

She had paced the room: it was 200 of her feet long and 159 of her feet wide. She guessed the high ceiling to be at least four Annies above her. The bed, as Ilmar deftly pointed out to her, was exactly the size of Annie's arms and legs extended. It didn't surprise her.

Ilmar took the chastity belt off that night and Annie was so grateful she climbed on top of him with abandon. Her cunt ached to be released, the pressure building in it had been horridly intense. She could not masturbate in any way with the chastity belt on. Her crotch was pounding since it had seemed more than a week since she had had an orgasm.

But it was hard to say really how long. Like being on a bad but sensual vacation with no schedule. She had begun to think only in moments. Moments when, in the night, Ilmar would undo the belt and Annie's sex could breathe. Moments of being strapped to the bed, of kisses and spanks. Moments when she almost came, to her surprise, when Ilmar locked the chastity belt on again. She had heard of men getting erections as they faced a firing squad – perhaps this was similar.

He had devised a set of wooden bars near his bed. They were smooth and felt good to her skin. On the top of the beam was a place to put her chin. Another beam came out to support her stomach. Annie could stand for hours like this. It was unbelievably comfortable.

But the catch to the whole thing was the gloves Ilmar had installed. Once Annie's hands were in, she couldn't even move her fingers. It terrified her and seemed to make Ilmar insane with passion. He must have loved her completely helpless. He would whisper in her ear, 'You can't move even if you want to.' Then he would spank her very hard.

Annie never cried out. She didn't want to give him that satisfaction. Yet, amidst her longing for freedom, she found perverse pleasure in all of this. She was not in control of her life. Annie came often in this position.

After some time, Ilmar did away with the chastity belt. He began looking at her a different way. She hadn't forgotten what Anya had written: 'He has done this before. If you want help, call me 312-534.'

Annie could not force herself to recall how often Ilmar referred to her blood, her *good* blood. Perhaps it was not a Slavic come-on but what it seemed to mean. Yet try as she might to consider that was the real reason Ilmar had 'kidnapped' her, Annie's mind fluttered away at the thought of it. Even after reading Anya's note. She had no reference to put it under, no rule to fight it with.

Something, however, appeared to be shifting in Ilmar. After a month, he stopped touching her in the same possessive way. He just stared at her with what seemed to Annie infinite sadness. When she dared to stare back, Ilmar's eyes had the accusing look of one who has been deeply betrayed.

The doors to most rooms were unlocked now and she wandered the house like an estranged wife. Ilmar was cold, observing. It seemed to Annie that without touching her, she didn't seem exist for Ilmar. Had this been what it was like for her lovers? When they looked into her eyes, away from lovemaking, and realised she was not there? Not with them? It was painful, this utter abandonment. Annie realised that she possibly only existed for Ilmar as sex. That had never quite been the case with any of her previous lovers. She had had a connection, not an easily definable one, but one she could now point to with hindsight.

Her day for freedom came unexpectedly. Ilmar walked in and said, 'Here is the key to your chastity belt.' She

211

understood that it also meant the door was open. She could leave.

How long had she been there? Why was she released now?

She dressed in the warmest clothes she could find, not knowing whether it was winter or summer outside.

The eyes above her bed beseeched her and Annie began to cry. A little voice cried its way along her veins. Annie didn't tell herself this was an illusion, this pinioned replica of herself. She went to the very still place in her heart, the place she would later call her soul, and listened.

She said goodbye to that creature, frozen in time. Floating without feeling, for ever and ever. Said goodbye to her portrait. Those idiotic eyes looked empathetic now, worried. She felt they were warning her. Saying to not let what happened to her, happen to Annie.

She told Ilmar that she needed a phone. She asked him for help to dial for a doctor. She told him she thought she was sick. Nausea, she implied.

He replied, 'I am a doctor.'

Annie thought fast. 'I would like to see an American doctor. I know it's crazy but I would like to see a female American doctor.' Annie was thinking more clearly and realised that if he thought she were ... well, he might just let her go without problems.

'As you wish.' He looked unhappy.

Ilmar called, speaking in Latvian. A few hours later, there was a hollow clang at the gate at the front of the driveway.

Three very large men entered, looking like Al Capone after having his head in a vice-grip for several hours. They were inviting Annie to get into their car. She grabbed her bag, the one with her passport, all the money she had, and followed them. She asked Ilmar if he were coming and he sadly shook his head, smiled, and said no. He was frowning and it made him look old and ugly.

She knew he had not bought the lie and its inference. Ilmar hadn't called for a doctor, though he had made an appointment for another type of operation.

The car was a sturdy older Volga. It looked inside like the one she had dreamt about when invaded by lesbians. But it smelled sweetly sick, like rotten gardenias. A funeral home on wheels.

The fat man at the wheel was cleaning his teeth through his glove. The shorter male was quietly telling a story that sounded at once like a lullaby and a horror story. It seemed like advice too. Bad advice. The tooth-picking man turned his right eye on him without seeming to move his head. Together with the small blobbish man in the back seat, they laughed. The driver spat on the windshield.

Her 'escort' started pinching her nipples. Annie yelled at him but it only made him laugh. He pushed her into the corner of the car and pushed up the hem of her dress. The driver turned his rear-view mirror to watch. The escort ripped off her underwear and put his nearly bald head between her legs. Annie hit his back over and over, and kicked at his legs. The man laughed into her crotch, putting her entire genital area into his mouth.

He pinched her thighs and grabbed her ass in his beefy hands. He poked both thumbs into a spot on the small of her back which seemed to paralyse her. Then he sucked her clit hard, laughing and sucking. Both of Annie's legs began to twitch and tears of shame rolled down her face. She willed her body not to be wet, but it was responding to the pleasure from the blobbish man. She felt herself grow more and more open, even as she prayed she would be too tense for him to do anything else.

He began licking from her cunt back to her asshole, as he began undoing his pants. He pulled Annie's legs far apart and she began to scream. 'Yah, yah, yah,' came encouragement from the front seat.

Thud. Thud. Then a little thud, thud. Her escort

stopped licking her and looked up. The car pulled over. Annie sat up and looked behind her. She saw a small family of some woodland mammals waddling off to the side of the road, a pile of blood and guts behind them. She wanted to vomit.

The driver seemed confused as to what had happened. He got out to check the tyres. Then the passenger got out to look under the car's hood. Then the blob got out too.

Annie could not believe it. The keys were in the car and the hoods were out now looking under the hood.

She jumped in the front seat, all doors still open and the car still running. The hood was still up but Annie figured that she would drive just a little way, jump out and close it. She clipped the driver as she drove by. She couldn't see in front but she could see in the rear-view mirror. All three men were chasing her. She thought she saw a gun.

Annie floored the car, nearly running into a tree. She put her head out the window to see around the hood and drove as fast as she could. Her own hair whipped her eyes and dust choked her throat but she kept going until she was sure the men could not catch up.

This is too easy. OK. Relax, Annie, she told herself. Go slow but not too slow. Her heart was madly skipping for joy. She pulled over, almost turned off the engine but remembered a movie where it didn't start again, so left it running. She shut the hood. Nobody. Not one soul on this road.

Annie really had no idea what to do next. She hoped she was driving away from Ilmar's, but she could not say. Somewhere, deep within, she felt Brad calling to her. It was too much like a novel she couldn't quite remember, and she ignored the voice just out of earshot.

She came up with a plan to find a big city, call her sister, and fly home. With this decided, Annie's tension eased up an erg. To have a plan, any plan.

Then she remembered Anya's note containing her phone number.

When she found the taste in her mouth again, she knew she would be OK. The way her pussy slightly quivered also told her that she would be OK. If she acted perfectly sane and like a good American (whatever that was), she would be OK. Without panic or any other intense feelings, she would be OK. Damn it! She still had on the floral peasant outfit.

'I am OK. I am OK,' she said over and over until lights of a small town were visible.

She drove the car into the half-village, half-town and called Anya. Tall grey cinder-block buildings masked small cottages with white wooden slats and dark green roofs. Everything seemed in some state of picturesque disrepair. Annie had doubted she would even find a phone here but she drove slowly through the town, chanting her mantra: OK, OK, OKaaey which worked for her – eventually.

Annie waited near the large cinder-block building they had agreed on. Annie had no idea how difficult it would be to agree upon a meeting place that was safe and recognizable. She was hoping to meet up in a café but Anya said they were all still private and too risky.

She saw a woman dressed in western clothes, a smart dark suit, trendy boots and a floral scarf. Her face looked intelligent and compassionate. It was Anya, at last.

Annie cried from relief. 'Please, Anya, get in the car. Help me. Those men . . .'

'They are bad men. Your friend too. Drive to my place.'

Annie had mainly spent her time fucking or working. This new companion put her at such ease, Annie instantly understood that she had missed out on something fundamental in life. She should have made some friends. Besides Nancy and Angelika.

They drove to one of the tall cinder-block buildings. Up ten flights of stairs, with apologies for the elevator being broken. The stairwells lay littered with cigarette butts and stank of cat urine. Annie hoped it was cat urine anyway. She guessed that stairwells were also places nobody in Latvia claimed to clean.

The apartment was small and crowded but richly decorated in tapestries and other colourful works. Anya made some tea which smelled of pipe tobacco and tasted like a sweet form of Latvia's earth.

Anya told Annie this was a secret home. Her special home. Where Boris could not find her.

'For money, I translate for the new business people. Americans like you, gangsters like Boris. And Ilmar. He is my boss, you know. And will be even after you leave. It will look suspicious otherwise. I don't like him but I try to undo as much of his harm as I can.' Annie nodded her head, so Anya continued. 'I studied to be doctor. Yet my real interest is something else. Something you know, Annie. I feel it.' Anya looked simply angelic to Annie at that moment. Most people do when they are rescuing you.

Annie wrote that down later in her rulebook as an addendum.

Annie told her everything. Anya explained the note. Ilmar had taken women before and just kept them like pets until he tired of them. Then there was a great danger. She told Annie not to feel stupid – Ilmar had an incredible magnetism and charm. It was unfortunately something Anya had taught him and that he exploited.

'My dear Annuchtka. You know this means, "dear, sweet little Anya"? Your feelings happen to many people who come to Latvia. They think it funny how everything is so similar ... no, familiar. I confuse those words ... Do you know why?'

Annie shook her head. She was unsure of the question. Anya intrigued her but Annie felt so sleepy. The adrenalin of running away was wearing off and her mind and body were exhausted. Anya didn't seem to notice.

'No, Annie. You must not do that. You do know. Try.'
Anya's eyes burnt into hers.

Annie tried to focus on them. She felt strangely dizzy,
a feeling of falling over backwards, being pulled out of
her body.

Anya pushed Annie's hair off her forehead and kissed
her. 'Dear, sweet girl, listen. This place special. Magic
lives here. My friends think it beginning of world here in
Sigulda. But not all beginning good.'

Annie looked at the gold-spun hair of her friend. Doe
eyes with an eagle's alertness. A very intelligent face. It
calmed her, the way Anya seemed to peer past all layers
of Annie's existence. And her face showed that she liked
what she saw.

'Annie, Annuchtka. You have other story. Your soul
crying out for you to learn something. You didn't learn it
last life.' Her green eyes kept Annie feeling hypnotised.
Anya's lips were not painted but they glowed a soft
warm pink. Her skin seemed to have no pores and it was
so hard to tell if she were fifteen or fifty. Her hands
showed that she was at least thirty. They were lined and
harsh-looking. Someone had told Annie once that you
can see the type of life a person leads by looking at their
neck and their hands. Anya's neck was still covered with
the scarf, but her hands revealed a very hard-working
woman who had not received much pampering.

Annie snapped herself out of the reverie. Was she
attracted to this woman? 'I'm sorry,' she mumbled.

'Nothing for you to make sorry. I can read cards for
you and you will know. You have friends, Annie. You
have soul too.' When Anya smiled, it seemed everything
in her crammed apartment lightened, making more space
and oxygenating the air.

'My soul search got me into this mess,' Annie said.

'It wasn't your soul, Annie. You have good soul. Old
soul. No ... What did it was something else. I don't
know word.'

'My cunt?' Annie whispered disparagingly

Anya looked confused, so Annie touched her cunt. Anya's eyes widened.

'Oh, Annuchtka! You know so much more than you know. Everything is everything. Your, how do you call? Cunt? It is you and you is you . . .'

Annie wanted to finish up the sentence with *And we are we and we are all together* but could not find the strength to put Anya off with laughter or any other means. Besides, a singular sort of truth was presenting itself and the knowledge was beginning to satiate Annie in a fundamental way.

Anya continued. 'Annie, Annuchtka, it is not your soul which is overwhelming you. Your borders hurt you. I know these things. Boris . . . that's why he pays me. Why he want but will never sleep with me. To learn things. He doesn't know I know he has murdered.'

Annie, awake again, not remembering ever being so curious before, asked, 'What is it you know, Anya? What is your specialty?'

Anya leant forward and whispered something which made Annie's cheeks flush.

Anya pulled back. 'But' – she paused, filling the tea kettle with water, ' – I now not do that kind of work. People need learn connect each other. Without me naked. I also walk in dimensions others do not. You one of few people who not think this odd. I feel it.'

'I know exactly what you mean.' Annie explained her walks on the cliffs, the hidden messages of the wind. 'I never doubted it existed but I could not integrate it.'

'Most people only doubt. Annuchtka, you are special. Good special. Ilmar special but bad special. He went to reach into other dimension but he pull out black – you pull out white.'

Annie shook her head. 'Not exactly. Do you know something about dreams, Anya?'

'Yes, I study them. I very much want to study you.

Unfortunately,' she gestured dramatically, putting her hand to her chest, 'my heart get in way. Latvian men always explain that is why women can only go so far with the science. My reply: that is why men can go only so far with the being human. Ilmar is not human. He wanted something from you. He did not ask you if you wanted to give it. He just saw what he needed and took it. He needed a new adventure, he took it. A new woman, new blood, he took it. He tries to take things one way then another. That is how he in your dreams. He make those dreams from other fabric, the one we all know is forbidden.'

'You make him sound like the devil.'

Anya laughed. 'You are very close. Anything which makes confusion like he . . . it is evil. And he wanted to take something from you, Annie. He wanted very much a part of you. Ilmar is terrible terrible man. That why no one here in Latvia for him. He has to travel far just to trick people.' She paused. 'Did he harm you?'

Annie began to shake her head no, but then she said, 'Yes. But he did it in such a way that it was connected to pleasure. It was amazing. Actually, I could not resist.'

'But, Annuchtka, you did resist. You never let him all the way with you. No, do not laugh. I not mean sex. I mean your soul. You keep it from him. That why he never inside fully.'

Annie pondered this. She had only been acting her normal self, not creating a vast inner resistance, but this seemed to have saved her. Sort of. At least it thwarted Ilmar's aim. Probably why he wanted to kill her. A coward's victory.

'Why did he say he was a doctor?' Annie asked Anya.

'Because he is. We went school together. But I chose other path allowed under Soviet law. You know para-normal medicine? We study it to hurt the West. Now no one want hurt West and no one study it.' Anya's face frowned. 'Ilmar! I've heard he's done this before but I could never prove anything. So, no scars anywhere?'

'No.'

'Too bad.' Annie looked concerned for a moment at Anya's sadness that Annie had no broken bones. Anya put her hand on her guest's and continued reassuringly. 'One of the judges in the area is a woman and we might get some help if she thought he had tried to kill you.'

'But he *was* preparing to have me killed off, after having me raped.'

'I believe you but we cannot show nothing. I think your first idea was the best. We must simply go to airport and get a plane for you. And we cannot use that car again. Give me keys, please.'

Annie handed her the keys. In the movies, this was when one found out that this woman was actually working for Ilmar. She hated the movies. For a moment, Annie panicked. But that emotion exhausted her. Besides, in accordance with her rules, What's done makes for what's done. No handwashing, no going back, no salty life.

She smiled wearily at Anya who slid out through the padded front door. The apartment was pindrop silent, with not a sound from the street permeating the inner sanctum.

During the hour of Anya's absence, Annie tried to think of nothing. Her cunt pulsed in its odd way. She felt shame rising up like a vapour. She had brought all of it on herself. Her aching need had drawn Ilmar to her, had opened a door to let him come in. But Annie couldn't follow any reasoning. Her mind lay like a river lined with bones of discarded ideas and aborted thoughts.

Yet her heart was expanding without her feeling its growth. Love – she had felt it. Really, it was the opposite of what Ilmar gave her. Perhaps she did know why she came here. To move a rock from her heart. To be so stripped, powerless, humiliated, threatened – was it worth this discovery? That she was alive again inside, feeling exploding like the flowers in Sigulda. Drunk on this over-abundance of feelings. Full for the first time.

And heartsick for Brad.

She jumped up and went near a knife when she heard the front door open again.

Anya looked nonplussed at Annie standing in a ready-to-stab position. 'It is OK now. I parked car near police station. This will make everyone happy. Unless, of course, they bribe right officers. So I bribe some officers to come tell me if they know someone else bribed. It is the only way,' she laughed, 'that justice really works in Latvia. We are not free long enough to appreciate impartiality. Annuchtka, it is night. I think it is best we sleep now. We leave in morning, yah?'

A diaphanous fear coursed through her body and Annie felt so ridiculous. This was a friend. A real friend. Better than the kind of friend one finds in greeting cards and movies. She was ashamed that she had thought, even for a moment, that Anya might be a foe. Annie tried to hide this and asked, 'But won't they have enough time to find me?'

'I will protect you. Relax. I will be our control.'

To give up control of her life again! She had read that to lose is sometimes to win. Perhaps . . .

Annie struggled to tell this kind woman something – maybe it was to ask forgiveness – but sleep circled like a vulture around her. She succumbed.

A little piece of grey shone before her eyes. Then white. Two white, flat eyes looking at her. Wet, with a smell of chemicals.

Annie tried to focus. She felt surprisingly refreshed. But what was this?

A photo. An 8½ × 11.

Hanging above her bed was a portrait of breasts. How bizarre to wake up seeing a portrait of body parts.

She looked more closely at the photo, wondering why

Anya would place something like that in front of her first thing in the morning. The breasts had a familiar roundness she well knew.

These were her breasts. To see this detachment of herself in the purifying light of morning was odd. Not confusing, not disquieting, but odd.

Annie had to admit, she liked her breasts. They were her favourite external part, round, begging to be cupped.

Or, apparently, photographed.

'Dobryo ootro, Annuchtka,' called Anya. 'Do not let your breasts disturb you.'

Annie didn't ask. Perhaps it was a Rorschach test of some Latvian school or a type of paranormal screening. Annie did not need to know.

Anya set thick, rich coffee in front of her. Next came a plate of beetroots, carrots, potatoes and onions in sunflower oil. Annie had never eaten vegetables for breakfast but she was famished. Anya gave her some black bread which tasted of coriander. All those vivid colours and tastes first thing in the morning swelled her heart.

It was the opposite of her austere mornings, waiting for secrets from 'the other side', alone. Here she was, waking in the companionship of someone she hadn't even slept with, and she enjoyed it. She felt so full. So free and so full. The secrets from the other side were here, clear and easy to see.

'Well, do you like your breasts?' asked Anya, without a trace of awkwardness or apology.

Annie was on her third piece of bread, piled with butter. 'They're beautiful.'

'I took picture. I'm sorry if not OK.' Anya looked confident that it would be OK.

'It's OK, Anya. I think everything you do is OK. You saved me. Really saved me.'

* * *

Unfortunately, the women could not walk together outside. Ilmar's men were watching. They had stopped Anya once to ask if she'd seen Annie. It was enough to throw Anya into a fit of cautiousness.

Being confined indoors, Anya instead painted all of Latvia for Annie from the kitchen table. She showed her pictures of Riga and its castles. Showed her a photograph of the Gutmana Cave near them where the poor beautiful woman was killed. How all the flowers grow there because of that death, especially pale pink, wild roses. The colour of Anya's lips.

Anya got out a deck of cards and asked Annie if she recognised them.

'Tarot?' Annie asked hesitantly, sure they were not.

'You are right. They are not Tarot but version our village folk play. You want play?'

Annie said she would and Anya asked her to hold the deck next to her heart.

Anya retrieved the deck, shuffled it, and then had Annie cut it. One of the cards gave Annie a nasty paper cut. She put her finger in her mouth and was intrigued to find Anya smiling.

'This is good luck, this thing you do.'

'Paper cut or the finger in the mouth?' asked Annie.

'Both these things, good.'

Six rows with five cards each were placed face down on the little red table. Anya indicated to Annie to turn over any five of the cards.

Annie turned over a king, a moon, a naked man, another moon, and a picture of a woman who resembled Angelika.

Annie laughed and pointed to the last picture. 'I know her,' she said.

'Is she a changeling?' Anya asked.

'I'll say. A damned good one.' But Annie didn't go into the details.

223

'Now I turn over five cards and we begin to tell our story,' Anya said seriously, green eyes glowing.

God, how Annie loved Anya right then. Her new friend made her feel so at ease because she expressed everything. Annie knew it wasn't a show of politeness – the way Americans feel compelled to animate their faces when they are most bored. 'No such thing as boredom, only boring people,' Annie's father used to quip. Anya had kept an unfathomably blank face at that first dinner – that long ago dinner when she dropped the paper in Annie's lap. Now her mask was completely off and Anya showed everything without restraint. Could any American do that? Well, except Angelika? Of course, that still involved a facade.

Anya turned over a king, a naked man, a hangman, flowers and a picture of a different woman who looked less androgynous.

'Are you ready, Annuchtka? This is your future.'

Annie was quite ready, and thrilled. The future – it did exist, didn't it?

'First, the dream with the king is not over. But soon it will be over. The moon shows this is good for everyone, not only for you, but the king too. The moon reflects the sun but only half of it with sun. The other half is in darkness. The king would be darkness.'

Annie could not stifle a giggle. This felt too much like a seventh-grade slumber party she had never had.

Anya didn't look at all upset with Annie's lack of solemnity. She continued. 'See this man you turned up. He is middle man, middle position. It means that the most important now in the life. He is a good man, surrounded by moons. He loves your light. Changeling knows him and loves him. Changeling loves you too. The changeling helps you now.'

'Now, my cards show – how do you say? – happy ending, no? I can no more do it, Annuchtka.'

Annie looked alarmed. Anya's face had fallen. She

224

asked her new friend what was wrong, so sad had she become, so suddenly crestfallen.

'Annuchtka, don't worry! I am sad I cannot to do it. I don't remember order. I forgot my girlhood and don't remember order for reading cards. Forgive me. I only gave you half story. But your story good. It is me who make mistake.'

Annie assured her that even half a story was enough. She would tell Anya the rest of the story after she lived it, either now or later, depending on which way the portal ripped or repaired itself.

In truth, this strange card play somewhat unsettled Annie. It was a game she had sworn never to partake of. She'd make her future or be damned trying. No Ouija board sealing a fate she'd step into. Plus, she had not completely bought Anya's story of losing her touch.

Wanting a friend and not a fortune teller, Annie decided to confide everything to Anya. Everything. Not merely the events but the emotions behind them. As she told her story, Annie realised that all of those actions she had taken had feelings behind them that she had only permitted, and only at times, to operate in hindsight. She was one step behind, a Cubist's holding tank of emotions and brushstrokes – nothing quite in focus with the place it emerged from.

Annie spoke of her aloneness and how she didn't really understand that she was alone. Anya's arm over her shoulder was reassuring, though it made Annie's sex pulse.

Why couldn't she control it?

'And Brad, Annie. He is a key for you.'

'Yes.'

'To what, though, Annie? You must consider, to what. He is a good man, I know.'

'I don't . . .' Annie stopped herself. She *did* know what Brad was the key to. He was her key to love. He was the one who connected everything together. Not exactly holding her together, but showing Annie herself. Showing that he saw that self and loved that self. He wanted to be a part of her. Not extinguish the light but add to it. He wholly loved her and she him . . . now.

Anya looked at her quizzically. 'It will be OK, Annie. Really. Ilmar will soon be gone for ever and this time you can easily go back to your heart.'

At Anya's funeral, Annie would say that this woman gave her the right path at the most important point in her life. Annie planned to look at Anya's mobster creep boyfriend, Boris, and freeze him with an icy stare. She'd hiss the one line she'd learnt to say perfectly in Latvian. 'You never understood even one drop of her.'

Chapter Twenty-Four

*T*he trip to the airport was close to uneventful. The airline officials told Annie that she had to pay cash, since a credit card transaction would take too long. Anya intervened and, with a few words and some American dollars discreetly passed on, the official said that a payment by credit card would work this time.

Annie gave Anya Nancy's address and telephone number since Annie didn't have either of her own at present.

Only after the plane was in flight did Annie realise that she had been very tense, worried that Ilmar might find her. She felt her jaw muscles stop clenching from fear and her belly start aching in a happy way from hunger, knowing the hunger would soon be relieved.

The man next to her smiled a I-can-reel-you-in-with-these-pearls smile. Annie smiled back. Harmless, she thought. Then he leant over and told her his name. Annie replied, 'That's nice.' He asked if he knew her, was she someone famous? She certainly, he was sure of it, looked familiar. Annie told him they had never met and began reading an article.

'Hey, I'm not going to hurt you or anything. I just

want to talk.' He leant her way as he said this, crossing the invisible boundary that Annie wished to keep around strangers.

'And I don't want to talk,' she said into the magazine.

Annie heard him mumble, 'Bitch,' under his breath but she couldn't have cared less. She could not stand even the pretence of a courtship. Her need to be desired or worshipped from afar had vanished. She wanted real connections.

Annie fought him. Fought the restraints. Ilmar kept saying, 'But I have your power. You gave it away so easily.'

That was my shame, said the face on the ceiling. Annie, you are free.

'Did you know that you talk in your sleep?' The smile hovered over her. Annie thought for an odd minute that she was at the bar where she and Brad had met, the bartender looking at her. She avoided looking at the face and, instead, focused on the airsick bag.

The man next to her leant over and squinted at her. 'God, you look familiar. Really! It's not a come-on. Would you like to know what you said in your sleep?' He held his secret over her like a score towards a final goal. Annie thought she just might use that bag. He wasn't ugly, but she could not play the flirting game any more. Not even a milligram of it.

'Did I say that I was madly in love with you?' The anger in her tone made the man sit back. Annie felt good. She had never really said an angry thing to a man that she could remember. It felt really good. She stared back at him and through him and thought about biting off his nose. The thought felt good. The aggression was pushing out the shame Ilmar had pushed in, and masking it: a piñata with candy on the outside. She had no need to bash away at an empty core. Hers or his. Annie was enjoying the whole new sensation. She was hot but not sexually. Back to being new and improved, panther-sleek, alive, lethal.

'Hey, I don't need to tell you anything. Just thought you might want to know. What's with you, anyway?' His square face had a vein going down the forehead. It pulsed with every word. The affront to his power was certainly angering him, Annie thought.

She was pleased. 'Why does something have to be with me? I said I don't want to talk to you. It's clear. If I have to, to use your word, be a "bitch" to accomplish this, then that's what I'll be.' God, how wonderful it felt. The man was at a loss. She saw the anger rise in him alongside confusion. Not Ilmar's quiet seething for control but a desire to spar without gloves. This man was not so calculating as her last lover, but the hint was enough to make her ill. He did not get what he wanted and now he was going to make her pay. She was happy not all men were like him, sorry too many still were.

Annie understood now that her strongest weapon ever had been surprise. But before she used it to attract men. Now she wanted to spurn them. They all rolled up into Ilmar for the moment.

No, that wasn't completely true. After everything, she could never think of Brad that way. Brad changed for her. She wasn't able to appreciate it then. For a moment her heart ached for him. His love for her was a bullet which cracked the green seed of her heart.

Annie, stop this, she said to herself. To stave off the hollow fear that was leaking back in when she imagined Brad had not waited for her, she tried to fill herself with the brightest thoughts: Anya's courage and cunning, the flowers in Sigulda, Rule 17 – *Love doesn't have to be 'whatever that is', never mind a certain prince.*

To alleviate her feeling of contempt for herself at having come full circle to discover the love under her very nose, Annie composed her second to last rule, Rule 21 – *Things do not have to move in order to make sense. Life is bread making; rising, kneading, rising.*

* * *

229

Her memory moved beyond the wing of the plane she was staring at. She and Brad had been walking in the woods. Annie had an overcoat on with nothing underneath. She had pushed Brad up against a tree and was impaling herself upon him like some driven sex priestess. A Druid doing rites to acquire life-fluid, she thrust, feeling his shaft as a monolith. Sacredness in defiance of order. She pushed at him wildly. His eyes were moist and urgent. He kept saying, 'You're so with me, Annie, so with me.' She kept thrusting into him because she thought he was talking about timing. Annie did feel very in sync with him, not realising something else was happening too.

The woods around her had seemed ablaze with colour, as if the whole sky had been washed and hung out to dry. Brad's eyes were melting into hers and, for a moment, she felt no boundaries. There was no difference between Brad and herself. They were as one. The air sat upon them and the silence purified even the birds. Trees, hair, pine needles, bird songs, sex scent: all felt as one. There was no separation from the animal act they did so joyfully and the nature surrounding them.

Annie's body then reacted to the lack of separation, fearful of the blurring boundaries. She couldn't look into his eyes, feeling her pleasure turning into something else which made her afraid. It had stunned her and she pulled away from him.

'You just don't get it, do you?' But Brad's words were not, as she had thought then, accusatory. They were sad and full of great pools of anguish and disappointment. He had held her close, stroking her hair. The lovemaking to her had ended, but not to Brad. Stroking her hair was part of it.

Don't get it. Those words sliced to her heart now as she looked out into the black sky outside the plane. We're like that, she thought. Each of us an utter nothing. The passions are layers but Brad knew something. He felt me.

He was there, inside. Not only my body but inside everything. Every pore and I was afraid. Smothered. I let Ilmar control me but this man, who changed his life for me, I could not. Too close, too close. There had been no room to lie.

The thoughts made Annie very tired again and she drifted off, flying into the black of her dreams.

'Look at him,' Ilmar screamed into her ear. He had thrust a bar between her legs. Suspended above her was Brad. Hanging. The white light everywhere like blood.

'Choose, Annie. He's dead. I'm alive. His love will kill you. Mine will set you free.'

'But I don't love you,' she sobbed.

'You don't need to love me. In fact, Annie, I'm not sure you can love. I think you are damaged goods. Somewhere, you got a scar on your heart that healed the wrong way. Now there's nothing there.'

She woke herself up with the noise. The face was hovering over her again.

'You're screaming,' the man said. 'Could I please help you now?'

Annie looked him in the face, wondering when this war was going to be over. This awful feeling that she couldn't let her guard down, awake or asleep. She stared her faultline stare.

It did not work. 'Let me buy you dinner and I'll show you how,' he tried again. The man eyed her and grinned in a way which made his jaw look like he had just placed two small tangerines inside his cheeks.

'Listen, when this flight is over, I hope to never see you again nor spend time with anyone who remotely resembles you. You just don't get it.' Brad's words. Right out of her mouth . . . but not the tone. 'Leave me alone. This is not the way to come on to a woman. Try conversation.' Her heart beat the way a fireman's must when he hears the alarm somewhere deep within his sleep: jolted in a crossover from one reality to the next.

'I tried. You didn't want to talk to me.'

'Try interesting conversation,' she snarled. 'Try to be interesting. Just that you have a dick in need is not enough for most women.'

'Gee. Thanks for the tip. I bet you haven't been laid in a long time.' And with that, he turned in his seat so his back was towards her.

It had taken an uncomfortable amount of rudeness to acquire the distance she wanted from this sort of man. Annie felt relieved and went back to staring at the blackness beyond. She had made herself invisible again. But not hollow. Should she call Brad when she got back? She really had been afraid of love. Of losing herself. Of having lost Brad.

He had given her a self she didn't know she had. Would he still be there? Would that self still be there?

Annie felt OK. If Brad were not there, she still had understood something profound. For Annie, the thought couldn't stay long with her but she managed to say to herself, Love is not fear. That simple and that important. Her final rule. She wished it didn't remind her of a book. Rule 22.

Chapter Twenty-Five

*T*he plane landed. Annie got off, knowing no one would greet her at the airport. Those expectant faces like half-opened presents. How she would have enjoyed seeing a friend stand there, waiting with puppy-dog eyes for Annie's face. Could she enjoy someone waiting for her, not for some fucking but just from love? Someone needing her, wanting to be with her alone or in a crowd. Not for torture nor manipulation nor to hide other needs too shameful to confess aloud?

She realised that she knew little about the safe, comfortable love some people experience. Not her sister's version of small packets of disappointments and a mortgage. Annie thought about how she only knew Brad through sex. But one *could* really know someone this way. It was possible. It wasn't the movies where clothes fall off at the minute people say they love each other. It was better than that. A movie cannot show a real connection, only permissible viewings on non-distinct body parts. Or like literature with its collapsed and elongated events, it shows the beginning or the end but not the long time significance in between.

She knew Brad had experienced real love through

making love to her. That was why he felt violated when she introduced Tom. Brad wasn't willing to share her, not out of jealousy but because it is something one cannot do when one truly loves. If another has your heart, someone else cannot have your crotch. If you really give of yourself. Hearts can't come together and then be ripped apart. She'd seen those people with too many scars on their hearts, Ilmar being a choice example. There was a point where so much sex and so little intimacy left one deeply unsatisfied. Lonely at the centre of the heart, mind, body and soul. Even a well-fed crotch needed the vitamins, the energy of love.

Up to now, Annie had been living her whole life at the halfway point without any understanding that things could go deeper. She had received love but had never abandoned herself completely to the control of love. She was always a bit on the outside of it. For her, loving had been an act of cowardice because she herself feared its power.

She decided to wait a while before calling Brad. From the arms of doom into the arms of a saviour. She didn't need to feel he was rescuing her heart.

Or, to be more honest, if he rejected her now, she would be utterly lost. She had to wait for that feeling to pass. She wanted to come to him whole.

The luggage came up the carousel and Annie noticed who took which suitcases. Vast mounds of black went to those dressed in black. Those with garbage type suits picked up the ugly bags and then there were those few women who actually believed luggage could have a feminine touch. All the handles were off those pastel-flowered cases, forcing the women to handle the bags like monkeys with crates.

Her unwanted travelling companion owned an imitation black leather garment bag. The straps were missing and it had an air of misuse. He seemed embarrassed to pick it up in front of her. He smiled bleakly at the door and then was gone.

She hailed a cab and snuggled into the back seat. She didn't even worry that the driver looked a little like one of her former assailants. Sigulda was a long way off and she was far from its cave. No tragedy for her life, for she had a choice now. As she had then.

The San José area revealed itself under a thin veil of brown haze. No one there, or in all of the Bay Area, would dare call it smog, for that was a term reserved for Los Angeles. Yet much of the architecture resembled southern California, where banks could be confused with movie theatres, supermarkets cloaked themselves as small fortresses, and every town bled into the next, creating an image of a thousand-mile ranch house with courtyards slyly referred to as 'parks' and 'open space reserves'.

Gertrude Stein was speaking of Oakland with her 'no there there', but in San Jose, there was no here here. So new was it that shadows still looked for places to reside and trees kept their leaves year round for fear of being seen by the wrong crowd. Annie couldn't wait to get back to San Francisco – when she could afford to. She needed the wind to whip secrets into her ears and the crispness of the air to keep them fresh. It was her city and she longed to speak to it once again.

Her sister's house leapt up to greet her on the left side. It looked smaller than she remembered it. Or had Annie's eyes grown?

Annie could not make sense of the feeling of purification. She felt large and light, as if there were no boundaries between herself and others. Had she become that transparent eyeball? Words of Emerson came into her head: 'Standing on the bare ground, uplifted into infinite space, all mean egotism vanishes, the currents of the universal being circulate through me.'

Her feet seemed miles away from her, walking

235

unknown territory. A beam of sisterly love seemed to shoot from inside her and out into the room.

Nancy noticed it. 'My God, Annie. Sunlight is pouring off you. What have you done to look so great after ... Uh, Annie, tell me what happened. I was really worried about you.' Acceptance. Had it always been there? Had she always been safe with her sister? Had a fear or a subservient boredom kept her from noticing? Younger sisters tend to find ways not to listen to the soundest advice from their older sisters. Not only a rule, but a law.

Nancy and Annie hugged and hugged, expressing the sheer gratitude one had for the other with the pressure of arms on the back and smiles upon the lips. We do not need to explain the mask Nancy dropped which made her face look strikingly beautiful or the language the siblings used to communicate their heartfelt relief and joy at seeing the other. Let us just mention that Nancy grew more powerful through seeing Annie and Annie settled back on the earth through seeing Nancy.

Phil came into the room. Short, barrel-chested – how did he manage to believe he was attractive? Had he done, not thought, just a little more so, he might have been. Something about him though smelled of entitlement. Like he was owed something. Her sister slumped a little when he came in and somehow, in one second, became a wife. Before, Annie was feeling that Nancy and she were equals and now, suddenly, she saw her sister disappear into the background. The woman above the bed, the voiceless other, the lesser. Hollow thou art born and hollow to the core. She willed Nancy to stop the act, to go back to being radiant and letting the universal being of love and largesse soar. In her mind, Annie undid the cords which bound the slave to the bed, the subject to her king, the victim to her captor. She projected this onto Nancy, to be full and overflowing with sentience, good-will, emotions, *love*. Her sister deserved it – to be full.

Hollow would not be Annie's end. Not this time, she

236

vowed. She'd like to make sure it wasn't Nancy's either. She wanted, figuratively, to get that doll and give it back.

'So,' Phil half-swaggered, 'you came back to little old America. Nancy tells me that you had quite a couple of months.' He leant back and tried to leer a bit, a Midsummer's Night fool in a tragic role. 'Was it worth it?'

'Of course it was. Everything in life has a purpose, even if the purpose is only to show you that things cannot get much worse. Nancy knows about that too.' Annie didn't know what had come over her, intimating conversations she and her sister held which portrayed Phil in a bad light. Speaking this way to him in his own house. It felt right though, knowing that she knew he did nothing to satisfy her sister's needs and yet believed he did. Annie wanted to take the power out of Phil but wisely figured that that was her sister's battle.

And what were those needs of her sister's? Nancy's home was secure but everything about her said, 'Afraid'. Afraid to move without Phil's consent, afraid to have her own opinion, afraid to be truly free. Afraid she was a prisoner and afraid to look and see if that were true. Afraid she would reach menopause before she ever had an orgasm. Afraid.

'Annie, have a drink. Anya called, you know. She has very good English.' Her sister spoke up, buoyant to relate a message from another part of the world. She seemed larger and lighter, just telling Annie. Shoulders back, eyes dreamy-looking. Nancy looked elated that Phil didn't receive the phone call. Phil looked undisturbed, bored. Yet, for a precious moment, it appeared to Annie that Nancy wasn't concerned with Phil's displayed attitude that his wife was somehow, as usual, wasting his time.

'Anya? Is she in this country?' Annie asked excitedly.

'No. I'm afraid it seemed like she was still in that 'L' country.' Nancy giggled a bit, not so much from embarrassment but from delight that they were in on a secret Phil could not understand.

'Livonia? Lithuania? Liechtenstein?' Annie had read about the other countries on the inflight magazine and was unable to resist throwing out the names.

'Right. One of those, I think. Anyway, she had something very interesting to say. Made me promise I would pass it on to you. She said that you are not to be afraid. Your past is finished and she was glad to help. She said that fear – am I getting this right? – yes, that fear is an allusion.' Nancy's face moved from right to left, recalling the words. She was smiling in a vague way and seemed to pull in some of the outside sunlight.

'Illusion?' offered Annie.

'Right. Illusion. "Love is the only constant if one is brave enough to trust". That is so charming!' Nancy exclaimed in a gush of admiration.

Annie knew what she would say at Nancy's funeral. She would say she was the most loving and giving sister a person could ever hope for. That there were certain people in Nancy's *immediate* family who could not possibly have appreciated the gift she had for being good – in the best sense of the word.

Nancy looked at Phil for a moment and his face hypnotised her back to the domestic trance. She said in another voice, a flat voice from a marionette controlled by Phil who opened his wife's mouth to make Nancy say, 'You really find them now, don't you?'

Annie might add, at the funeral, that Nancy was at her best when left to her own devices. And that certain people in the *immediate* family never understood that.

'Yeah,' chimed in Phil. ''Member the people she used to work for? Them freaks who managed to make a livin' outside of the circus. Amazin'.'

'Nice to see you two again to remind me of what's normal. Nothing has changed for you.' Too bad, she added under her breath. After a pause, she relayed with

enthusiasm, 'But you know, I like people on the edge.'
As she said it, Annie realised that was true. Would
probably always be true.

'Problem with the edge,' and Phil poked a finger into
Annie's upper chest, 'is that sometimes ya just fall off.'

Annie thought, When you start on the ground, there's
no falling – just getting up.

Nancy gave her the letter. 'I'm sorry. I told Mom that
you went to Latvia and she asked a lot of questions.
Anyway, I think she wrote it a week after you left.'

Annie opened the letter, written on onion-skin, and
read the following.

Dear Annie,

Been informed that you've gone off to Latvia. Good for
you. Do not know what possessed you, Annie dear,
but thought you might want to hear a theory.

A long time ago, there was a child. A very sweet
child who knew very well how to dig. She dug, holding the spade in her hands, imagining it were a doll.
How could she know it was not a doll? How did she
know that the dirt under her fingernails was not chocolate? That the shrivelled tubers she put into the earth
were not the eyes of her mother?

She dug for it was her job. A tiny spade for the tiny
hand to wedge a deep turn of the earth and put the
potatoes into their coffins. She did not know they
would grow for she did not know what they were or
what was their purpose. Had no idea things could
change or evolve. Or that one day, this soft mouldy
rock could be dug up and digested, after boiling. It is
hard to understand tasks, my daughter, when they
were born with you and seem as natural as bleeding.

In a long building with chinks in its wood, this child
listened to the wind howling and she thought it the
ocean. Her stories of dolls, chocolate, the sea, con-

vinced the other girls (By God! There were many others!) that if they believed enough, it was as good as if it were true. She told them that energy lived in the air and if they swallowed enough of it, they would not need or want food. Their stomachs which did not know what it meant to be full would be so full that an idea of food could burst them. Oh yes, you would be surprised that she knew how to talk and talked all the time to any person who would listen.

This hungry child knew how to imagine a world outside the green woods which surrounded the long building. She dreamt a great palm came down and asked her to climb aboard. She stepped into the mighty hand and it carried her away to a place with real oceans and mountains of chocolate whose richness flowed through her like a mighty stream. She woke with her mouth swallowing air and tasting something she knew was waiting for her.

Think I was five when they took me. Remember being so happy that I was chosen because I knew I would be chosen and so I was chosen. Other girls wanted to know who would tell the stories. I did not care for they were already dead to me. The stories. I had been chosen, see, and these girls, the only people I knew in this world, had not. It was a victory to which only this day do I feel estranged from the spoils. Those girls. Whatever happened to them? Do they still dream of chocolate and warmth in the winter?

Wish I could tell you more, for this is all I remember. When your grandparents brought me back to San Francisco, they said that I would make digging motions whenever I was distraught. I could not speak English at all and the children laughed at me in school. I did not even know 'yes' or 'no'. Your father says that, from time to time, I still I dig in my sleep. Until your departure, I did not believe him. 'Why would I be digging in my sleep?' I asked him, sure he was lying. Thought he wanted a dog.

Annie darling, perhaps you are wondering why you went to Latvia. It felt like it was your destiny, yes? A burning in you that could not be resolved. You imagined it before you ever got there, for I am sure it came with the milk in my breast. I am sure that I fed Latvia to you for I am sure that is my homeland.

Never wanted to see it for I am happy here. I really had forgotten everything. That is why you made me so angry, asking about my past. Had no past, was not even certain that I did not make up the one I could to prove I lived here. The one in our city, my past down the road from our Richmond home, that was the past I saw. It still looks to me like broken bottles over so many years of wreckage, so imagine how distant my distant past truly is.

But when I heard you went to Latvia, everything came back to me and I wanted to talk to you.

I know you've said that I was not a good talker. You have even accused me of not being adopted. Annie, I was most surely taken away from that place of greenness and hunger. Words come to me that I have no idea what they mean. Perhaps you do. Perhaps your man can help me. Nancy said you went there with a man. Perhaps you will marry him and we will come full circle and I will see myself in your child's eyes. But this does not seem possible. Yet why would you go to Latvia with a stranger? Weren't you afraid?

Daughter, I wish that we knew each other better. I hope that you return and that we can begin a relationship. Please tell me everything you saw. I need to hear it. Do not tell your father. He cannot understand that I want anything to do with a memory of starvation. But it was more than that. It was my imagination. I left it there.

Please, Annie, be my eyes. Florida laughs at me with

its sunshine and well-fed people. I need to see that green, need to feel that dirt, if only through your eyes. Let them be pearls, Annie.

Understand if you do not wish to tell me. You have always been secretive. It is probably my fault somehow. No, I do not think you blame me but secrets have been a commodity that I am afraid I passed on to you.

If nothing else, please let me know you are OK. Nancy promised to give this to you when she knew where you were. She does not know its contents. Do not tell her. I have no secrets for Nancy. I'm sorry.

Love,
Your mother

Nancy asked what was inside the letter, amazed at the expression of bewilderment on Annie's face.

'I really could not say what it is about,' was all Annie was able to answer. She desperately wanted to crawl away for a few hours to process the meaning. Her mother and Latvia. Then who was Ilmar?

She began to worry that her life was beginning to resemble the novels she had read. That after her mother's letter, she would find another secret which would explain to her all her actions for the past five years. At the funeral, Fred would come forward and say, 'I was sent here from Planet Z to initiate Annie into her body.' Everyone would nod and her father would say, 'And you did a good job, just like I asked you to.' Charles, Jeffrey, Tom would get up to explain themselves and their part in the divine plan of Annie. Brad would be Irish and her father's best friend's boy. Son that is.

No, this was not the time to imagine death in her life. She needed to be there for it. She willed herself to be present and not slip off somewhere, either physically or mentally.

* * *

Nancy had the day off and was delighted to take Annie up on her suggestion that they hike the cliffs of San Francisco.

The story, told once to Anya, seemed much simpler to tell to Nancy. Yet more difficult too, for now it sounded completely unreal. A photograph you've carried of a person who has since grown aged and you cannot reconcile the image in your hand to what is before you. A crossover from one portal to the next.

The cliffs, the sun hitting the Golden Gate Bridge – it was July and that tender pink of the sky played upon the red metal. A patient etherised upon a table, said Annie to herself. How glorious to walk the cliffs with a friend. Nancy was her friend. Annie supposed she had had to go to Latvia to find that out too. Take away all your comforts and one finds her true values and needs. And loves.

They stood at the top of the hill. Annie heard the voices but did not try to tell Nancy about them. *Undone, undone, undone.*

Annie wanted to put words to what she and Nancy had felt so she told her sister that she loved her. Nancy did not seem surprised by the information. She said quietly, 'I know.' That was that. It left Annie wanting to open up her heart and be a beacon of love for her sister and the universe.

When Annie finished her story (she had left out many of the sex details she had related to Anya, figuring that withholding information is not the same as being secretive – she even planned to tell Nancy the contents of Mother's letter), Nancy clasped her sister's hand and said, 'Bless your soul.'

That word made Annie stop. 'Nancy, I need to ask you something, You're the spiritual one . . .'

Nancy interrupted her. 'I'm the religious one. *You* are the spiritual one.'

That hadn't occurred to Annie, but it seemed true. The

243

more she considered it, the more she knew it to be true. How on earth had her sister come to that realisation? Perhaps Nancy had some psychic abilities Annie should look into. Certainly Anya would have something to say about it. Yet it didn't answer what she needed to hear from her sister.

'Nancy, what do you think a "soul" is?'

'See, you *are* the spiritual one. You don't ask about what church you should go to or clarification on a Bible passage. You want to know what a soul is.'

'Well . . . what do you think it is?' Anne was afraid that the whole tone of their walk was about to change and suddenly Nancy would be pouring down advice Annie needed a shovel to get out from under. Oh well. She should take it. Nancy had been there for her much more than vice versa. Not that Nancy had ever indicated that she needed help.

'I'm not sure I can say, Annie. I think it is what exists without our bodies or our minds. Something like our essence. If you stripped away everything, down to the bone, that would be your soul. It lives beyond you. It's music for ever, hoping to reach for something which cannot be described but can be understood. A longing that you feel somewhere out there lies a completion of yourself and that you know deep down resides within yourself if you only recognise it. It's when you stand and you know that you are standing and in some sense you will always be standing and that which is you, truly you, will be there long after the beautiful body you possess crumbles away under the heel of God. Stripped and peeled away until there is only you. The you which has always been you and will continue to always be you.' Nancy was quick to add, 'That's just my opinion.'

Annie grinned. She had been stripped. Left bone naked to the universe.

Chapter Twenty-Six

*T*he problem with encountering your things in storage is you realise how useless they are. A bunch of stuff you paid to have kept in a musty hole with a poor lock. Once put into boxes, any semblance of elegance your possessions might have had is completely lost. Cram all the boxes into a six-foot by fourteen-foot space, and it's junk.

But not her diary. Her rulebook/journal was at the top of the first crate she encountered. So quietly had it rested in this self-storage area south of San Francisco, while she had traversed miles in order to find out information which had been there all along. That if she had slowed down, she would have realised that.

It was quiet in that self-storage unit, with its view of the Oakland Bridge disappearing into the fog. This place was like one of those wasteful cemetery plots 'with a view' for twice the price. What had Nancy been thinking?

Those boxes filled with her books looked very heavy. Nancy said she had not hired movers so who had done this stacking up to the very ceiling? Phil had not, she could see. It was too neat and nothing looked damaged.

The mattress of the bed was covered in the sheet which

had been under Brad and her the last time they made love. Strange, since that had been tucked away in a corner of her closet. Lying upon it had made her too sad.

With journal in hand, she suddenly did not mind the extra price for the storage unit. It was very quiet on the grounds. Quiet enough to hear the birth of new thoughts, ideas.

She began to write:

I'm moving into *my self*. I am not *my self* but greater than *my self* for *my self* will live beyond me. It is contained beyond the storage unit of my heart.

Annie ripped the page out. To put words on her soul would be to diminish it. She would not take diminishing in any form. Plus, at the moment, she had no stomach for bad writing.

Looked to her like someone had dropped the journal. Part of the binding was broken and one of the pages was terribly dirty. Touching the book longer, Annie sensed that someone had also read it. She hoped the anonymous reader had enjoyed invading her privacy, the jerk.

Annie was tempted to not even get her stuff out. All these things we carry with us to prove that we had the power to buy them. Did she need the extra baggage in her life? She thought she might leave the lock off for a day and those people who were actually living in their storage units could come in and make her things their own.

Instead, she left her boxes there, locked up, and asked her sister if she could stay a while longer at their San Jose house. Nancy had been thrilled but Phil worked hard at making her understand that she wasn't welcome. He ate all the food Annie bought and cooked, even the organic vegetables he mocked. He watched horrible TV. He swore. He belched. He farted. Annie didn't care. At times, she could look through him as if he were invisible. Annie tried to imagine what she would say at Phil's funeral but kept coming up speechless.

Nancy tried from time to time to bring up the subject of Brad but Annie would not discuss it. 'I'm not ready yet to hear that he's gone,' she kept telling her sister.

'I'm sure he is not gone,' replied Nancy.

Kerri, the green-eyed manager, gave Annie back her job at the bar, letting Annie work double shifts to catch up on finances. Angelika was overjoyed to see her again. Saturdays had not been the same since Annie left. Annie was invited over for a barbecue to tell all about the handsome Latvian man. And to gossip about the one she left behind.

'Annie, look at these people. They aren't even from our hood. Wanna guess where they're from?' John was John now, standing in his backyard, flipping veggie burgers and drinking freshly squeezed lemon juice with vodka.

Annie did not recognise anyone except the Skunk lady. John saw her look in that direction and giggled. 'Recognise anyone else?'

Annie did not. Then John pulled a banged-up greeting card from his back pocket. 'Recognise them?'

It was a picture of Annie and Angelika dancing on the bar. Annie had a rose in her mouth and was holding the boob which said, 'Mean it'. Angelika was kicking a leg out into the crowd.

'Like it?' asked John.

'It's hysterical.'

'Really like it?' He giggled.

'Sure. Are you going to give it to me?'

'Oh yeah. Hon, I'm really gonna give it to you. Here.' He pulled another piece of paper from his back pocket. 'These are yours.'

Annie read 'Certificate for 350 Shares of Comesquat.'

'You invested for me?' she asked incredulously, won-

247

dering what kind of intrusion into her livelihood John had made this time.

'Not exactly. You own it. We – our silent partner and I – decided it was your picture too so why not have you own a piece of the action.'

'You're selling our picture?' she asked, even more surprised.

'Calendars, greeting cards, stationery. On the web. You should see the home page. I stole some of your very designs for it. You always did have a better eye. But,' he said in a low confidential voice, 'I did have the better brain. Guess what you're worth.'

'But I didn't *do* anything though.'

He giggled. 'Neither did we. Your friend and I. Just posted a notice and they're selling like hotcakes. Happy you came back to help now. We're sure to sell even more. Can't keep up now, as it is. So, what do you think you're worth?'

'I don't even know what a share is,' replied a bewildered Annie.

'We went public. You own some of our company. Get it?' He giggled. 'Ninety-eight dollars a share.'

'No way.' Annie sat down. This was too much like an ending to a Dickens' novel for her to believe it was happening. Things like this never happened in the real world. Mothers do not write letters explaining their connection to your wild hair. Friends don't just decide you need some money and set up an account for you.

'Yes. Oh ho ho, yes! And these people here are some future investors. *Major* investors. Ready to do the routine?'

Annie did not need any more coaxing. She leapt on to the picnic table. John said, 'Hit it,' and Dolly Parton music came on.

For a moment, she missed Angelika. She'd never danced with minimally clad John. But he fixed that. Out came a blonde wig and heels. John peeled off his jeans to reveal fishnet stockings and half a corset. He took off his shirt and strapped on the famous boobs.

And they danced. He pulled her under him, Annie pirouetted. He flipped her. She dipped him. She rudely pretended to be groping him like in a seventh-grade dance. The last strains of 'Best Whorehouse in Texas' died down and the applause rose up.

'Count me in, John,' said a deep voice from the back of the crowd.

'Me too,' piped in others.

John giggled. 'It's money for our video, Annie. Kerri has already taken over two hundred orders.'

After her time in Latvia, nothing seemed fantastic any more. Annie smiled and John hugged her. It was Thursday so there was no pain. He whispered, 'And you'll never guess the other surprise. So don't you dare even try.' After that, a large man with curly dark hair pulled John by the bra straps into one of the alcoves of the house, so Annie could not even badger John to tell her.

Annie had no idea what she'd done to deserve a John Cunha in her life and she wasn't going to fret herself to death trying to find out. She'd keep him – or it looked more like he would keep her. His funeral was going to be spectacular – she'd see to that. Boobs passed out to everyone and a wake with food from a leftover office party. He'd love that.

She hadn't called Brad yet. She wanted to be certain that her motives were not misplaced. She wanted to call out of love, not out of a strong yearning between her legs. And the novelistic events needed to die down. She needed her meeting with him to feel real. She wanted to be there without any atom of her wondering if she weren't making it all up.

Yet, seeing a strong jaw line, a touch of sandy blond hair, an exposed Adam's apple, drove her crazy. She finally understood unrequited love and all the courtly love poems she had read.

One day, she smelt him. Grassy and lemony. Someone was drinking a margarita with some Thai food brought over from next door. Another day, she heard his sorrow in a tale one young man was telling another about the girl who got away. On the bus, the curve of a stranger's hand wrenched her heart.

But it wasn't a stranger! Brad was getting off the bus and she couldn't get to him. Her face pressed up against the window, she willed him to turn around, to see her.

His body stiffened. He seemed about to turn when a delivery truck pulled its white side up against the bus, blocking the view.

Annie forced the bus driver to let her off and she searched wildly right and left for Brad. Gone.

Dr Zhivago's theme played annoyingly in her head. It wasn't even a real Russian theme, just Americans pretending.

She prayed Brad was merely around the corner and not lost for ever.

Chapter Twenty-Seven

'*H*ello. Is this Brad?'
    'Annie, where are you?' The voice thick with . . .
sleep or recognition? Annie couldn't decide.
    'I don't have a right, but I'd like to see you. I don't
even know how long it's been but something has happened to me. Something with demons I only half understand. May I come over?'
    'I could come over, Annie.'
    'Well, I'm staying at my sister's so it isn't very private.'
    'Do we need privacy?' He sounded hesitant.
    'Should we meet tomorrow?'
    'I think that would be better, Annie. This is such a
surprise. I thought you were gone.'
    'I was.'

They met at the first place they met alone, having horrid
burnt coffee reheated from the previous night. The cream
floated, another oily surface on some plankton-filled
water.
    The bartender was there and eyed both of them as a
threat to his establishment. This was not a place for love
or reconciliation. Most of his clientele had forgotten that

tender feelings could exist and instead opted for the more vital producing emotions like fear, anger and the morning-after nausea. This couple looked like an old married couple after separate vacations. They held hands and cooed over the coffee. The bartender didn't know that as they were cooing, both of them were fighting the urge to give up. All seemed so bizarre. They regretted coming to the place and went out to another coffee shop around the corner.

'Whew,' said Annie, sliding into the booth. 'We've moved from Betty's Brothel to Disneyland. Good choice. I'm ready for a little good old American fun. I've had enough darkness for one lifetime.'

'What would that be, Annie? Which lifetime? I'm not sure what happened.' Brad's Adam's apple was poking through the collar and he glanced down several times as if catching it in its conspicuous place. 'Why don't you tell me what happened.'

'I can in time, Brad. What I wanted to tell you, what I must tell you, is that I understand you.'

'OK.' He sounded confused, reluctant.

'And that I love you. I mean really love you. I had to travel around the world to discover it. I had to be controlled and to take back that control to discover it. I had to live some other lives . . .'

'What do you mean by other lives?' He sat up and was visibly agitated.

'I have had some. I don't know if they were dreams or realities but I was continually betraying myself in them. I had to have many of these before I could see it . . .' Her voice trailed off and she looked a little crazy to Brad. He unconsciously moved a bit away.

'OK,' she continued, 'there's time for those later. I met my other self, my soul.'

Brad's eyes watered, his chest rose and didn't fall. 'Did you fall in love in that country?' he asked.

'Yes. I mean, no. Brad, I have only really fallen in love

once, only I didn't understand it. And it's the same person, before as now. It's you. My Mary Magdalene.' She surprised herself with the metaphor and, in her enthusiasm, pressed her hand to his knee under the table. He didn't move.

'Annie, a lot has happened since then. I'm, um, involved with someone.'

Annie's heart leapt and then took off as fast as buck-shot in the open wind. She scattered everywhere. How stupid, she thought, to believe that Brad lived in some constant, waiting for her to return. He is an active man, not a photograph. Not a negative of herself. She had merely awakened something inside him.

'Brad, tell me that you are not sleeping with anyone for money.'

'Goddamn it, Annie. You said you understood me. You understand nothing. You changed me, don't you get it?!' He got up to leave but she pushed her hand down harder on his knee.

'Brad, I do get it. We are not the same people and yet we really are. My sweet love. You gave me back my soul. I didn't even know it was missing.' Tears came to her eyes and she let go of his knee. The tears kept coming and coming and she sobbed a big, gulping, snot-filled cry in the coffee shop. If the soul stuff had not been enough for the Disneylandish customers and tourists who'd been fascinated by the passion conveyed, this surely was. She didn't notice and Brad didn't either. He put his arm around her and pulled her head to his shoulder.

'Shh, Annie. Listen, sweet Annie. There is no one else. There is but it has only been a matter of wasting time. I felt so hollow. You are my spirit. My air. Shh.' He stroked her hair over and over again, making her laugh when his hand stuck to it. Apparently, Brad had touched some syrup beforehand. He laughed too and now they laughed as much as she had cried. A great relief swept over them and they stared into each other's eyes, past each other's eyes and into each other.

The kiss in the coffee shop should have shattered the window. Annie thought she might have died because a brilliant flash of light played inside her mind – the past united with now. Her former lives culminating in this moment of epiphantic splendour.

We do not intend to tell here the reuniting of the lovers or the quieting of two hearts which still kept beating in their respective cages. Do not need show the music playing quietly beyond their range of hearing but in perfect harmony with every feeling shared. Suffice to say that when Brad looked into Annie's eyes, he knew she had come back to him without a ghost of her remaining somewhere else. Suffice to say that when he held her hand, even Annie's knuckles knew that she and Brad would be fast in bed before long and that he wanted her love as much as she wanted his. Suffice to say that both knew they were in America and, consequently, they were due a happy ending.

When Brad suggested they go back to his place, she did not hesitate. But they boarded a train going the opposite direction.

'Did you move?' she asked.

'Sort of. You'll see. You'll find it very familiar.' A glimmer of mischief hung in his eye. 'Oh, look, Annie. There's the Chinese Roseanne.'

Annie started. 'How do you know John? Or do you know Angelika?'

'Both. He, or they, is a good friend of both of ours. A very good friend. The best of the best.'

They got off at her old stop. They walked to her old apartment. Before opening the door, Brad said, 'When I stopped by your apartment to see what had happened to you, Nancy was there. She said the apartment was still up for rent. So I moved in. It was a bit like being inside you again. I missed you so much. I just walked around in your energy.'

He opened the door and added, 'Still, Annie. Understand that I did not know you were coming back. I prayed for it but did not feel it. If I'd have known, I would've waited.'

She noted with some jealousy that some women's things were lying around. Brad hurriedly put them under the bed. He disconnected the phone line. Locked the door and put a chair under it. He said to her, somewhat embarrassed, 'I don't want anyone having the chance to find us.' She knew that it was the us he was concerned about. The him. He had begun another life which now seemed a dream, and Annie the dream within the dream.

They held each other that night, their naked bodies pulling in each other's heat. Annie could imagine a thin cord connecting her to Brad and he to her. It pulsed with various colours and sent shivers up to the top of her head.

Brad kissed her hair, her neck, the soles of her feet. They did not let their touch leave one another's for the entire day and the entire night. On Annie's old bed in her old room they lay, bodies impossibly close, pressing each other in an attempt to break past the skin and bond their molecules. She cupped his balls, he let his hands palm her breasts. Their lips mingled and drew in the other's breath. Their nipples touched, erect and searching. She nuzzled his chest hair and let the little piece of hard flesh part her lips. Brad smoothed her back then pressed her close in to him with something akin to a mother's embrace. The suckling so peaceful, so still, so magical.

Annie discovered that this was the most erotic love of all – this complete connection with another. For between her and Brad lay no space for lying nor did she have any desire for there to be. They were completely open to one another and with one another. She would surely die at

Brad's funeral from the separation. 'I loved him completely,' she'd say to the multitude gathered to mourn his death. 'His was the greatest love I'd ever known. Not just fucking but really loving.'

Annie felt herself relaxing into Brad. They talked, really talked, about the past. She told of potatoes and tarantulas and voices on the cliffs. Brad listened without any sign of judgement. He wanted to hear it all. Annie wanted to fill him with her stories, with her past, with talk of their future and, of course, with her love.

Brad told of his life in Chicago, how he started doing what he was doing when they had first met. Told of Tom and some of the strange manipulations he'd seen going on. He also told Annie that he was now a pilot and she could travel anywhere she wanted. He told Annie of all the things he wanted them to do together – even half-imagined crazy ideas he did not know existed in his head until his mouth formed the words. Anything was possible, anything.

Brad also told Annie how John had stopped by, hoping to meet up with her but instead finding Brad. John told Brad about the Latvian man. Her lover and her friend soon were spending all their time together, using their concern for Annie as a basis for friendship. That was how Brad became the 'silent' partner of John's greeting card venture. John taught him how to do all the follow-up work necessary for their business venture to soar.

So it was a Dickensian ending, thought Annie. She gave in to the notion that it was fine to read one's life if one lived it at the same time. And that her life could be a novel. That miraculous things could happen which summed everybody up and sent them off in a prosperous direction. That the good succeeded and the evil – well, who cared what happened to Ilmar. That wealth from some benevolent friend had suddenly materialised and made their lives, and their love, easier. Not that she wouldn't have been willing to suffer, to do the old 'Even though we ain't got money, I'm still in love with you, honey'.

Yet, if given the choice, choose wealth. That's what her father always said, and for once, she agreed.

She felt an expansiveness rising within her from Brad's ferocity. Annie's eyes widened, she mumbled, 'Own me.'

'But, Annie, you've never been owned.' Brad was deep inside her netherworld, tangled in the seaweed of her womanhood. Drugged, lucid, conversive then taciturn, he could not quite place where their lovemaking was. It felt like a philosophical conversation.

'Own me, Brad. Do it. Like you'll never let go.'

'I will, Annie.' He thrust deeper, picking up her long steely legs and pulling them above his shoulders. He watched his cock disappear in front of the heart of her ass. 'There,' he sighed when in as far as possible. 'Do you feel me now? Do I own you?'

'Yes.' Annie's voice was clear and present. He looked into her eyes and saw that she was laughing. 'Except you can't own me.'

Brad started laughing too and started thrusting steadily. His cock was slick with Annie and he felt, even in the moisture, that it had love in it. He came in a few minutes and fell down beside her.

She looked at him, her eyes full of water, her pupils impossibly enlarged like mirrors reflecting mirrors. She stroked his back, smoothing his spine, pushing his sweat off him.

He loved her cool hands. They made him feel sleepy. He remembered that, at some critical moment, he had wanted to say something. The words held themselves in front of him but he could quite see them. Then he remembered.

'Annie.' He turned over to look her fully in the face. 'Annie, you've never been owned. It's only by your

257

choosing. I can't own you. It's only for a moment, not for ever.'

She saw in his face the face of her groom in the dream. The face forgave her. Her insides felt larger, as if her womanliness were growing and filling her from the inside out. She felt sated, full of desire and yet absolutely complete. Before him, after him, she would still have her soul.

No fragmented poetry buttressed her, no rules clanged about her mind, no funeral scenario presented itself as the lens through which to experience this, nor did any literature try to span the gap between living and perceiving. Almost, anyway. Aristotle came to mind to agree with her feelings: 'When there is no separation between the action and the actor, the vocation and its doer, one has found joy.'

She didn't need to touch Brad to feel him or to feel alive. And he lived for her like a completion she could join, had joined. And she joined it, whole and wholly.

Epilogue

*R*eader, she didn't marry Brad. That is not the point. (They did, however, promise to stay with each other eight years or for ever – which ever came first.)

You might wonder: did Annie find love? She found it again and again. Love flowed from her soul, for she knew she had one. And this soul wasn't much further from where she thought it was the very first time. At last, she had connected all her parts.

LOOK OUT FOR THE ALL-NEW BLACK LACE BOOKS – AVAILABLE NOW!

All books priced £6.99 in the UK. Please note publication dates apply to the UK only. For other territories, please contact your retailer.

SLAVE TO SUCCESS
Kimberley Raines
ISBN 0 352 33687 0

Eugene, born poor but grown-up handsome, answers an ad to be a sex slave for a year. He assumes his role will be that of a gigolo, and thinks he will easily make the million dollars he needs to break into Hollywood. On arrival at a secret destination he discovers his tasks are somewhat more demanding. He will be a pleasure slave to the mistress Olanthé – a demanding woman with high expectations who will put Eugene through some exacting physical punishments and pleasures. He is in for the shock of his life. **An exotic tale of female domination over a beautiful but arrogant young man.**

FULL EXPOSURE
Robyn Russell
ISBN 0 352 33688 9

Attractive but stern Boston academic, Donatella di'Bianchi, is in Arezzo, Italy, to investigate the affairs of the *Collegio Toscana*, a school of visual arts. Donatella's probe is hampered by one man, the director, Stewart Temple-Clarke. She is also sexually attracted by an English artist on the faculty, the alluring but mysterious Ian Ramsey. In the course of her inquiry Donatella is attacked, but receives help from two new friends – Kiki Lee and Francesca Antinori. As the trio investigates the menacing mysteries surrounding the college, these two young women open

Donatella's eyes to a world of sexual adventure with artists, students and even the local *carabinieri*. **A stylishly sensual erotic thriller set in the languid heat of an Italian summer.**

Coming in June

WICKED WORDS 6
A Black Lace short story collection
ISBN 0 352 33590 0

Deliciously daring and hugely popular, the *Wicked Words* collections are the freshest and most entertaining volumes of women's erotica to be found anywhere in the world. The diversity of themes and styles reflects the multi-faceted nature of the female sexual imagination. Combining humour, warmth and attitude with fun, filthy, imaginative writing, these stories sizzle with horny action. Only the most arousing fiction makes it into a *Wicked Words* volume. **This is the best in fun, cutting-edge erotica from the UK and USA.**

MANHATTAN PASSION
Antoinette Powell
ISBN 0 352 33691 9

Julia is an art conservator at a prestigious museum in New York. She lives a life of designer luxury with her Wall Street millionaire husband until, that is, she discovers the dark and criminal side to his twilight activities – and storms out, leaving her high-fashion wardrobe behind her. Staying with her best friends Zoë and Jack, Julia is initiated into a hedonist circle of New York's most beautiful and sexually interesting people. Meanwhile, David, her husband, has disappeared with all their wealth. What transpires is a high-octane manhunt – from loft apartments to sleazy drinking holes; from the trendiest nightclubs to the criminal underworld. **A stunning debut from an author who knows how to entertain her audience.**

HARD CORPS
Claire Thompson
ISBN O 352 33491 6

This is the story of Remy Harris, a bright young woman starting out as an army cadet at military college in the US. Enduring all the usual trials of boot-camp discipline and rigorous exercise, she's ready for any challenge – that is until she meets Jacob, who recognises her true sexuality. Initiated into the Hard Corps – a secret society within the barracks – Remy soon becomes absorbed by this clandestine world of ritual punishment. It's only when Jacob takes things too far that she rebels, and begins to plot her revenge. **Strict sergeants and rebellious cadets come together in this unusual and highly entertaining story of military discipline with a twist.**

Coming in July

CABIN FEVER
Emma Donaldson
ISBN O 352 33692 7

Young beautician Laura works in the exclusive Shangri-La beauty salon aboard the cruise ship *Jannina*. Although she has a super-sensual time with her boyfriend, Steve – who works the ship's bar – there are plenty of nice young men in uniform who want a piece of her action. Laura's cabin mate is the shy, eighteen-year-old Fiona, whose sexuality is a mystery, especially as there are rumours that the stern Elinor Brookes, the matriarch of the beauty salon, has been seen doing some very curious things with the young Fiona. **Saucy story of clandestine goings-on aboard a luxury liner.**

WOLF AT THE DOOR
Savannah Smythe
ISBN 0 352 33693 5

30-year-old Pagan Warner is marrying Greg – a debonair and seemingly dull Englishman – in an effort to erase her turbulent past. All she wants is a peaceful life in rural New Jersey but her past catches up with her in the form of bad boy 'Wolf' Mancini, the man who seduced her as a teenager. Tempted into rekindling their intensely sexual affair while making her wedding preparations, she intends to break off the illicit liaison once she is married. However, Pagan has underestimated the Wolf's obsessions. Mancini has spotted Greg's own weaknesses and intends to exploit them to the full, undermining him in his professional life. When he sends the slinky, raven-haired Renate in to do his dirty work, the course is set for a descent into depravity. **Fabulous nasty characters, dirty double dealing and forbidden lusts abound!**

THE CAPTIVE FLESH
Cleo Cordell
ISBN 0 352 32872 X

18th-century French covent girls Marietta and Claudine learn that their stay at the opulent Algerian home of their handsome and powerful host, Kasim, requires something in return: their complete surrender to the ecstasy of pleasure in pain. Kasim's decadent orgies also require the services of Gabriel, whose exquisite longing for Marietta's awakened lust cannot be contained – not even by the shackles that bind his tortured flesh. **This is a reprint of one the first Black Lace books ever published. A classic piece of blockbusting historical erotica.**

Black Lace Booklist

Information is correct at time of printing. To avoid disappointment check availability before ordering. Go to www.blacklace-books.co.uk. All books are priced £6.99 unless another price is given.

BLACK LACE BOOKS WITH A CONTEMPORARY SETTING

To find out the latest information about Black Lace titles, check out the
website: www.blacklace-books.co.uk or send for a booklist with
complete synopses by writing to:

> Black Lace Booklist, Virgin Books Ltd
> Thames Wharf Studios
> Rainville Road
> London W6 9HA

Please include an SAE of decent size. Please note only British stamps
are valid.

Our privacy policy
We will not disclose information you supply us to any other parties.
We will not disclose any information which identifies you personally to
any person without your express consent.

From time to time we may send out information about Black Lace
books and special offers. Please tick here if you do <u>not</u> wish to
receive Black Lace information.   ☐

Please send me the books I have ticked above.

Name ....

Address ....

....

....

....

Post Code ....

Send to: Cash Sales, Black Lace Books, Thames Wharf Studios, Rainville Road, London W6 9HA.

US customers: for prices and details of how to order books for delivery by mail, call 1-800-343-4499.

Please enclose a cheque or postal order, made payable to Virgin Books Ltd, to the value of the books you have ordered plus postage and packing costs as follows:

UK and BFPO – £1.00 for the first book, 50p for each subsequent book.

Overseas (including Republic of Ireland) – £2.00 for the first book, £1.00 for each subsequent book.

If you would prefer to pay by VISA, ACCESS/MASTERCARD, DINERS CLUB, AMEX or SWITCH, please write your card number and expiry date here:

....

Signature ....

Please allow up to 28 days for delivery.